BLACK RAID

THE JACK OF MAGIC BOOK 3

BLACK RAID

ALEX LINWOOD

GREENLEES PUBLISHING

This is a work of fiction. Names, characters, organizations, places, events, and incidents are either products of the author's imagination or are used fictitiously. Any resemblance to actual persons, living or dead, or actual events is purely coincidental.

Published by Greenlees Publishing, contact@greenleespublishing.com

ISBN-13: 978-1-951098-11-7

Cover design by Dominic Forbes

For Pumpkin,
my tiny Monster

Portia ducked as the pieces of wood exploded, sending fragments flying throughout the room. One large chunk of wood hit her hand and drove into the open palm, sending a streak of pain up her arm. She tucked in, gasping and holding her hand.

She couldn't hear anything, not the drumming that had filled the room a moment before, or even the sound of the wood falling like snow around her.

One chunk of wood remained on the kitchen table, burning brightly, flames licking upwards. The ancient table discolored as the finish heated and its old varnish blackened.

"That was not correct," a dry voice said, cutting through the silence in her head.

Portia looked up. Across the room, through the still falling debris, Lord Fife sat in his chair, the drum silent on his lap. He stared at her.

She awoke with a start, and sat up, her bedclothes soaked

and sticking to her skin. The darkness of her room confused her at first with the nightmare of her most recent failure so fresh in her mind. Her heart raced and felt constricted in her chest. If her magical abilities were getting worse and not better, how could she save them all?

PORTIA STOOD outside the small cottage where Lord Fife and Merit, his companion and caretaker, lived. The front yard was a riot of plants and herbs growing together in a tangle. Despite its random look, it was far from undesigned. Symbiotic plants grew together, and medicinal plants filled every open spot.

Taking a deep breath, she opened the gate and walked up the path to the front door. Before she knocked, the door was opened by the tiny elf, Merit, who smiled at her and bade entry. Merit was short, even for an elf, and only reached Portia's shoulder—but then Portia was tall for a fourteen-year-old human. Portia followed her into the kitchen where Lord Fife waited.

Lord Fife was bent over in a wheeled chair by the fire. His eyes, surrounded by wrinkles and wild long white eyebrow hairs, shone with intelligence and spirit. They burned in Portia's direction. The gentle smile softened his face but did not completely banish Portia's nervousness.

"Welcome back, child. How is your hand?" he asked, solicitous.

"It's fine," Portia said. It still stung, but there was no

lasting damage. She hid the bandaged hand behind her back. It was a mortifying reminder of her failure.

"No matter. You will succeed today," he said. At Portia's skeptical look, he continued, "You must."

Portia nodded and looked to the table. Merit had left the kitchen, leaving the two of them alone.

On the table were the items for her work that day—a ridiculously large swan egg, a tiny plant clipping in a crystal cup, a miniature rose bush, and an enormous log of wood.

Portia's heart sank. The log took up half the table. It had been broken over a rock in the yard and was larger than the one that had exploded. Why not try a smaller piece after what happened? As if in response, her palm throbbed. Lord Fife had not taken that option.

Lord Fife took a piece of paper off his lap and ripped it in two and then placed it on the table.

"We'll do a warm-up first," he said, nodding at the paper. He meant to get to work immediately.

Portia stepped forward to face the piece of paper.

Picking up the drum on his lap, he beat out a complex rhythm Portia knew by heart. It haunted her dreams and hounded her throughout the day, but it was also reassuring to hear it played for her. She focused on the rhythm first, then looked to the paper.

She sang.

The sound of the drum faded away in her hearing as she concentrated on the paper while singing the Elven words. The pieces vibrated with her efforts. Using only magic, Portia nudged the paper pieces closer together so they just touched.

A tingle ran down her spine from the power concentrated in the room. She ignored the hairs rising on her back and her shaking hands and only thought of the paper, of how it would look whole and unmarked.

The paper's vibrations increased, the two halves fluttering next to each other until their torn edges joined from the top to the bottom in a rapid motion. It was whole. She had succeeded. She had cast the splinter healing spell and not faltered. Still singing, she checked the paper for any mark upon it where it had been ripped. There was none.

Portia stopped singing and released the spell, hanging her head down. Sweat dripped down the back of her neck and into her shirt. The drumming stopped.

"Well done, child, well done," Lord Fife said quietly, setting down the drum on the table next to him, his breathing ragged. Even playing the drum for as long as it took her to sing the spell exhausted him. Portia wished, not for the first time, that she was faster with the elf magic. At least this time she had completed it.

"Thank you. Finally, it worked," Portia said. Lord Fife raised one eyebrow at Portia's comment. "I don't usually have trouble doing magic." Portia's face turned red. "And, well, it's a little off-putting when things explode when you don't do them right. And I messed up your table."

Lord Fife waved that away. "I suppose human magic doesn't have such hurdles. How uninteresting."

Portia squinted at the elf master. "Yes. Don't you think that's preferable to exploding?"

"No, because I think that means it's weak. Maybe the

spell should explode or evaporate the idiot attempting it incorrectly or do something else terrible if it's misused. You think there shouldn't be consequences?" A brief twinkle shone is his eyes before Lord Fife's face became drawn and serious. His twisted sense of humor had made the long hours of studying go by much faster and had helped when she had failed time after time—especially now with the stress of all that had happened within the last few days.

"Consequences?" Merit said as she entered the kitchen. The tiny elf walked to the hearth and swung the kettle over the fire to make afternoon tea. "What do you know about consequences, you old elf?" Merit was formidable even though she looked nearly as old as the elf master of magic sitting in the chair by the fire. She took good care of the old master.

Lord Fife waved his hand dismissively at Merit. Portia turned away to hide her smile. "I know all about consequences," he said. "That's why I am teaching this young human what she needs to know to save all our skins."

Merit grunted and pulled mugs down from the shelf. "Tea will be ready soon." Smoothing her dress, she exited the room without giving either Portia or Lord Fife a backwards glance.

"Relentless," Lord Fife mumbled under his breath.

Despite his complaints, Portia had never seen him turn down a meal break from Merit. Nor would Portia ever do so, for Merit's cooking had no parallel. Her mouth watered just thinking of the small sandwiches and seed cakes to come.

"Now. You think too much. We are going through all the spells I've taught you. Quickly. No arguments," Lord Fife said, picking up the drum once again. "We have little time before our kings and queens move you around like a chess piece to the front of the war coming our way."

Portia shifted on her feet. What time she had here learning from Lord Fife after the hourglass had reached zero—the gigantic hourglass that told when the next splintering was upon the world—was precious. They'd sent word to Queen Lorica of the human kingdom of Haulstatt, but no message had come back yet. A twinge of guilt knotted Portia's stomach about not returning right away to her queen, but there had been little choice. She needed to be fluent in the splinter healing spell to be any good to humans or elves. The magic was critical to protecting them all. And no other human had the ability to cast it, so the duty fell to Portia. Failing would mean death and hardship to those she cared about.

Her hand throbbed again.

"More doing, less thinking," Lord Fife commanded over the thud of the drum. He hit with great force, its reverberations filling the kitchen. The commanding noise forced the thoughts out of Portia's head.

Nodding, she turned to face the row of items on the table.

First, she attempted the basic elf healing spell. Picking up the smooth white swan egg, she cracked it against the table—hard enough for a thin line to appear on the shell but not so much as to open the egg. Setting down the cracked egg, she sang the lilting song of healing. As with all elf magic, it was music based. The spell did not need the drum that Lord Fife played, but it helped Portia match the correct rhythm with her singing, which kept the magic flowing. If she had been more talented, she could have strengthened the spell by playing an instrument, but she lacked that skill. Too bad there was no magic powered by thieving skills, at least none that she knew of, since that was the skill she had practiced most in her life.

After several moments, the egg wobbled on the table and a silvery shimmer flowed over the surface; the magic started to take hold. Portia concentrated on hitting the high notes in the healing song and allowing her throat to relax. Pulling her shoulders back helped with both her singing and banishing the tension in her back. Healing was a complex and exhausting spell, somewhere between the ease of fire magic and the draining effort needed for cryomancy.

After one last decisive wobble, the egg stopped moving. Portia looked it over carefully while still singing to maintain the spell. The crack was gone with nothing left in its place to give away it had ever been there. Portia stopped singing and held her breath. The egg remained stationary on the table. She breathed out a sigh of relief.

Lord Fife did not stop his drumming. He nodded at Portia to continue.

The next spell was one of her favorites. Picking up the crystal glass holding the tiny clipping that only had two leaves on it, Portia looked at it closely and blew on it for good luck. She then sang to it the Elven words for growth and happiness. The vine vibrated in response. Portia imagined she could feel its thanks as she sent it energy. The vine trembled for several seconds then grew rapidly, expanding out of its container, new leaves appearing as it lengthened and thickened. Portia quickly put down the glass and the fast-growing plant. It had become too heavy to hold.

"Enough, child!" Lord Fife admonished, laughing. "How is Merit to get that out to the front yard?" He motioned to the large vine now covering the table, its body as thick as Portia's wrist, with just the last bit of one of several large roots still in the tiny glass that had once held the entire thing. Portia's face turned red. Pride at her accomplishment mixed with embarrassment at having gone so far overboard.

"I'll help her, don't worry," Portia assured him, turning to hide her embarrassment.

"The next one, now!" Lord Fife commanded.

Portia concentrated on the second plant on the table, a tiny tea rose bush. It was all of five inches tall but had nearly three dozen tiny buds on it. Portia sang a fast little tune to the plant. It was a quick burst of music, closer in tone to a flute than a human voice. Even without the drum, the rhythm was perfect. The plant responded by instantly sending each bud into full bloom, packing the blooms into a tight sphere of ruby red petals. Portia laughed in delight.

"'Tis well done." Lord Fife beamed at the flowers. Just as with all other elves she'd met, he adored roses. "But keep going. Hurry."

The last object on the table now lay partially hidden beneath the leaves of the huge vine: the large broken log. Long, thick splinters and fibers on each half showed where it had been forcibly separated into two pieces. A shiver ran down her spine and her palm stung with sympathetic pain.

The spell began in a low register. Portia used the bottom

of her range to give herself room to reach the high notes without exceeding her own natural singing range. The notes began deep in her chest and resonated there, adding to the power of the spell. The first time that had happened, it had scared her. Now it was a comfort. It meant the spell was being sung correctly and was working its magic. Building in both volume and pitch, she progressed through the song of the spell.

The two pieces of log vibrated and moved across the table towards each other, ever so slowly.

Exhaustion pulled at Portia. The heavy pieces of wood resisted moving. The other spells had pulled upon her pool of magic already.

Portia's song faltered. The vibrations shaking the logs became erratic, bouncing the wood all over the table.

"Concentrate!" Lord Fife called.

Portia pushed thoughts of the other spell out of her mind and instead focused on the jagged edges of the log, on where each fiber had been ripped from its place in the wood. She willed them back together.

The vibrations in the wood once again calmed and slowly moved the pieces closer, the wood fibers intertwining as the two pieces nested, finding where they had once grown as one. This was the most dangerous part of the spell where the energy poured into it was the highest, but there was as yet nothing to hold the energy in except the spell itself.

Portia pushed that worry out of her mind. She must concentrate on action. She tapped the rhythm on her knee with her hand along with Lord Fife. Each time she hit her knee, it helped reinforce where she was in the spell. A change in the vibration within her chest told her the pieces were mending with each other. She kept the vibration harmonic with the pitch of her singing. Any dissonance now would create a weakness in the wood.

Such a weakness in a healed splinter between worlds meant it could open up again and cause more troubles. That was what she was learning this spell for—to heal and shut off a gate between worlds. She must heal this wood without a scar, just as she must heal the splinter without a defect.

The air around the wood blurred, hiding what was happening at the exact jointure. Portia felt the progress. The vibration within her resonated for a moment and then faded away until it was just her singing left.

The spell was over, and the magic had done its work. Lord Fife nodded. Tentatively, Portia stopped singing, backing up at the same time. It was cowardly, but getting hit by the exploding pieces of wood on the previous occasion was a powerful incentive to get some distance.

The log lay whole upon the table. There was not a mark upon it to signify that it had once been damaged in any way, much less broken into two completely separate pieces. Portia breathed out a sigh of relief.

Lord Fife stopped drumming. "Excellent work. See? Less thinking. You approached it differently this time. And just in time, because here comes our taskmaster."

Merit entered the kitchen again. "Oh hush, no one tells you what to do and you know it. Unless you need to hear it, of course," she said, checking the kettle to see if the water was hot enough.

The contents of the pot steamed as Merit poured it into the teapot on the dried leaves within. She set a cup down by Lord Fife and one for Portia on the table.

Portia pushed aside part of the vine and sat on the bench in front of the table, picking up her cup of tea. She sipped it thoughtfully. "Why do things explode if the spell doesn't go right? I'm still unclear on that."

"The spell needs to pull the pieces together, which takes a lot of energy." Lord Fife picked up his own cup and held it for Portia to see. "A crack in a cup is easy, the pieces are right next to each other, which makes it easier. But the edges of a splinter are far apart—they must be for creatures to pass through—and you need to force them together and then run the healing spell to keep them together. That is why the spell is so dangerous if you do not complete it. If you do not bind the energy it takes to move the pieces together with the second part of the spell and make the object whole, then the pieces will fly apart... or a fire will start, or some other unexpected event will happen. The energy is there and must go somewhere if you do not use it in the healing."

Lord Fife wheeled his chair closer to Portia. "I'll admit, child, I'm glad you're here." Portia looked up at him sharply. "No, I'm not afraid. That's not it. I'll travel to the splinter, if I have to. Dying to save my people doesn't scare me. But you're younger and stronger. You have a better chance of succeeding than I. You will succeed. We all need you to." He patted her on the arm.

Earnest sincerity shone in his eyes, but still her stomach clenched with doubts. It was a lot of pressure to be the one to close off a portal to another world—for that was what a splinter was, a portal between worlds, and there would probably be chaos around her while she cast the spell. The invaders would not stand aside and let her do her work unhindered if they knew it was in their best interest to stop her.

Suddenly light-headed, Portia exhaled. Her hands and feet tingled. "What if I get anxious when I need to be calm?"

"It won't be a problem. What did you do on the streets of Valencia when thieving and someone almost caught you?" Lord Fife gazed at her impassively.

"I ran. And fast. And got someone between us so they wouldn't catch me," Portia said, sitting up and taking a deep breath. That world seemed so far away now. It was nearly two years since she'd been in Valencia as part of the orphan gang Black Cats. It had not been an easy life.

"You acted decisively... enough to save yourself and do what needed to be done."

That much was true. A lot of orphans did not make it to adulthood. And yet here she was, alive.

"Yes, but—"

"Stop thinking so much. Just practice. Make it as reflexive as your rules of thieving."

A knock sounded at the door. Merit left to go answer it and returned a few moments later with a letter sealed with bright red wax. Even from her seat, Portia recognized the royal seal from the human kingdom of Haulstatt, her home. Her throat tightened as Merit brought the letter. Lord Fife and Merit busied themselves as she opened it and read. The letter was from Queen Lorica. It bade her to return and with all haste, mentioning a change of circumstances but giving no details. Further, it directed Portia to speak to King Magnus and Queen Ceola of the Elves for arrangements of travel home.

"I'm to return immediately," Portia said, her throat tight. While she missed her friends there, the stinging in her hand was a constant reminder of her failing with the splinter healing spell. More time to practice would be helpful.

"Not surprised, my child," Lord Fife said, wheeling his chair closer to the table where Portia sat. "These last few weeks were a welcome bonus. We cannot get greedy and ask for more. Besides, you're much improved. It will be enough." He put a hand on her arm.

Portia reminded herself to not despair; she'd had extra weeks to practice, and friends and supporters awaited her back in the Magic Academy in Coverack.

She placed the letter on the table and picked up her cup of tea. Her hand shook only a little.

ONCE SHE HAD RETURNED to the Elven palace, she made her way to the audience chambers rather than her small room in the tower. She needed to talk to the king and queen about her return. A guard escort, or at least the use of a fleet Sika deer mount, would be helpful. Even a horse, as slow as they were, was preferable to walking that long distance.

Sergeant Lyren was guarding the entrance to the audience chamber that day. This was surprising since her duties rarely fell within the palace walls. She was a sergeant of the city guard. Her unexpected appearance made Portia's heart race. Had something happened?

"Greetings, young human," Sergeant Lyren said to Portia as she approached the door.

Portia nodded at her. Sergeant Lyren was an ally; perhaps she would tell Portia what was going on. "Has something happened?"

"Many things have happened," Sergeant Lyren said with a twinkle in her eye. Portia waited, but the sergeant did not share any more information.

Portia sighed then pushed forward. "I mean has anything happened today?"

"I'm sure something has happened today." When Portia smiled at the joke, Sergeant Lyren relented. "They have called me to be here for you."

"Oh." Did this have to do with her journey back? "I'm here to request an audience with the king and queen. I've had news from Haulstatt." Portia held up the letter she had received from the queen.

"Indeed, as have they. You are expected. Please enter." Sergeant Lyren held open the door for Portia, who entered and was promptly announced by the steward standing just inside the door.

Much to her surprise, Lord Fife was already in the audience chamber despite her having just left his house. He gave her a wink which both amused and irritated her. Even as her teacher, he clearly was not teaching her everything he knew, such as how he could travel the city so quickly. Ignoring the provocation, Portia smoothed her face and concentrated on executing a somewhat decent curtsy. Her skills had improved in the last few weeks with practice.

"Come forward, Portia, Friend of the City," the king said, using the title Portia had earned. Its use caused some in the audience to mutter. Portia was used to this by now and barely heard it.

"Thank you, Your Majesty. I have a letter from my queen stating that I must return."

"We have had similar word and understand the urgency."

Portia gave him a quizzical look. He must have gotten more information from Queen Lorica than she had, but she dared not ask for it explicitly. Her expression must have been transparent, for the king further stated, "They will share more upon your return. Meanwhile, Lord Fife will give us a report of your progress so we can understand how prepared you are."

Upon being mentioned by the king, Lord Fife spoke. "She knows all the healing spells she needs to know, though perhaps not as fluently as one could wish for. I taught a few spells beyond those that might be useful. The only thing now for her is to practice more and often. These are difficult spells."

"Very well," King Magnus said. "We have also had a report from a librarian that she taught you a learning spell."

Learning spell? This was confusing. The only librarian Portia could remember meeting in the Elven kingdom of Rocabarra worked a spell upon her, more of a gift, then having taught her anything. "I didn't learn to cast that spell," Portia tried to explain, "but rather she cast it on me so I may read Elven. With this I was able to read textbooks in your library. But I do not know if I can cast this spell on anyone else."

"I see the distinction. But you can read Elven now?" the king asked.

Portia nodded.

The normally quiet queen spoke. "That could be very useful. Especially if we are at war."

War?

"Indeed," a voice said behind Portia. She turned to see Sergeant Lyren standing behind her. The sergeant turned her attention to the king and queen. "My apologies, Your Majesty, for the interruption. I've received word that the preparations are complete."

"Excellent. I expect that you will leave as soon as possible."

"We will, Your Majesty." Sergeant Lyren gave a small bow. Despite her words, Sergeant Lyren did not move after her bow, waiting for something. Behind her, a guardsman stepped forward carrying a small bundle.

The king motioned for the guardsmen to continue to the base of the dais. King Magnus rose from the massive wooden throne and descended the steps, opening the bundle the guardsman held. Portia gasped. Inside was the sword she had admired in the armory. She recognized the green leather scabbard and knew inside lay the shimmering copper-colored blade that had called to her—the blade she had wanted but dared not take because she had been more comfortable with her own knives.

King Magnus picked up the scabbard with both hands and turned to Portia. She stared at the beautiful weapon then up at his eyes. "This is a gift from the kingdom of Rocabarra to you, young Portia, Jack of Magic. Please accept it and use it to protect us all."

A few unhappy mutters sounded through the watching court.

Portia's skin tingled all over. This was too beautiful a gift. She did not feel worthy. Some in the audience agreed.

Sergeant Lyren leaned in towards Portia and whispered loudly, "Take it, young human. Do not offend our king."

Portia quickly moved forward and bowed, then held out her hands to accept the sword. The king chuckled but didn't admonish his sergeant.

With the sword in her shaking arms, Portia felt the familiar tingle—the vibration that had called her to this blade. It felt like it was a friend to her, although she had only held it but once before. Her fingers curled around the sheath. She wanted to pull the blade free and give a few test swings but didn't dare until she was out of the throne room. Professor Aelric would be interested in seeing it. Perhaps he knew some special techniques for the shorter reach of this elf-designed blade. "Thank you, Your Majesty, thank you."

"You're most welcome, young Portia. Use the knowledge well that we have shared with you. Much depends on it." The king waved her away, dismissing both her and Sergeant Lyren.

As soon as they exited the throne room and the audience

doors shut behind them, Portia turned to Sergeant Lyren. "Did you do this? This sword?" The sergeant glanced at the ceiling and whistled. "You did, didn't you? Thank you. Thank you."

The sergeant gave her a sly smile and then a wink. "Enough of that now. You've got a lot of work ahead of you. Save your energy for that."

Portia's smile dropped a bit at that. "Are you coming with me? Is Lady Harper?" Lady Harper, envoy to the king, had been Portia's guardian of sorts for her entire time in the Elven kingdom. She couldn't imagine leaving without her.

"Sorry to bear bad news, but you only have me as a companion to get you to the border with Haulstatt. The king has another task for Lady Harper. And no, I do not know what it is. But he has promised us two of his fastest sika deer. We should reach the border within two days."

Her heart fell at this news. Lady Harper was not always the friendliest, but Portia had become accustomed to her presence. She had not known the depth of her attachment until now.

"Enough with the long face, young human. I'm sure Lady Harper will find an opportunity to harass you again."

"Harass!" Portia protested, but Sergeant Lyren waved her off.

"Harass, befriend, it's hard to tell sometimes. But enough philosophizing. We're leaving first thing in the morning. There is no sense spending two nights in the road. I for one prefer my warm bed. Be ready to go at dawn. I'll come get you at the tower."

Sergeant Lyren turned away then halted, turning back to Portia. "I almost forgot. This, too, is a gift from the kingdom." She tossed a bag of coins to Portia, who caught it one-handed, careful to not drop the sword she carried.

Nodding at the sergeant, Portia shoved the bag into her own coin purse at her hip. She'd investigate the bag later; first, she wanted to practice with her new sword, the unbelievable gift from King Magnus and Queen Ceola.

The next morning Portia waited, her bags packed, sitting on her bed and watching through the open window as the sky grew light in the east. The sun had not yet risen, but the birds were already awake and singing while the pink and red streaks in the sky grew lighter and lighter.

The metallic clinking of hardware and bridles and saddles drifted up to her window. Portia went to the window. Sergeant Lyren led two saddled deer to the base of the tower. Grabbing her pack, Portia took one final look at the small room she had lived in for several months in the Elven kingdom and then shut the door firmly before racing down the stairs and exiting.

With their bags tied firmly to the saddles, they mounted the deer and exited first the rich inner-city of Rocabarra, the city of royalty and rich merchants, and then passed through the outer city where all others were consigned, the lower-class elves and the scattered humans. Portia had been one of the rare humans ever allowed into the innermost portions of the city. Finally, they exited the outer gates and reached the forest that led to the pass through the mountains and out of the kingdom of Rocabarra.

They traveled through the forest for the rest of the morning, the deer quickly climbing the ever-increasing slope. Finally, after several hours, Sergeant Lyren motioned for them to stop. There was a stream there and a place for the deer to graze. Portia's stomach rumbled as well. She'd not eaten breakfast, and her body was now complaining.

"Always hungry, young human. It must be inconvenient to have to eat so much," the sergeant said. Despite her ribbing, she pulled out two cloth-wrapped packages and tossed one to Portia. Inside were several sandwiches and a few pieces of fruit. Before Portia sat down, she shoved one of the sandwiches in her mouth, took a huge bite, and chewed. It was an especially tasty cheese layered with vegetables and a smooth spread she couldn't name the flavor of. She looked down ruefully at the small sandwiches and wished there were more than just two—her hunger demanded more than that. At least five. Perhaps Sergeant Lyren would not eat all her food. It was amazing how little food the elves got by on.

Before she got a second bite, a snap sounded in the woods next to their resting spot. A bolt knocked the rest of her sandwich from her hand. Portia ducked down and scrambled to get low to the ground. Out of the corner of her eye, she saw Sergeant Lyren do the same thing.

Another bolt whizzed over Portia's head and buried itself into the ground before her.

A scrambling sound alerted Portia to an elf up high in the trees behind them, revealing one of the attackers. Anger welled within Portia as she eyed her sandwich spread out in the dirt. It was too much to not only be shot at, but have her lunch taken away as well.

Singing quietly, she directed her magic towards the elf in the tree. Quickly, the tree's branches wrapped around the elf and grew thicker, the strength of the branches knocking the bow from the elf's hands and pressing his arms tight to his body. He squeaked as the tree hugged hard, the branches tightening.

A branch snapped in the bushes at the base of the tree, giving away the location of a companion. Sergeant Lyren ran into the woods towards the noise. Portia looked around but spotted no others, so she followed the sergeant, pulling her familiar knives from their sheaths as she ran. They were not needed. Sergeant Lyren sat on a second elf attacker and grinned at Portia, looking well pleased. A bow and arrow lay scattered on the ground as well as several knives.

"All under control here, young human. I think this is the only other one."

Portia nodded, too surprised at the situation to think of an immediate response. Standing still to listen, only the faint scrabbling of the elf under Sergeant Lyren reached her ears. "No others?"

Sergeant Lyren pulled herself to her feet and yanked the elf up as well, twisting one of his arms behind his back to keep control of him. "None that I saw or heard. They are arrogant little jerks to come after us with just the two of them. Or just unlucky to pick us to attack."

"You think they would go after anyone?" Portia asked, slipping her knives back into the sheathes at her waist.

"How would they know we'd stop here? Unless..." A dark look crossed Sergeant Lyren's face.

Portia's scalp tingled. "You told someone we were resting here, didn't you?"

"That I did, young human, but it is not proof conclusive. Many take their break here. So, it is impossible to know if they were lying in wait for us in particular, or for any passersby."

"Are there many travelers that pass by here?" Portia was under the impression that not many were allowed into Rocabarra. This wasn't a well-traveled path.

Sergeant Lyren shook her head, confirming her suspicions. "Not many, that is true. Certainly not many humans such as yourself."

A squeak from above caught their attention. The tree whose branches contained the elf had continued to grow even after Portia had stopped singing. His eyes were barely visible over a branch that had grown across his face. He was able to pull in enough air to make some noise but if the tree did not stop growing soon he would suffocate. Portia sang a quick little ditty, inviting the tree to stop and rest, which it obliged. The elf wrapped in its boughs stopped squirming and just lay there panting.

"Didn't work out well for them, did it?" Sergeant Lyren asked, not expecting an answer, while frog marching the elf back to where their deer were tied. Portia followed, gathering up the weapons on the ground as she went.

"Nice work on the growing magic. I take it you learned that little piece of elf magic while in Rocabarra?" the sergeant asked over her shoulder.

Portia could hardly deny it, having used the magic in front of the sergeant, but was loath to admit it. The fewer that knew of her talents, the safer she would be. Luckily, the sergeant was willing to let the question go without an answer.

Tying the prisoner's hands behind his back, Sergeant Lyren then kicked his feet out from under him so he landed on the ground with a thump. "Okay, so where's the rest of your stuff?" She leaned in menacingly. The elf turned away and refused to meet her gaze. Sergeant Lyren pulled a knife from her belt and held it to the prisoner's throat. Portia sucked in her breath at the sudden aggression. "Is your bedroll really worth your life?"

Silence greeted that question. Even the woods, it seemed, was holding its breath waiting for the reply. Finally, the elf slowly turned to meet the sergeant's gaze and shook his head.

"Excellent choice. Shows lots of promise and common sense for such an elf... a surprising amount, considering you're stupid enough to try to rob us. Now speak," Sergeant Lyren commanded.

The elf reluctantly spoke of where their packs were. And riding deer. The attacker that the sergeant had captured had holes in his tunic and breeches, and yellow stains in the armpits of his tunic. His cheeks were gaunt—extremely so. Sergeant Lyren raised her eyebrows at Portia over the prisoner's head when they found the attackers' deer mounts. The saddles were unmarked but of fine quality leather, and the deer themselves gleamed with grooming and good feed. Someone was financing the two attackers, for surely they did not have the funds to buy such deer. More than likely they would have bought food for themselves first.

Sergeant Lyren took the knives and weapons from the two attackers. It had taken nearly half an hour of Portia's efforts of singing a spell to the tree and regrowing the branches in a different direction to free the elf trapped above them. It happened slowly enough that he was able to grab a branch and not fall to the ground. The arrow Sergeant Lyren aimed at his heart was enough of a deterrent for him to not attempt to run. Instead, he climbed down the tree to join his companion in having his arms tied behind his back and sitting in the dirt.

Digging through the attackers' packs, Sergeant Lyren pulled two bundles of food and dropped them in front of the prisoners, as well as a few coins from the full coin purse she'd found within one of the packs, stashing the rest of the money in her own bag much to the furious looks of the prisoners. She then removed the saddles from the deer and slapped them on the hindquarters, sending the animals scurrying off into the forest without riders or hardware.

She turned to address the glaring prisoners. "I don't have time to take you back to the guards, something for which you should be grateful, but I won't allow you to continue to harass us or any others who might come after us. Be thankful you have your freedom today—and your lives. Now I'm going to untie you, and what you're going to do is, you're going to pick up your food and your coins and you will travel in any direction but east. Do you understand me? Because the only other solution I can think of is to kill you both, and I really don't want to have to wash my knife today."

The prisoners' eyes opened wide at that speech. They were afraid enough of Sergeant Lyren to believe she would coolly murder them while they sat there tied helplessly. Portia doubted she would do any such thing, but how well did she really know the sergeant? She chewed her lip and thought on the possibility.

"Now nod if you're going to be good prisoners and scurry off like I told you to." Both prisoners nodded vigorously. As soon as their bonds were removed, they scrambled to their feet, grabbed the food and coins, and ran off into the woods.

"Was that really a good idea?" Portia asked. They had another day and a half of journeying to reach the gate and she did not like the thought of those that meant to do them harm at large. Perhaps they could have tied them up and left them until Sergeant Lyren made her way back again.

As if reading her mind, Sergeant Lyren responded. "Well, we could have left them tied up, but if anything happens to us, they would die just as surely as if I stabbed them right here and now. I don't want to be responsible for that, and I'm not willing to just straight-up kill someone for trying to take our food or whatever they were after. That one had the chance to kill you outright and did not. It would be too much of a coincidence to think it was just because he was a bad shot."

That was probably true. There were many who wanted Portia and any others who were fighting against the splintering stopped, but at least these two had not seemed murderous. But their attack made her feel even more urgently the need to get back to the human kingdom.

The rest of the journey for the next day and a half was uneventful. They raced through the dense growth that marked all the Elven land Portia had seen. Two tall trees were the perfect sleeping place once Portia used her magic to grow secure boughs for their rest.

Finally, they emerged from underneath the dark overhang of the trees to face large green fields spread out before them. Barely visible in the far distance was the Eternal Wall, the elf-made structure designed to keep invaders out of Rocabarra. It looked tiny from where they sat, but Portia knew from experience that it was massive—the largest structure she had ever seen. They spent half a day journeying across the fields on a narrow hard-packed dirt road to get closer to the Wall and the nearest opening in it, which was named the Moss Gate. Much to Portia's dismay and surprise, the double-walled structure looked even larger. It had been fortified extensively in the short time she'd been in Rocabarra.

She wondered at the worth of the elf king's promise to allow human refugees inside that wall if needed, for it looked as if they didn't plan on letting anyone through.

2

When they approached the four arches of the Moss
Gate other changes were apparent. There were
humans, a long trail of them, walking on the road on the inner
side of the wall. Many more than she'd seen the entire time
she had been in the Elven land.

Several elves rode from the gate to join them and ride
escort back. When they drew closer, Portia could make out
more details of humans and elves walking along the inner
barrier of the Eternal Wall. Some carried large packs. A few
pulled small wagons behind them loaded with belongings.
There were children, old men and women, and mothers
holding babies. Even a dog or two. These were not merchants
but families on the move.

Portia looked to Sergeant Lyren for an explanation, but
the sergeant merely shrugged her shoulders. She did not know
what was going on either.

The same elf commander Portia had seen when she had

first entered Rocabarra with Lady Harper greeted them at the wall. He nodded respectfully and addressed Portia. "Was the mission successful?"

His good memory threw Portia a bit. She stammered, "We shall see; it is not yet complete."

"Very good, very good." Turning to the sergeant, he continued in a more familiar manner. "It is good to see you again, although I was hoping there be more reinforcements than just yourself."

"Reinforcements?"

"The soldiers I'd been promised by the king. You will have to do until they arrive." The commander motioned for a soldier to come and take the bridles of the two deer after Sergeant Lyren and Portia dismounted. Portia quickly pulled her pack off before the deer was taken away.

"Ah, that makes things awkward. I was hoping to escort this young human, with the help of a few guards, of course, to Coverack." Sergeant Lyren blocked the commander from walking away.

The commander looked at Sergeant Lyren in surprise. "Coverack? I could hardly do such a thing. We don't have enough bodies here for what the kingdom needs. You will stay and help, Sergeant Lyren."

"Beyond assisting Portia, my superior is expecting my return—" Sergeant Lyren flapped her arms.

"And you will, as soon as I get some help. The situation is dire here. We will send word," the commander said, walking around the sergeant and striding swiftly towards the guard-house. Portia and Sergeant Lyren scrambled after him.

Portia looked uncertainly at Sergeant Lyren and then spoke up to the commander's back, "But I need an escort. It's royal business."

The commander turned at her words, forcing Portia and Sergeant Lyren to skid to a stop to not run into him. "Royal?"

"Queen Lorica—" Portia started.

The commander turned again and quickly walked off, calling over his shoulder, "Human royal business is no business of mine, except perhaps for getting them to do something about all these humans flooding our land."

"But... but..." Portia thought furiously. She needed to get help.

"Go ask the human commander who is squatting in my second guardhouse. *She* can take care of you."

She? Human commander? Things had changed here, for Portia could not remember a human commander when she had passed through before, much less a female one.

When they got closer to the guardhouse they were jostled by all the humans and elves walking quickly by. The commander disappeared into the guardhouse without a backwards glance at either Portia or Sergeant Lyren. Several guards tightly controlled the traffic of humans coming into Rocabarra from the gate separating the inner and outer walls marking the boundary. Portia was loath to exit in case she couldn't reenter again. She wanted to set up a meeting with the other commander before leaving Sergeant Lyren.

"Can you get word to the human commander?" she asked Sergeant Lyren.

"Possibly. Probably. But it will take some time. Meanwhile, you need to be out of the way and not swept away in the crush of this crowd." Sergeant Lyren motioned for Portia to follow her as she walked towards some stairs hidden in the wall some distance from the gate. They climbed the shadowy stairs, dampness seeping into Portia's hair and clothes even though it only took a few minutes to climb the four levels of the Eternal Wall and reach the rooftop ramparts.

"Hang here for a bit, young human. I'll see what I can do," Sergeant Lyren said and then disappeared back down the stairwell.

Portia walked to the edge of the rooftop passageway. It was open to the sky above. A breeze smelling of dense greenery and the smoke of an open cookfire passed over it. Beyond the second wall—the wall facing away from Rocabarra—a ragged line of humans and elves came down from the mountain pass.

One family in particular caught her eye. An elderly man pulled a small cart, trailed by two little girls that could have been twins. Neither of the girls had shoes, and the old man's footwear had holes so large that Portia could see them from her perch on the wall. A blanket moved on the cart, startling Portia. The cover flung down and there was a woman lying on it, clearly ill. The elderly man struggled to control the path of the cart as the slope grew steeper closer to the Eternal Gate. One of the little girls looked up anxiously at the woman in the bouncing cart and reached up for her, holding her outstretched hand.

Portia looked away, anxious for the family and ashamed of the jealousy she felt for the little girl. How could she envy someone so poor and in such dire straits when she had a letter from the queen in her bag and a beautiful sword from the elf king? Still, she wished for a mother's hand to hold.

When she looked back, the family had disappeared into the crush of people further down the road.

It was not a simple journey for these people to reach this gate. How desperate they must be to come here! From what she had recently learned, it was far from a certainty that any refugees would find shelter in the Elven kingdom of Rocabarra—at least human refugees.

Sergeant Lyren was gone for several hours. Portia's stomach growled, but she dared not eat freely of her rations, instead nibbling on a piece of stale bread and the tiniest bit of cheese that she broke off from the hunk in her pack. Her food must stretch since it was a long way to Coverack.

Eventually, an elf guard came and tapped Portia on the shoulder, pulling her attention away from the refugees. "I'm here to escort you to the human commander."

"What about Sergeant Lyren?"

The guard shook his head. "That I do not know of. I only know my orders."

Portia nodded. The day was drawing on, and she needed to make progress on her journey back to Coverack. She would have to trust that all was well with Sergeant Lyren, for surely she was the one responsible for the guard coming to get her.

They descended the dark staircase, the light even dimmer now that the sun was setting. The guard walked her to the interstitial area between the walls marking the end of Rocabarra's land and the beginning of the human domain.

They pushed against the tide of humans coming in the other way and turned the corner to walk along the shadowed area between the inner and outer walls to the guardhouse.

Curiosity finally got the better of Portia. "Who are all these people? Where are they coming from?" The guard did not answer her except to give a halfhearted shrug before knocking on the door to the guardhouse.

A scruffy and sleep-deprived human soldier opened the door and nodded at the elf guard. He must have been expecting Portia, for he did not ask her name, instead shutting the door after she entered and turning and waving for her to follow him as he walked back through the long narrow guardhouse to a dining room at the end. He cleared his throat to get the attention of the occupant of the room.

A formal dining table filled most of the space, but only one place was set. Many dishes were laid out on the table around its sole occupant, a female human commander with gold bars on the shoulders of her uniform. She was bent low over her dish and eating bites of a roast quickly.

The commander motioned for Portia to take a seat near her while the soldier left the room. "My apologies, young lady, but it has been a long day and I'm only just returned. I hear that you have a reason to meet with me?"

Portia stared at the commander. Her age was difficult to discern, but her hair was dark without gray and there was a long scar on her cheek that moved as she chewed. The smell, too, of the roast—well-done and swimming in gravy—was overwhelming. Portia's stomach growled in response. She hoped it was not audible to the commander.

Speaking quickly to cover the noise, she answered the question. "Yes, sir... ma'am." The commander stopped chewing, looked up, and raised her eyebrows. Portia tried again. "Commander."

"General, but commander will do. Don't have the time to wait here for you to get it right by guessing." The general shoved another bite of roast into her mouth, this time topped with carrot and potato.

Portia stared at the food as it disappeared then quickly turned away. "Yes, Commander... General." Her heart pounded. She wasn't sure why she felt so flustered.

"Well?" The general stopped chewing and stared at Portia, taking her in for the first time from head to toe. "How old are you, child?"

"Fourteen, soon to be fifteen." Portia said, lifting her head and straightening her back.

"A blooming teenager. Here, alone. Well you look well-armed. That is impressive. But if you're anything like my nephews, the only teenagers I know, you must be starving." The general rang a small bell that was sitting on the table next to her. A servant appeared at the door, inclining his head at the general and awaiting her orders. "Another plate, please, and glasses and all that. I am being rude to my guest here, and we must correct that."

The servant left the room and soon returned with a plate for Portia and helped dish food from the many platters on the table onto Portia's plate.

The general leaned back in her chair, sipping on a glass of red wine as she watched Portia eat. She pulled a small toothpick from a case on the table and casually used it. Portia snuck glances at her while eating.

All too soon, Portia's plate was empty. The general leaned over the table, picked up a platter of green beans—one of the few plates that still had food left on it—and dumped the contents in Portia's plate. The remainders from the other dishes quickly followed. Portia's face turned red, but she did not protest and gladly acquiesced when the general motioned for her to continue eating.

Finally, all the food was gone, and Portia felt that she could think clearly again. Her thoughts were no longer overwhelmed with the aroma of food and the desire to eat.

"Okay. Let's try this again. Why are you here and why do you need to meet with me? I don't normally take meetings with teenagers, but I have been suitably convinced by an official representative of the royal house of Rocabarra that it is in my best interest to do so with you. Please explain." The general steepled her fingers and stared at Portia.

Portia squirmed for a second then forced herself still. No matter how nice the general seemed, it was not wise to share everything about herself. All the times she'd been attacked was proof of that. Pulling the queen's letter from her pack, she pushed it over the table to the general.

The general opened the letter and scanned it quickly and then looked over at Portia "It is most impressive that you have a letter from Queen Lorica; however, this still does not tell me who you are."

"My name's Portia. I was sent to the Elven kingdom to learn... stuff to help the kingdom. Even I don't know why I'm to return so quickly. Does it have something to do with all these people here?"

"Now is my turn to tell you I don't know," the general said, refilling her glass. "I did not expect to be here, that is for sure, and I'm still trying to gather what's going on. We are expecting an update from Coverack soon. I, for one, cannot figure out why the elves have changed their stance on letting humans inside their gates. I've not seen anything like this in my life." The general pushed the letter back to Portia then leaned back in her chair. "That piece of business also doesn't explain why Rocabarra considers you so important. What are you to the elves?"

A chill settled over the room. Shifting in her seat, Portia suddenly felt unable to make eye contact with the general.

"As a commanding officer here, I expect my questions to be answered."

Still looking down, words poured out of Portia. "The king called me 'A Friend of the City'. I was able to help out a few important elves. And in return I was given some knowledge and granted a favor. The king, King Magnus, said he would allow humans into the country if they needed shelter."

"You? You want me to believe that a child convinced the king of the elves to allow all these people shelter after eons of warfare and distrust?"

I don't care if you believe it, Portia thought but bit her tongue against saying it out loud. It would not help her case. "Perhaps they had already planned to do so. They did not tell me why."

"I should think not. Affairs of state are complex matters."

The general paused, looking up in thought. "But you do have their regard, as well as Queen Lorica's. That is a significant accomplishment for anyone." Portia held her breath, and the general tapped her fingers together in thought. Finally, she looked to Portia again. "You have my respect for that alone. Well, you have your meeting with me. To what purpose?"

Trying to still the impatience she felt, Portia intentionally adopted a soft tone in her voice, "I am requesting an escort to Coverack. And a horse. My only goal is fulfilling the queen's request of my return as quickly as possible."

A barking laugh greeted that speech. "A horse? And an escort? Child, I can give you neither of those things right now. Have you seen what is going on outside? I do not have enough soldiers as it is. Thieves, the dirt of the earth, are preying upon those poor people out there, making a bad situation even worse. Our supply wagons are being attacked near constantly. We can send word to Coverack and request more help from them, and they will give it if you are so important to them, but that is not something I can provide you." The general leapt to her feet and paced the room, agitated.

Looking down, Portia's face burned with the reference to thieves as the dirt of the earth. Thieving was not a good thing, she could see that, but sometimes there was no choice. Starving was worse. Had this general never been hungry a day in her life? How about for a week or month? The room closed in, the air feeling scarce; the urge to run out the door was almost unbearable. But she would not run. She had done nothing wrong, not here anyway. There were those who were depending on her return. Letting them down was not a choice.

"Could I not even buy a horse? Or rent one?"

"No, sadly. The resources cannot be spared." The general's expression softened. "It would take under two weeks for an escort to reach here, and you are welcome to stay for the duration. You would be useful helping with the refugees."

"That is too long. I must get back."

"If you leave on your own, you might not make it back. Surely you are aware of that?"

Portia nodded.

When Portia did not speak further, the general huffed and then rang the bell on the table. "You will stay the night at least. I'm sure even you can see the folly of setting off at sundown. We have a bed and can spare you some food for the road."

"Thank you," Portia said, rising from her chair and gathering her pack. She followed the servant out of the dining room and down the hall to a small room the size of a closet. There was only a small wooden bed with a pallet on it, hay sticking out from a few holes in the ticking. Exhaustion from the day's events overcame her, and she was asleep moments after laying down on the mattress.

A RIPPING SOUND tore across the night with a booming echo. People camping on the land below screamed, running from their tents as the ground shook violently, tossing many of them from their feet.

An enormous shadowy face filled the black gap in the night sky, its red eyes burning like two small stars. Fingers reached down impossibly far until they touched Portia's shirt and lifted her, pulling her up and away from her world while frantic people grabbed at her feet to hold her back.

Portia awoke with a start, drenched with sweat and her feet tangled in the lattice work of the foot board. Her heart raced. It was another dream of the splinter between worlds, the opening that would allow others to come into their world. It was not something Portia or anyone alive had ever seen, and Portia fervently hoped it was nothing like her imagination.

The room was still dark, but since there were no windows it was impossible to tell what time it was. She grabbed her bag and exited the room to find someone or the exit. She needed to go.

The dining room was dim and quiet with no evidence of any recent use. Even the bell for the servants was gone. The glow of sunrise shone through one narrow window. Remembering her route from the previous night, Portia exited the dining room in the direction she hoped was towards the main door, nearly knocking over a servant who held a large package wrapped in muslin.

Quickly reining in his irritation, he gave her a small bow and then held out the package. Surprised, she took it and peeked inside. It was provisions: bread, dried fruit and nuts, cheese, and even some meat. A note was enclosed, *'Travel safe — Gen. A. Bancrot.'* The day was already going better.

The servant led her to the front door without her even requesting it. She gave him a small bow, unsure of the protocol in that situation. He held the door while suppressing a smile at her awkward acknowledgment.

The morning was cool, with the sun just above the horizon. Dew soaked the grass. The dust from the dirt road was temporarily gone in the still air but would more than likely return with the heat of the day. There were no travelers yet coming down the road from the mountain pass. Only a few soldiers paced the gravel pad in front of the gate.

Portia checked her belongings one last time before setting out: her knives were all in their sheaths, the precious sword securely strapped to her back, her coin purse tucked within her tunic, and the pack with everything else slung back across her shoulders, sharing the space with her sword. Adding the food to her pack made the load uncomfortably heavy. Portia resolved to walk slower to reduce the strain on her back and knees. There were worse problems than being weighted down with provisions. It would be several weeks' journey to Coverack if she had to walk the entire way. Hopefully, carriages were still running through Holne, the small hamlet on the road before Coverack, and she could purchase transit from there.

The guards at the outer gate nodded and opened the gate without her having to say a word.

Inhaling the fresh morning air deeply, Portia set out on the road leading over the mountain to the human kingdom.

As the morning wore on, the cool air gave way to a brilliant sunny day. The road sloped more steeply upward to meet the mountain, passing through tall rock outcroppings with sections cut into the rock that offered brief respites of shade. Sweat poured down Portia's back. The faint tinkle of water over rocks spoke of the river running along the pass. If the journey had been less urgent, she would have swum in the crystal-clear waters.

Groups of travelers came from the other direction. Most looked to the ground, with only the occasional child meeting her gaze with a smile. The adults were subdued and would not greet her even after determining Portia was not a threat. Anxiety increasingly gnawed at Portia as yet another family passed by in a cloud of despair, their mood dark.

In one stretch between upward slopes, where there was little other than rocks and a small copse of trees, the whinny of a horse cut through the air, an unusual sound. None of the travelers she'd seen that day had been mounted. Curious, Portia walked to the copse. A flicker of a horse's tail moved within the trees.

She stepped within the trees. Two horses grazed on the sparse undergrowth, no one else around. Portia reached out to grab one of the horse's bridles, for they had tack and saddles, but jumped back again when a boy jumped down from the tree above. He jabbed a small knife in her direction and crouched, ready for a fight. Portia cursed herself for not having seen him first.

"What cha think you're doin'?" He scowled and tried to look fierce. The boy could not have been more than twelve and did not even reach her shoulder. But Valencia had taught her that even small ones could be deadly so she gave a respectful distance.

"My apologies, I did not see anyone around," she said, keeping her voice low and relaxed. The boy was at least as dirty, if not as thin, as other travelers she'd seen on the road. "Would you be willing to sell the horse?"

He squinted at her, eyeing her clothing and pack. "I dunno. They be my Granpapa's. You'll have to git with him and see un' he says."

"Okay. Is he here?"

"Ay, that he is," a deeper voice spoke from the copse. An elderly man stepped from behind one of the trees and faced Portia. "So you want to buy a horse. They're the only thing we rescued in the mess, so it'll come dear, missy." He wore the deep velvet waistcoat of a merchant, but it was dirty and torn. The britches below were equally filthy. It was an odd sight to see such fine clothes unclean and in disrepair.

"I can pay." Portia stood taller under their scrutiny.

"We'll see. Four platinum."

Portia sucked in her breath. Four platinum was two hundred gold pieces—more money than she'd ever seen in her life. But she needed that horse.

Stalling, she checked her purse and found only a few gold amongst the silver and copper, and the small bag that Sergeant Lyren had tossed to her in Rocabarra. She'd forgotten about it in the rush to leave. Pulling the thin leather strap that held it tight, she pulled it open. It was full of platinum coins!

Stopping her gasp, she kept her face impassive, even as a

tingle of shock ran over her scalp. It would be unwise to give away how much the purse held to these two. They did not look aggressive, but even so, desperation could make people do strange things.

"That is a steep price. How about two platinum?"

The boy's eyes widened. "How be you have two platinum?" He looked her up and down, reevaluating. If it had just been the boy, Portia probably could have talked him into it, but the elderly gentleman shook his head.

"We lost everything, Missy. Four platinum. If ye do not have it, best be on your way." He waved her away, but a rack of coughing gripped him, and he bent over double, spitting blood onto the ground. Panic crossed the boy's face.

Portia looked past the old man and saw a small fire with a tiny pot on a stand over the flames. A small pile of bedding sat nearby but no food. "Have you eaten today?"

Waving her away again, the old man sat down on the ground until the spasms left his chest. The boy gave Portia a dirty look and sat next to his grandfather.

Biting her lip, she looked down the road trying to figure out what to do. Horses were few and far between. The old man was sick, that much was clear, but she needed to get back to Coverack. Many more lives possibly depended on it. They had two horses. Buying one would not leave them abandoned.

"All right, four platinum but on the condition that you break your fast with me." At the boy's hostile glance Portia quickly continued. "My supplies will provide our meal. And he must drink some tea." She motioned to the old man, and the boy slowly nodded in agreement, a little stunned at their good fortune.

Luckily, there were herbal bushes growing in the copse that would help the old man's chest spasms. The same bushes grew in Merit's garden in Rocabarra. Gathering up some leaves, she crushed them and put them into the small pot with some water from the nearby stream. While the tea brewed, she passed around food from the muslin packet she had been given that morning, giving especially large servings to both the boy and the old man.

They ate quickly, almost against their will, for they looked down and would not make eye contact while eating. This behavior she understood from having been hungry in the past —it was near impossible to eat slowly with a stomach so empty that filling it consumed all thoughts. Looking away for their dignity's sake, she chewed her own lunch. She could afford to share now that she had a horse to travel quickly.

"So why are you going back?" the old man asked when he had finished his meal. He poured tea for the three of them, moving slowly.

"I don't know what you mean," Portia said.

"Back." He gestured up the trail towards the mountain pass.

Portia squinted at him, trying to understand the question. "I'm going to Coverack. I have business there."

The old man nodded. "Brave girl."

"Or stupid," the boy muttered as he kicked at the ground.

"Hush." Putting his hand on the boy's head briefly to quiet him, the old man sat down again.

Portia stared. "What's going on? What is back there? No one at the gate knew—or would tell me anyway."

The old man nodded. "Ay, ye don't know. That be explaining it."

"Will you be so kind as to tell me what you're talking about?" Portia forced her voice to remain soft and patient.

"They took Jukhnovo. Them others. Our home. People fleeing, the city in flames. We were looted of cash and easy goods by those fleeing. Luckily them horses were hidden in the woods on our grounds or they would have gotten those too."

"Others? What others?"

"I dunno, to be honest. We never saw them, just the destruction they caused. Didn't seem the smart thing to stick around to greet them."

Jukhnovo was the human kingdom to the north of Haulstatt. It, too, bordered the sea. Portia's lunch was heavy in her stomach. Could '*the others*' mentioned by these two be from the splintering? If so, would they be as bloodthirsty as the author of the book she held in her bag?

"Where did the others come from?" she asked finally. At their puzzled looks she clarified. "Did they come from the sea?"

"That's what a bunch of them fleeing told us. Said we should run, and fast," the boy said, kicking at the ground. Rising suddenly, he paced a few times then walked quickly further into the copse.

The old man hunched his shoulders. "Seems that's the case... their being from the sea, or that direction a'how." He rose and kicked dirt over the fire, gathering the few cups and knives they had.

Taking that cue, Portia rose and packed her belongings. Thoughts raced through her head of what could be happening in the kingdom of Jukhnovo, and what might now be happening in Haulstatt, her own kingdom. Coverack, it's capital, lay right on the sea. Was it still safe? Were her friends safe? Was the queen?

Desperately, she wished for her friend Mia's knowledge right now, for she couldn't recall any of the geography of Jukhnovo except that it was somewhere north of Haulstatt. She didn't even have an idea of how far north. Mia though, one of the nobles at the Magic Academy, had an in-depth knowledge of nearly everything. Her father had paid for the most learned of tutors, and had ensured they took their jobs most seriously, much to Mia's chagrin.

Returning, the boy approached Portia. Tapping her on the shoulder, he turned away awkwardly to avoid eye contact and spoke in a rush. "Sorry to call you stupid. Be safe. Thank you for feedin' us."

Portia could not help but smile. "You're welcome. Now let's all get out of here before the day is gone."

Returning her smile, he gave a nod then went to retrieve the horse he still owned.

Before she left, Portia helped the boy tie two of the coins in his hair so they lay hidden at the nape of his neck, and then did the same for the old man. She gave them a few loose coppers in addition so they wouldn't have to use such a valuable coin as a platinum for a small purchase. She planned on doing the same with the other platinum coins when she had some distance from them, not wanting to pull out the remainder of the coins in front of them.

The last thing she did was to tell them to mention her name to General A. Bancrot if they needed any help. It was only a few hours by foot, and much less by horse to the Moss Gate and the Eternal Wall. They should be able to make it unmolested that short distance.

Watching them disappear down the pass towards Rocabarra, she felt some melancholy. The horse beneath her shifted uneasily, perhaps missing its mate that was leaving with the boy and old man. Portia turned to face the pass leading up the mountains. Once again, she was alone, but at least this time she had a horse.

3

Even sparing the horse by keeping a moderate pace, Portia still made good time and reached Holne in less than a week. Truthfully, she could have pushed faster but wanted the animal fresh in case they had an urgent need of speed. Better still, she was not exhausted and felt able to defend both herself and the horse in the event they were attacked. Luckily, there had been no such ill fortune. The only other travelers on the road were refugees going in the other direction. They looked too drained by their own ordeal to cause her any problems.

A few of the more prepared travelers had let her buy evening meals from them. She paid with coins from her regular purse; the platinum coins were hidden, tied in her hair and scattered within her clothing. She did not dare pull out something so large unless for the most dire of circumstances.

From a distance, Holne looked the same as she remembered it. It was a small town on the road to the capital city,

Coverack, and she'd last passed through on her journey with Lady Harper of the Meadows, an elf envoy, on her way to the Elven kingdom. It had only been a few months ago but somehow felt like a year. While the town still had its finely trimmed houses and greenery, the town square was now crowded with people, wagons, and horses when Portia rode into it. The Inn was so busy that coaches backed up in front of it, the coachmen waiting for an ostler to come. People poured in and out the front door. Most were well-to-do, but there were groups of more disheveled and dirty folk who carried their belongings in sacks slung over their shoulders.

Looking longingly at the Inn, Portia thought of a hot bath and a meal to follow, but she had business to do before then. Her first job was to get back to Coverack, and for that she wanted an escort as protection against any ambush, such as the one she had experienced on her last journey from Coverack. Nine elves had died in that fight, and another one nearly so. She felt lucky to have survived. For that reason, the ride to Coverack was not one Portia wanted to make on her own.

Dismounting, she walked her horse through the crowd towards the guardhouse. When the face of the building was finally visible, the difference in its appearance stunned her. Previously, it had been the most rundown building in the town. But now... now it had fresh paint and patched walls; newly forged bars protected the windows. Soldiers walked in and out in groups, many more than had been present during her last visit.

Tying her horse to a post outside the door, Portia pushed her way into the entrance. There were so many people inside that it took some time to scan the crowd for the close-cropped white hair of the older captain or the dark hair of young Lieutenant Jassock. The younger man had led the escort on the journey from Holne to Rocabarra. She would have even welcomed seeing Zeck, the surly old guard who gave her nothing but grief on the journey to Rocabarra.

After several minutes, she finally located the white hair of the captain. Pushing her way through the room and edging around soldiers, she reached his desk near the back wall.

He looked up as she neared and nodded acknowledgment but his eyebrows drew together as he looked around her. "Where is Lieutenant Jassock?"

"I... I don't know," Portia said, confused. "Should I know?"

"Of course you should—after escorting you through the pass. Or is he off coddling that horse of his again?" The captain looked at her expectantly, but his words made things no clearer for her.

"That was many months ago. He could be anywhere now."

The captain eyebrows shot up. "Are you saying he did not escort you here?"

"No." Portia shook her head. "There was no one for me. There wasn't even a horse. I had to buy my own on the road and was lucky to do so." Alarm set her arm hairs upright. Where was the lieutenant? What had happened to her escort?

The captain stood. "That's not good. But at least you're here, safe." He scowled and looked around. "You need tending to, but I need to find out what has happened to my men. To Lieutenant Jassock. He is not the sort to take his duty lightly."

Portia nodded her head in agreement. Jassock had been amiable but also run through with steel when it came to carrying out his orders. It would have been good to have him by her side.

The captain waved over an assistant who approached quickly and nodded respectfully. "As of now, our escort to Rocabarra is missing. Summon the lieutenants for a meeting." The assistant ran off to do his bidding. Turning his eyes once again to Portia, he motioned for her to sit down. "Well, now we must get you to Coverack, no?"

"Yes. I was hoping for an escort after last time." Portia shifted in her chair. Looking around at all the people and commotion in the room, she turned back to the captain. "What is going on? Is it the bandits? Have you found more cult members?"

"Ay, that we have, but that is not the worst of our problems. We are inundated with refugees. I must leave those in Coverack to tell you more, if you don't learn of it on the road." At Portia's questioning look he continued. "My orders—my very specific orders—are to tell no one more details than needed. And I'm afraid that includes you. We'll get you to Coverack as soon as we can, and you'll learn what you need to know." He looked slightly abashed but firm.

Portia pushed down her indignation at being kept in the dark. It would do her no good. She would find out as much information as she could along the way. There were too many refugees and eyewitnesses to keep anything much of a secret.

Nodding, Portia smoothed her breeches to break eye contact.

"We'll be able to go in the morning. There's no sense leaving at this time of day, not with the bandits still active—and they are. You should go see about a room for tonight if the Inn has any left. We have nothing here. I can barely house my own men."

"I'll do that." Portia rose to leave.

"Sunrise. Don't be late," the captain called after her.

Portia waved but kept walking. The room felt suddenly overfull. She hurried with the need to get outside to breathe some fresh air, even if it was nearly as crowded. At least there was blue sky and somewhere close lay open spaces.

Outside the guardhouse, she glanced down the street to the clothier she had frequented several times before. A group of women were just exiting. On impulse she strode down to the shop, leaving her horse tied up in front of the guardhouse. It would be fine for now. No one would dare molest it in front of the soldiers though, she would still need to be quick since it did need feed, a good rubdown, and some water.

Somehow, miraculously, inside the clothing shop was just as calm and quiet as it always was. Even though there were more people inside it than on previous visits, the stillness of the air was the same. The voices inside were muted, leaving it remarkably peaceful.

Alice, the owner of the shop, walked towards her, recognizing Portia immediately. Her gaze took in Portia, who did her best to hold her chin up: she was dirty from the road, which seemed to be her constant state when entering the shop.

"Greetings, child," she said warmly.

"Good afternoon, ma'am." At Alice's sharp look Portia quickly corrected herself. "Alice."

"Much better. So, the greens agreed with you this time? Were they useful?" Alice asked solicitously.

"Yes, they were. Unfortunately." The last time Portia had visited the shop she had purchased a doublet, jacket and breeches of a sturdy green canvas, specifically chosen for ease-of-use during fighting. They had come in handy, leaving her better able to defend herself than if she had been encumbered in a kirtle with its long skirt and tight bodice.

The clothier's eyes lingered on the sword strapped to her back, squinting a bit at the high-quality sheath and hilt. Conscious of Portia's notice, she moved her gaze onwards and pretended to not be surprised by the fine weapon. "You come back bearing prizes?"

"Yes, of a sort, though it does me little good strapped to my back. Would you have anything here to place it in a better position?" The question felt awkward. "To use in a hurry if I need it." Surely there was a proper name for the gear she needed to hang the sword by her side where it could be drawn quickly in an emergency. Perhaps it was something she should be buying from a saddler.

"May I see?" Alice asked, holding her hand out.

Portia nodded reluctantly. She only had the sword for a short time, but already it felt like a part of her own body. It felt odd to remove it from its position and hand it over to another person. Ignoring the slight chill that ran up her arm, she placed the sheathed blade in Alice's palm.

Alice weighed the weapon in her hand and tested the balance. She was taller than Portia so it could not have fit her well. The blade was perfectly proportioned for Portia, surprisingly so, considering it was from the elf kingdom. But then some elves were taller than she'd thought possible.

Nodding approval, Alice handed back the weapon then walked to a cupboard in the corner of the shop. Returning, she held out a dark leather baldric that was nearly the same color green as the sheath itself. Putting it over Portia's head, she laid it along her chest and showed her how to strap the sword's sheath within the adjustable sleeve designed to hold it fast.

Stepping back for room, Portia reached for the sword with her right hand and withdrew it quickly, the rasp of the blade leaving its sheath attracting attention from others in the shop. The baldric positioned the sword perfectly, and the motion had taken little effort. Suppressing her smile with effort, Portia downplayed her joy in front of the unwanted audience now surrounding her. Curious eyes looked at the fine copper-colored blade and then at the small girl holding it.

One set of eyes belonged to a tall man in well-worn linens, who took on an especially greedy look that made Portia regret her indiscretion. He flexed his thin fingers and eyed the sword appreciatively while stepping towards Portia.

Backing up, she quickly returned the blade to its sheath and then walked out of the circle of people now around her. Thankfully, she would have an escort tomorrow. Even so, it would be better not to let anyone see where she was sleeping tonight, if at all possible.

Drawing Alice aside, Portia said quietly, "It is a beautiful piece of equipment. What's your price?" She pulled out her money bag.

"For you, two silver." Alice winked. "You're turning into a regular customer."

The price was more than fair, and Portia handed over the two silvers, thinking it strange to find herself a regular customer of anybody. It made her feel more like an adult than anything else she had done in her life. The only regulars she'd had in Valencia were the regulars she stole from. Her face turned a little red even now at the memory. But when one was starving, one did what one must.

"Anything else I can do for you, young friend?"

"No, no. Not today. I must go." Many of the others hovered uncomfortably close by. The tall man was still staring, but at least he had not approached again. She would have to make sure he didn't follow on the street.

"Very well. Until next time." Alice waved as Portia exited, then quickly stepped in front of the tall man, asking what she could do for him while effectively blocking his exit.

Portia trotted back down the square towards the guardhouse, breathing a sigh of relief as she spied her horse still tied up in front. Unhooking the reins from the pole, she walked back to the Inn, glancing behind her occasionally to see if the tall man was following her. He was nowhere in sight, but that did not mean he was not there.

Leaving the horse with an ostler and strict instructions for his care, she ran up the stairs to the main room of the Inn. The innkeeper was behind the bar, wiping it furiously and looking harried. Servers ran back and forth between the kitchen and the tables. Portia pushed her way to the bar to get the innkeeper's attention.

"Room for tonight, please," Portia said.

"Ha! Good luck with that. I don't have room for half these folk. You think I'd be happy, but no, sad surprise to find there is such a thing as too much business." At Portia's crestfallen look, he relented. "Sorry, lass, shouldn't be taking it out on you." He squinted at her and stood back to get a better look at her. "Weren't you here with that important elf lady?"

"Yes, that was me." Portia nodded with relief, feeling a bit hopeful that some space could be made for her.

"That 'twas strange to have an elf here, but she was a good tipper. Any chance she's coming back? Ah, I don't know why I am asking; I don't have room for her either." The keeper moved away down the bar, not waiting for an answer from Portia.

Portia pushed along the bar, squeezing through the crowd in front of it and trying to keep the innkeeper's attention.

"Sir, do you at least have space for my horse and some hay and oats I might buy?" she called after him. "Sir!" she called louder when he did not stop, drawing irritated looks from others, some of whom pushed back at her in response to her jostling.

The innkeeper stopped and turned back to Portia. "Ay, you're in luck, lass. So many on foot there's room for your horse. It'll cost you though. We're running out of feed even so."

Portia nodded. She could and would pay to keep her mount in good condition. It had calmed down after initially leaving its mate outside of Rocabarra, but the chaos in town and the smell of fear from many of the refugees caused a great deal of agitation. A stall, if nothing else, was a quieter place.

"I'll pay double for permission to sleep there too. And meals."

Her offer won a small smile from the innkeeper. "Dinner only."

"Agreed." Portia shoved a silver coin over the bar to the innkeeper, who quickly stashed it on his person.

"He'll show you a spot," the innkeeper said, pointing to a servant standing at the rear of the room.

Following the servant out the back door, Portia breathed a sigh of relief with the sudden quiet and space around her. In the back courtyard were several horses being washed and brushed, but otherwise it was blissfully empty of people. The servant showed her to the pump, who to ask for feed, and found the ostler who was now watering her horse.

The stall itself was well cleaned out and laid with fresh hay. Being located at the far end of the barn, it was quieter than being in the middle and further from the Inn. More importantly, it was close to a door, the barn itself having the rare luxury of an entrance at each end. The thief training in Portia valued access to a quick exit.

After attending to the horse's needs, which included a long brushing with the fine tools the inn stocked, Portia looked around the stall considering security that night. She had already attracted too much attention in town and must assume that someone with ill will knew where she was and intended no good that night. She considered laying nodes of light magic as a trap around her but knew that magic would startle the horses if set off. Panicked horses were no small matter—they could kick out and cause direct injury, or worse yet, run and knock over a lantern and cause a disastrous fire.

No, she needed something less flashy but still enough to stop a possible intruder in the middle of the night.

Finally, she settled on using ice magic. It was more difficult for her, especially so since she would have to conjure the water as well, but it would be worth it to stop an intruder without frightening her animal or the other animals in the building. Laying nodes around her stall, she concentrated on the floor by the entrance as well as the top of the stall all the way around to the back wall. This would prevent someone from entering a neighboring stall and climbing over the wall. There were too many servants in and out with horses to lay any magical traps by the main doors. The ones around her stall would have to do.

Dinner was a hot cabbage stew and some crusty brown bread. Portia ate it quickly in the crowded main room. Her eyes were drooping as it was; it would be only harder to stay awake once her belly was full. Escaping the loud room as soon as she was finished, she made her way back to the stable and the quiet of the stall where her horse was standing with his eyes already closed.

That night, her sleep was disturbed by her frequent nightmare of the sky opening up. Even sleeping she recognized it was a dream, having experienced it so often, but it was still terrifying. This time, cold poured out of the sky and booming noises permeated the dream.

Portia woke with a start, a chill passing over her body. She lay shivering, trying to remember where she was. A rooster crowed in the background and the gentle shuffling of the horses in the stalls brought her memory back to the barn in the inn yard. Her own mount leaned down and nuzzled her.

Rubbing his forehead, she breathed in the clean smell of the horse.

"Good morning, sunshine." He nickered in response.

A cold drop of water landed on her head and ran down her neck. Portia jumped at the unexpected chill, then looked up and focused at the stall wall. There was melting ice at the top of it. A magic node had been set off!

Scrambling to her feet, she felt around herself for her knifes and her money belt. All was there. Reaching under the bed of hay she found the sword and baldric still safe. Her bags were unopened in the corner. Whoever or whatever had set off the magic had not taken anything from her.

Examining the stall wall, she found a few spots of blood on the other side. The intruder must have panicked when the ice encased their limbs and struggled too hard to free themselves, causing injury in the process. But it had not been enough to keep them there. Only the horses looked at her curiously as the morning light started to filter in the slates of the barn. The intruder was gone.

Portia blew out hard and rubbed her arms. It was bad that

she slept through the whole thing. She was lucky indeed. It would have been bad if they had found her sleeping with no defenses.

She couldn't help but feel as if she was still being watched as she gave her horse breakfast then ran into the inn to buy her own. They only had fruit and bread and a tiny slab of cheese she talked the barmaid into letting her buy. It would have to do.

It didn't take long to saddle her horse and make it over to the guardhouse. Luckily, not many travelers were up yet so it was easier to cross the square. It was also easier to watch for any attackers. Portia felt silly, but she couldn't stop looking around. Even as a thief in Valencia she hadn't acted nervous. Perhaps it was the thought of getting attacked again on the road to Coverack.

The guardsmen were waiting outside for her, their horses tied to the post in front. She didn't recognize any of them. The man in charge stepped forward and waved at Portia.

"You must be our charge," he said. "I can't imagine there are many girls with such a fine mount leaving at dawn. I'm Lieutenant Royck."

"Hello," Portia said, looking around at the men. They were well-armed and fit. She had some misgivings that there were only four but tried to push those feelings aside.

"There's no use dallying. If we hurry, we might yet have our supper in Coverack tonight. I've no appetite for sleeping on the road," the lieutenant said.

Mounting the horses, they rode out of Holne.

It was a beautiful morning. Portia was glad to be out in the sunshine and away from the town. The birds were singing, and the fields shone with dew under the morning light. The only thing marring the view were some rags on the road left by travelers. Refugees.

Portia glanced at the lieutenant as they rode, trying to judge if he would share information. He had an easy open smile and seemed completely relaxed. The other men rode in silence around them.

"Thank you for the escort," Portia said. "It was not an easy journey the last time."

"So I've heard," the lieutenant answered. "Jassock warned me about you. You do know, don't you, to not run after any bandits we might see?"

Portia whipped to face him, feeling defensive, but before she could say anything, he laughed out loud.

"Don't worry, we'll take care of everything," he said, mirth still in his voice.

Portia's face burned. She had not done anything wrong, and certainly she had been much quieter than Lieutenant Jassock's men in their encounter with the bandits. This man's arrogance grated unpleasantly on her nerves.

"Lieutenant Jassock wasn't with us when we encountered the bandits on the way from Coverack. That was Lady Harper, the Elven convoy from Rocabarra, and two Coverack guards. They killed everybody but Lady Harper and I, and that was close." She couldn't help herself from further saying with some venom in her voice, "There are only four of you."

The light in his eyes went dark at that and he nodded. "That is true. We are well aware of our danger. All I'm saying is that you have some spirit." He locked eyes with her. "That's not a bad thing."

Portia nodded and looked away, mollified.

They rode in silence for the rest of the morning. The road, initially so empty, soon filled up with refugees coming from Coverack. She had not seen any going their direction. Since they were on horseback, they would have overtaken any on foot. There just were none.

Sometimes when they passed the refugees, she could hear them speaking. They spoke the common tongue but their accent was unfamiliar to her. It lilted in a way she couldn't remember hearing in Coverack. The snatches of conversation were tantalizing, but they rode by so fast as to never overhear more than a few words here and there.

Taking a break from the noon sun, they stopped under the shade of a few trees by the road and had lunch. Portia's breakfast was long gone, and she was glad the guardsmen had some provisions for her. Their resting point had only a few trees, surrounded on all sides by plains for lengths around; it would be difficult for anyone to sneak up on them.

After watering her horse at the small stream by the trees and setting it in front of a fine patch of grass, Portia sat down to eat the sandwiches the guardsmen had handed her. Lieutenant Royck was nearly finished with his meal already since one of the other men was busy taking care of his horse.

"The refugees have an odd way of talking," Portia said.

Lieutenant Royck nodded but didn't take her bait. He chewed his sandwich and looked out at the scenery.

"Where are they from?" Portia asked, giving up all

pretense of disinterest.

Lieutenant Royck stared at her, raising his eyebrows at her boldness. Finally swallowing, he answered as he rose. "Jukhnovo. North Jukhnovo. The seaside villages." He brushed crumbs from his britches and rose. "No more questions. I think you know our orders," he said then walked away.

Portia stared after him. Jukhnovo. That matched what the old man had told her, but he had been from a city, not a seaside village. Whatever had happened there was widespread. Again, Portia wished that Mia was with her. Mia knew so much history that surely she would know about Jukhnovo. But she would be back to Coverack soon enough and could ask Mia in person.

To her great relief, Portia's fears about the journey were unfounded. They rode through the rest of the afternoon passing more and more refugees, and even some refugee camps set by the side of the road, but encountered no bandits. The peaceful quiet of the morning gave way to the clank of pots and metal tripods on fires, kids running, and parents calling after them.

But the worst camps were the ones that were quiet, where no kids laughed, and the folk were so tired and worn they didn't even speak. Portia's stomach tightened in anxiety when they passed by those, the urge to stop and help nearly overwhelming. But they were on a schedule, and she doubted the guardsmen would halt even if she had asked. Their task was to get her to Coverack, and they wished to do so before nightfall for their own opportunity to sleep in a bed, as well as discharging their duties.

It was well after dark before the city rose up against the sea that had been in their sights for several hours. The market outside Coverack was many times larger than she remembered from just a few months past. It was filled with tents for living quarters as well as market stalls. Irate city guards strode through it yelling and trying to keep order.

They reached the gate as the ninth bell rang. Despite the gate closing in an hour there was still a long line of people trying to get in. The smell of bodies pushed tightly together overwhelmed Portia. Her horse shifted side to side and blew out his nostrils.

Lieutenant Royck motioned for Portia to join the line along with several of his men while he and another rode to the front to see what was going on. He was back within only a few minutes and motioned for her and the other men to ride with him to the front of the line.

"Show the guards your letter," Lieutenant Royck said to Portia.

She pulled the letter from her bag and handed it over to a guard. The guardsman was not familiar to her and his look unfriendly. Examining the broken seal carefully before reading the letter, he handed it back to Portia with more respect than he had shown when he had grabbed the parchment from her hands.

"All right, you all can enter," he said curtly, motioning Portia and the men to enter the gate.

But their way through the gate was blocked by other city guards processing people in line. Most were getting turned away and refused entrance to the city. One burly city guard pushed a small child and mother, stumbling, into the people behind them.

"No entrance. You've 'eard the commander. Stop trying," he said roughly. The small child whimpered and tried to hide in his mother's skirts.

Portia's horse whinnied and tossed its head against the reins. Portia loosened her grip on the leathers and breathed in deeply, trying to keep calm while watching the scene, her back stiff with fury at the guardsman. The woman and child disappeared back into the darkness of the market outside the city. Portia fervently hoped they would be all right.

"I said enter!" the city guard who had read Portia's letter said, impatience and anger in his tone. Portia whipped around to face him again, then glanced at the other guardsmen who had escorted her. They looked as nonplussed as she felt. Biting her lip from saying anything rash, she merely nodded, and they rode around the unhappy refugees in the gate entrance and into the city of Coverack. Whatever had happened in her absence had changed the city she remembered. Something was very wrong.

"Come on, we have orders to go directly to the palace," Lieutenant Royck said, his face serious. The happenings at the gate disturbed him as well.

They rode quickly through the near empty streets of the city towards the palace.

Much to Portia's surprise, the full court was present in the throne room. Angry faces and mutterings gave away that a conflict had been argued there that evening, something that was still not resolved.

After Portia and her guards were announced, she was motioned to approach the throne. Dark circles showed under Queen Lorica's eyes, and she sat a little less straight than Portia remembered. King Consort Aldis leaned to one side of his throne, his eyes glittering as he looked around at the muttering nobles.

"Welcome back, Portia, Jack of Magic," Queen Lorica said.

"Thank you, Your Majesty," Portia said, uncomfortable with the tension in the room. Looking around, she couldn't quite figure what was going on. No one was happy. And the queen was exhausted.

"Did you learn what you needed to, young Jack? We hope so, for we have great need of you now," the queen said.

"Yes, Your Majesty, I believe I did learn it." Portia bit her lip nervously. She had *barely* learned the magic. Just enough. It would've been better to stay longer and become stronger in her abilities. But she dared not say so to the queen. "I need to practice though."

"We expected as much. We had no choice but to call you back. You saw the conditions of the road?" The queen touched her forehead for a moment before straightening up again.

"I did. All those people from Jukhnovo. Who would do such a thing as to attack them?"

The king consort's eyes shifted to Portia. He gave her a small nod.

"Yes, you are perceptive. Or at least alert. That is good,"

the queen said. "As to who, we do not know. Only that they came from the sea."

"I apologize for my boldness, Your Majesty, but how is it unknown who the attackers are?" Portia asked, her curiosity once again overriding her manners.

"Because no one who has seen them has survived. Not a single refugee that has come through this kingdom knows what they look like," Queen Lorica said.

Anxiety gripped Portia's stomach. Coverack was directly on the sea.

Mutterings floated through the nobles around Portia. At last she understood their anger. They were scared, but it was coming out as rage. The longer she was in the room, the more she could smell it. The children's gangs in Valencia had much the same reaction when things were not going well. It was a shock to realize adults could act the same.

"This is why we called you back," the queen said. "The elves are all inland. We are not, and as such, we need our champion. Their assistance in other ways was also requested, but we have not yet had word on that. The first need was to get you here."

"Is my task set then?" Portia asked.

"No. We are in counsel now." The queen motioned to the full court.

Portia wondered how much of a counsel it was and how much was the queen letting the nobles vent their unhappiness. Better to do it here now, to her face, than to have them scheme behind her back. Surely she had better advisors than the rich landowners in the city.

"We will send our orders when they are ready. Meanwhile, your task is to continue training. Go back to the Magic Academy. Work hard, for all our lives might depend upon it."

A shiver ran down Portia's back. "Yes, Your Majesty." An image of the woman and child at the gate flashed in her mind. If she was to protect them, didn't it mean all of them? Before her brain could stop her, the words flowed out of her mouth, "If we are in danger why are so many being turned away from the city gates?"

The queen stared at Portia, shocked at her effrontery. Quiet descended over the room as the court watched.

Queen Lorica straightened and looked down at Portia, her eyes glittering. "This city might not be secure, despite our best efforts. We cannot pretend to offer shelter when we might be the next to go. For their own good, these refugees must move further inland. My Lords here demand that we offer them guarantees that we cannot. Guarantees to protect their lands and their castles and their *gardens*. But at the very least we can offer refugees the one piece of advice that might help them—that they must continue inland. The refugees, at least, can be more tractable."

The queen looked around the room, sparing no one her anger. She rose abruptly and left the throne room, followed by the king consort and her advisors, leaving the rest to stare at each other and then down at the floor. No one rose up to speak in the absence of the queen. Silence fell heavy upon the room.

All quickly exited.

4

Portia returned to the pyromancy house, expecting it to be full at the late hour. Instead, it was deathly quiet. There was no one in the common room having a late-night snack, nor were there any students running through the halls comparing homework for last-minute assignments. The silence unnerved her. She would've enjoyed it if she knew where everyone was.

After tossing her bags on her bed in the room she shared with Ella, she went back to the common room to grab a cup of tea and think about what to do next. Going to bed sounded like a wonderful idea, but she was too wound up after the long day and witnessing the scene in the throne room.

As she was pouring water for her tea from the large kettle near the fire, Professor Hilda Griffiths walked in.

"Welcome back, Portia," Hilda said, a broad smile on her face. She held out her arms for a big hug, and Portia gratefully walked into them, squeezing her professor and house mother tight. "You must be exhausted."

"I am... but where is everybody?" Portia asked. "I've never seen it so empty at night. It's weird."

"Nothing has felt normal for a while." A dark look crossed Hilda's face. "Things are a bit different now. They're all in night training."

"Night training?"

"Battle training."

Battle training. This was something new. Her Magic Academy classes had never talked about using magic in war settings. The students understood it could be done, but no teacher had acknowledged it. Until now. Portia's eyebrows drew together. The Magic Academy had not escaped the changes that had overcome the city.

"You could probably take the night off considering you just got back." Hilda's voice interrupted Portia's thoughts. She eyed Portia up and down. "But you're probably too worked up for that. The energy of youth, I envy you that. You'll find them all down in front of the main hall. The yards look a bit different now."

Putting aside her tea, Portia left immediately for the main hall. She couldn't imagine they'd be working much later that night and didn't want to miss whatever they were doing.

'A bit different now' did not do the change justice. The lush green lawns in front of the main campus where admittance trials were held every year were no longer wide expanses of grass. Instead, there was a dark spread of water reflecting glimmers of moonlight. The air was moist from spray thrown up as waves hit the stone embankment around the pool. It must be deep; the amount of water in the pool was impressive.

It had taken great effort to construct this.

Walking closely towards the sounds of voices on one edge of the large pool, Portia spied buoys and other targets floating on the dark waters. There was at least one rowboat that did not move from its spot in the middle of the pool. It must be anchored there.

Suddenly, a flash of light streaked over the practice lake towards the rowboat. It landed in water, twenty feet or so shy of its target. Unhappy yelling carried over the water towards Portia. The students were on the far side of the pool.

Other light streaks followed. Most missed the boat, but one landed with a light green burst on the prow. Cheers arose after it hit its mark.

Whoever had done it had thrown their magic further than she'd ever seen before. How were they accomplishing that?

Portia walked around the pool to get closer and see who was there. Were there others training besides the pyromancy house students, perhaps more advanced mages? There were no streaks of ice, bolts of electricity, or wind gusts that the other houses could do. Perhaps each student house had a different practice night.

"Hello?" she called. The moon was only a quarter full, leaving it difficult to see in the darkness.

Suddenly a voice cried out, "Portia!"

Before she could react, she was swallowed in a bear hug and nearly knocked over by Ella Schulz, her boisterous roommate at the Magic Academy. "You're back! Just in time for all the fun." Ella held Portia by the arms and looked at her. Ella's golden hair and broad smile warmed Portia like sunshine.

"You have a strange idea of fun," a deep voice behind Portia said. She turned to see Richard Virtanen, twin brother to Liam Virtanen. Liam joined them and pushed Richard out of the way to hug both Ella and Portia. Ella slapped him away.

The two boys could not have been more different. Richard was the serious one, with messy brown hair and even more rumpled clothes. Liam groomed himself conspicuously. It was too dark to see what color Liam's hair was, but even in the dim light Portia could make out bleached tips.

Portia extracted herself from their embrace. It was good to see them, but the close contact was unsettling after being away from it for so long.

Mia Roux, the one noble in their close group, waved to Portia, too shy to hug her. Portia had a ton of questions for Mia, but those could wait for another time. First she wanted to find out what they were doing there—and how.

"Portia, our long-lost Portia." Liam pulled at her arm. "Come join in the fun."

"What are you doing?" Portia asked.

"Target practice," Liam said, a jaunty lilt in his voice.

"You could have fooled me, considering your lobs just ended up in the water," Ella said, trying to pull Portia away from him.

"Oh, like you were doing any better, village girl," Liam responded as he deftly slipped Portia's arm from Ella and pulled her towards the water.

Portia's mouth dropped at the insult. Was he serious?

Ella blew out air and followed, along with Richard and Mia. The rest of the house was crowded at the edge of the pool. There were no instructors around.

"This isn't a formal class?" Portia asked.

"No. Just homework. Oh so much homework," Richard said in a quiet voice.

"Exciting homework." Ella bounced up and down. "They've taught us *all* some new node magic. So we can throw our magic further. We've been given the week to get it down. Also, morning classes have been moved back so we can work late."

"Thank goodness." Liam patted his hair. "I need my beauty sleep."

Ella grunted. Liam's good looks and impeccable routine irritated her, not the least because he wouldn't share any of his beauty secrets with her, such as how he got such wild colors for his hair. Teal or magenta were not unheard of for him.

New node magic? That was exciting. Node magic allowed a user to set the magic into a small ball which could then be triggered by motion or some other condition to go off later. Learning node magic her first year had allowed her to lay a trap for her enemies and stop their harassment. It had also probably saved her life in the Elven Kingdom of Rocabarra.

They reached the edge of the pool and looked out into the dark waters.

"But why at night? And what is so different about this node magic?" Portia asked.

"You can throw it instead of just laying traps," Mia said,

quietly. "I'd read about it but didn't know anyone still knew how to do it. It seemed like one of those arts lost in ancient times."

"'Tis not lost at all." Liam showily formed a ball of fire above his right hand. He waved around the fire with his left hand, and a thin blue wisp of smoke wrapped around the fire and seemed to spin it like a top. He waved again and the fire responded, spinning faster and faster. Finally, he threw the fire with his right hand and sent it over the waters towards the boat. It missed, falling many lengths short.

"Ha!" Ella crossed her arms.

"Never mind her. We'll get it," Liam said sheepishly.

"Mia already has it," Ella said.

Portia looked to Mia, who shyly created a fireball of her own. Mia repeated the wrapping motion with blue smoke that Liam had done, but with much smaller motions of her hands. She flicked the fireball over the water to the boat and it hit neatly on the prow with a bright green flash. It had been Mia who had done so earlier.

"Can you throw all magic like that?" The second question she wanted to ask but dare not was, could other types of magic be thrown too? No one in the house knew she was capable of anything other than pyromancy. In the human world most people could only do one sort of magic, or at the very most, one tree, such as all fire magic or ice magic. Those rare ones that could do many sorts were Jacks of Magic.

She was the third Jack in all recorded history.

They didn't know that.

"As far as we know, but our lessons of course have been

pyromancy. We haven't seen the other houses much this week. Everyone is assigned in shifts. We're the lucky ones." Ella elbowed Portia. "Our shift is before midnight."

"I'd stay away from Magisend if I were you," Richard said quietly. "She's been in a rage. There's a rumor cryomancy is the—"

"Pre-dawn shift," Ella said triumphantly. "It gives the ice time to melt during the day. And we don't have to see them."

The cryomancy house had a high number of nobles in it, including Magisend Lucy Gwynn of the House Riddlepit. Whom Portia had once robbed. Lucy nearly killed her in that encounter. Her fury at Portia's presence in the Magic Academy was common knowledge.

Portia turned to Richard. "Are you using the nodes too?" Of all the students, Richard was the only one that breathed fire. The instructors might have shown him a different technique that could be used for Portia's different sorts of magic.

"I am, but not in the same way. I can use it to support my fire... but I still can't throw it," Richard said.

"Yet," Liam said, putting his arm around his brother and squeezing. "We'll find a way."

Portia looked between the two of them, puzzled, but then realized why it was so important: If Richard couldn't find a way to use his magic at a distance, then he would have to go into close combat. As cavalier as Liam acted, losing his brother would be no small thing. She looked down, embarrassed to realize that she'd been staring at them.

"Can you show me how you do it?" Portia asked Richard, anxious to move the conversation on.

Richard shrugged then stood, legs apart, facing the boat. He breathed in deeply then exhaled a plume of blue-white fire. Using his hands in circular motions, he elongated the plume. It streaked towards the boat, reaching several lengths longer than she'd ever witnessed but still falling far short of the target. He stopped suddenly and stood at the edge of the pool, panting. The downfall of his magic was that he *had* to stop for air.

Voices carried around the pool from the rest of the house. Balls of fire and light flew over the water towards the boat. The whole house was there, but out of all the efforts so far, only Mia's had succeeded in reaching the boat.

"You should try it," Ella said, prompting Portia and pointing at the boat. "I'll tell you the incantation and movements."

Portia nodded. Ella spoke the chant that Portia was to think and demonstrated the hand motions that went with it.

Facing the boat that bounced on the waves, Portia conjured her light magic, the one they'd seen her perform the most often, a skill firmly in the Pyromancy magic tree. Doing as Ella had instructed, she flung the magic towards the boat. The throw was far from controlled though; instead of flying towards the boat directly, her magic shot up, nearly vertical, and exploded at the top of the arc. Bright light flooded the yards and surprised faces turned to her as the sky became nearly as light as daylight.

"Dang," Liam whispered.

"That could be useful," Ella said, her voice unusually quiet.

The other students came over to greet Portia, now that she'd so clearly announced her return. Before they could reach her, Portia repeated the question that no one had answered yet. "But why at night?"

"Because the attacks came at night," Mia said, serious. "We've heard of two so far, both under new moons. This," she waved at the quarter moon, "is probably too light by far. But it is better than practicing during the day."

Any further talk had to wait until the greetings from other house students were met and many questions answered.

———

THEY DECIDED to eat after practice since the mess halls were open for late meals due to the unusual training sessions. The group loaded up their trays and met at a table in the far corner. Portia was grateful the table could only fit their small group. It was near the middle of the night, and her day had started long ago in Holne.

"So, who is being spotted in these night attacks?" Portia asked as she shoved in a mouthful of steaming fried fish. Oh how she had missed fish.

"No one's gotten a close look for sure," Ella said authoritatively. "At least no one I've talked to has heard a good description. There's lots of talk of their boats. They are unlike any others."

Portia raised her eyebrows and waited for more. Ella leaned in conspiratorially. "They don't use oars or sails."

The looks on the others' faces confirmed what Ella said.

How could a boat control where it was going without oars or a sail? Did it just drift aimlessly and hope for the shore?

Not to be outdone, Liam leaned in. "But the ships go fast. Very fast. The defensive clippers in Jukhnovo could not intercept them. That's how they were able to attack the city—at least that's what they think. Only one of the Jukhnovo's ships survived. It's rumored most buildings along the shoreline are destroyed."

Ella elbowed Liam to get him to back off. Portia wondered at their sitting next to each other considering they got along so poorly. Ella used her hand to block Liam from speaking further then continued. "They are trying to figure out what sort of magic they use for these ships. They pulled the best professors from the Academy, but we've heard no word yet of their findings."

Liam looked at Ella's hand in irritation then leaned in and licked her fingers, drawing a cry and a dirty look from Ella.

"Mmm, honey on those fingers," Liam said provokingly. "You are a messy eater, village girl, to have so much food all over your fingers."

Normally mild-mannered Richard glared at his brother from across the table. "Enough, Liam."

Liam gave his brother an abashed smile and sat up. "My apologies, brother. I will be on my best behavior. I promise."

"Too bad we can't get better than that," Mia said dryly. The entire table looked at her in surprise then burst out laughing. Mia was so quiet and proper, it was easy to forget she could also be funny.

"In all seriousness, Portia, we've only had one report of a

spotting of the creature on the ships," Richard said. "It was said to be humanoid but not quite right. Something was off. They said it looked like a lizard mated with a human. But sadly, it is hard to check the veracity of this report—"

"Because the person reporting it is a known drunk," Ella burst in.

Richard sighed at Ella's interruption but said nothing. Liam rolled his eyes at Richard's meekness.

"Well, well, well. I thought we were well rid of you, *thief*," an icy voice said from behind Portia's back.

The hair on Portia's neck rose. She knew that voice.

Magisend Lucy Gwynn of House Riddlepit.

She turned slowly to face Magisend, who stood behind Portia with her arms crossed and her weight on one hip, her face etched with a scowl. The cryomancy cronies flanking her stared at Portia with derision.

"Good evening, Magisend," Portia said, keeping her voice even.

"It was a good evening until we found you here," Magisend spit out. She flipped back her black hair then stepped in closer to Portia so she could look down on her. Magisend was a tiny girl, so if Portia had risen, she would have towered over her, but somehow Magisend felt intimidating nonetheless. Portia consciously kept her back straight so she did not cower. Magisend's black eyes burned into her.

"Surprising that I would have so much power over your evening," Portia said congenially.

A frown crossed Magisend's face while her cronies muttered angrily. Invectives directed at Portia prompted those sitting at her table to rise in response, but Portia refused to stand.

"Things have taken an urgent turn, and we don't have the resources to waste on a charity case, *thief*. You don't belong here. You should leave," Magisend said, leaning in so closely that spittle flew and hit Portia in the face.

Portia stared back, then calmly wiped her face with a napkin taken from the table. Magisend was trembling with rage. Portia stared at the napkin and then back up at Magisend.

"If things are that urgent, perhaps your time would be better spent practicing and not harassing others," Portia said calmly. She knew she should not be provoking Magisend, but she was tired and not in the mood to deal with this.

Magisend hissed in displeasure at Portia's admonishment.

"Yes, isn't cryomancy supposed to be practicing now? Doing all your fancy ice magic," Liam taunted. "You know, drowning them in ice cubes and making pretty little snowflakes."

"We start in an hour, as if it's any of your business. At least our magic does more than make fancy light shows for little children," Magisend said contemptuously.

Ella pushed back from her chair and lunged towards Magisend. Mia grabbed her by the wrist, pulling her back, and nodded at the entrance to the mess hall where several professors in flowing blue robes were staring at them. Ella stopped pulling.

Lucy and her cronies turned to see what Mia had nodded at. Magisend's body language changed immediately; she gave the professors a smile and a wave. Turning back to Portia, her smile turned to a grimace and then a glare. She flicked her fingers at Portia before walking away with her crew.

"Goodbye for now, commoner."

Portia forced her shoulders to relax. She had hoped Magisend's hatred had abated. The last time she'd seen Magisend, she had helped Portia mount a horse. Maybe she wasn't trying to help Portia at all, but rather Magisend's desire was to get Portia out of the Magic Academy as quickly as possible. Perhaps she thought Portia's trip away was permanent.

At least Magisend was gone. For now.

Turning back to face her dinner, Portia picked up her fork to eat more of the fried fish, only to find the remaining food on her plate encased in ice.

All their meals were frozen and ruined. Lucy must have done it with her last gesture. Liam threw down his fork in disgust.

THEY ARRIVED BACK at the Pyromancy house far past midnight.

Portia finally unpacked her bags while Ella sang from the bathroom, preparing for bed.

A knock at the door startled her, but it was only Mia holding out a letter for Portia. "This came for you last week."

Portia took the letter. She didn't recognize the stamps on it.

"Come in." Stepping back, Portia motioned for Mia to enter. "How have you been?"

"I'm fine. Don't let me stop you. Open it."

Portia gave her a puzzled look.

"Okay, fine. I'm curious," Mia admitted. "I don't recognize some notation on the outside. Who in the world is writing to you?" Somehow, even when she was being sneaky, she still looked dignified.

Portia gave a small laugh. "That admission deserves some information in return. Fine. Have a seat."

Pulling open the small black seal on the letter, Portia unfolded the sheet to find Mark's familiar handwriting. She checked the outside of the letter. The handwriting there did not match the interior handwriting. Outside, the lettering was jagged and rough, as if someone had written it with their opposite hand, while the inside held the familiar square printing she was used to seeing from Mark. Her stomach clenched. He would have had a reason for disguising his writing.

"It's from my friend Mark. We grew up together in Valencia," Portia said, not sharing the rest of the story with Mia.

They had indeed grown up together in Valencia, but it was not an idyllic childhood. Portia had been an orphan living on the streets. Luck had been on her side, and a sympathetic gang leader, John, had taken her in. She in turn had convinced John to rescue Mark when she had found him on the street at five years old, crying over his mother's broken body.

Mia settled on Portia's bed, pulling a pillow from its head

and placing it behind her back as she leaned on the wall. "What does it say?"

Portia scanned the letter quickly. He talked about the weather and oncoming storms. He said the harvest would be coming in early and the fall colors would be beautiful. He invited her to come visit the farm in Lusatiana before it was too late.

Last she had spoken with Mark, he was working for a mysterious outfit as a page. He had never been on a farm in his life, as far as she knew. Likely the only true things in this letter were that he needed her to come visit and that he was in Lusatiana.

Portia checked the seal. It looked as if it had been unbroken, but there were ways to hide that.

Mia looked even more curious. "Well?"

"He's in Lusatiana. He wants me to come visit," Portia said. That was true enough.

Mia laughed. "His timing is excellent. That is in the opposite direction of Jukhnovo. You could get away from the attackers."

Portia gave her a dirty look. "You don't really think I'd run away, do you?"

"No. Of course not." Mia shot Portia a hurt look. "I have always been curious to see that kingdom though. If you do go visit sometime, I want to come with you."

"There is a kingdom you haven't seen? I thought all you nobles were toured around everywhere so you knew what you were talking about."

"Somehow, that kingdom never made the schedule. Something about low profit margins. My father was off-put enough about the gold for the tutors," Mia said, with a touch of her own bitterness.

Gold. They had gold just to pay for her schooling. Portia shook her head. She never thought to be here amongst those who had so much money.

Mark's letter worried her, though. He would not have risked writing, especially if he thought it would be read, unless the need was urgent. He must need her help. But there was no way she could leave now—not when the queen had called her back explicitly from her important task in Rocabarra. The kingdom of Haulstatt needed her too.

Even so, turning her back on Mark was a betrayal she couldn't stomach. There had to be a way to assist in whatever he needed. First, she would have to find out what that was. There were return directions on the letter. She would write back at the very least. Hopefully, there was time for the correspondence and his need wasn't urgent. A shiver ran down her back. An image of Mark as a child crying over his mother came unbidden into her mind.

Mia stared at her, an unreadable expression on her face. Portia waited for her to say something, but instead Mia turned away. The strange moment hung in the air, broken by Ella returning from the bathroom while singing at full volume.

"You do know that people are trying to sleep, don't you?" Portia asked, grateful for the diversion.

"Blessed girl, stop being so ill-mannered. We all just got back. No one is sleeping yet." Ella hung up her clothes, unperturbed by Portia's chiding.

"Because you won't let them," Portia retorted, facing Ella with her arms crossed. Mia had the same expression.

Ella looked back and forth between the two of them.

"Oh fine, you two. You are too much." Ella turned and put away her toiletries, now humming nearly as loudly as she had been singing.

Mia exchanged a look with Portia and shrugged her shoulders. It was probably as quiet as Ella would get until she passed out in sleep. And even then, she would most likely snore. Loudly.

Portia shook her head. Having Ella as a roommate was not a silent affair.

Mia slid off the bed to return to her own room.

"Wait, Mia. Is there a way for me to mail a letter back? I've never done so," Portia asked before she could reach the door.

"Yes, they'll take mail directly from the house. The messenger comes by in the morning... or maybe it's afternoon. I can't remember. I'll show you where to leave it on the morrow."

Portia nodded. Mia disappeared out the door before she could ask the second question. "How much does it cost?"

5

Portia woke long before dawn. The room was dark, and no light was leaking in from around the shade over the window, the moon having set hours ago. Ella snored in the bed across the room. Nothing short of the din of the morning bells would wake her.

Using a flick of her magic to light a nearby candle, Portia drew back the covers and got out of bed. She pulled out Mark's letter and read it one more time. On the surface, it was the words of a relaxed boy on vacation enjoining a friend to come visit. But that could not be the case. What was really going on with him? Was someone overlooking him when he wrote this letter? A stab of pain shot through her heart as she realized how much she missed him. He'd been a constant companion for most of her life, near all of it that she could remember, and even the joys of learning at the Magic Academy were not always enough to forget what she had lost.

If only he had stayed and tried to get in himself.

No, she shook her head. If they ever discovered his role in the attack on her or Elyas, they would never let him in the Academy. More than likely, they would throw him in the stocks never to see daylight again.

Or release him to meet the noose.

Portia paced at the thought.

Going to her trunk in the corner, she pulled out the faded leather pouch she'd saved from Elyas's house after he had been murdered. He had been so kind to her. Withdrawing the locket with the engraving of Elyas and his daughter, Chenna, Portia ran a thumb over the raised likenesses. What would it have been like to grow up with a loving father? Was there something about her that was ill luck for the paternal figures in her life? Her real dad was more than likely dead, for how else would she be an orphan? John, the gang leader that took her in, was dead as well, and worse still, it was because she'd... Portia couldn't even think it. It hurt too much even after all this time. She pushed her thoughts on, but they were not any cheerier. Elyas was dead. And now Mark was in trouble.

Then there were the deaths of the convoy elves and the human guards from the attack while journeying with her to Rocabarra.

So much death. All around her. Was she bad luck?

Could she be the opposite of a Jack? Not a being destined to save them all, but one destined to bring ill fortune and oblivion to all so stupid as to be around her?

The darkness of the night seemed to answer yes, she was all those things. And worse. Portia rubbed her arms vigorously, trying to warm up, but the motion did nothing to dispel the chill around her heart.

Maybe Magisend was right and she was just a drain on them all. Her skill with the Elven magic was far from masterful. It was just as likely she'd blow them all up than successfully seal the splinter to keep further invaders away. She shivered and then turned to look at Ella's trusting face.

Ella, who believed all was good in the world. Ella would not give up.

Her gaze fell upon her new sword, given to her by King Magnus and Queen Ceola of the Elves. They would not give up. Furthermore, they had put their trust in her, as had Sergeant Lyren and Lady Harper.

Would she let them all down by turning and running?

The answer came in a flash. It was as if someone spoke directly into her mind: No.

She would not give up.

She refused.

Elyas's last words to her were to not run, and she had promised she wouldn't. She would keep that promise. She would stay and fight, no matter how scared she was. No matter what the outcome.

Portia shoved the locket in the bag and put it back in her trunk, shutting the trunk lid harder than planned.

Ella snorted in her bed and turned over but did not wake.

Grabbing parchment and quill, Portia sat down at the small desk to write to Mark. The letters appeared to dance on the paper in the flickering candlelight. She forced herself to breathe in deeply, then to write more slowly. It would do her no good to write so fast as to make it unreadable.

When the letter was sealed and ready to post, light was coming in around the shade over the window. The sun was about to rise, but they had been allotted extra hours rest due to the night practice. Portia crawled back into bed. Sleep finally came.

THE NEXT DAY felt oddly normal. Despite all that was going on, classes were held on campus as usual except for the morning sessions. The vast pool in front of the main hall remained, but all else on campus was unchanged.

The first course of the afternoon was pyromancy. This was the house's main specialty, so all the house members walked together to Professor Hilda Griffith's class. Hilda was not just their house mother but also their professor, at least for the first few years.

Portia found her normal seat vacant and took it. It was as if she had never been gone.

"Good afternoon all. I have a report from last night's practice; thank you, Mia," Hilda said, nodding at Mia, who had written down the results and given them to the professor upon entering. "Improvements are there, but you must work harder. We need accuracy and forcefulness upon impact. I know this is a lot to ask, but there is no choice in the matter."

No one asked for clarification. Students fidgeted in their seats.

"Portia," Professor Hilda said as she shuffled papers on the desk. "You'll have extra homework until you're caught up. Under normal circumstances you would have more time, but I'm asking that you hurry. All the information we've covered is important. Mia can help you. Here's a list." Professor Hilda put several pieces of parchment on Portia's desk.

Portia groaned inwardly, trying to keep her face straight. The list was in tiny writing: three full pages of readings and magic practicals for her to learn. It was an enormous amount of work, probably three times the length of a normal syllabus. As calm as Professor Hilda appeared on the outside, there must be panic at the school if they were pushing the students this hard. Could they really have covered all that in the few months she was gone? Now she was expected to learn it all even more quickly. Glancing up, she met Mia's sympathetic eyes. If anyone could learn all this so fast, it was Mia, not her. At least Mia was going to help her.

"Now most of you," Hilda said, motioning to the class, "have some form of fire magic, not just light magic. That means you have the ability to create heat, with varying degrees of control amongst you. Not all things burn at the same temperature. It is helpful to know just what you're aiming for. Does anyone know what would require more heat between parchment and wood in order to set it ablaze?"

A voice from the back yelled out, "Parchment."

Parchment? How can that be? Wood is so much thicker than paper. Portia's eyebrows drew together.

"Excellent, excellent," Professor Hilda said. "Someone has done their homework. Yes, wood burns sooner but it's hard to tell because there is usually so much more of it, pulling that much more energy."

Portia slumped down at her desk as Hilda continued on about the various ignition temperatures of items. Ella leaned over and gave Portia a poke. She was laughing.

"Serves you right for running off on some vacation while we're all working hard," Ella said.

Portia scrunched her nose. Ella had no idea how hard Portia had been working, but she couldn't tell her the truth, not yet anyhow. "So, you'll get a perfect score on the tests, right?" It was a low blow, but she knew Ella worried about failing tests.

"Don't be a jerk," Ella replied testily.

"Don't start it."

"Since you two are having a private conversation, may I assume that you know all the material we are about to cover on heating metals?" Hilda asked, leaning down over Portia and Ella. The rest of the class watched.

Portia looked around at the other students and sat up straighter in her chair, self-conscious. Her face turned red and her ears burned. What did she know about heating metal? It took a lot more in energy from her than light magic, that much she knew, but that was probably not what Professor Hilda was looking for.

"No, Professor," Portia said.

Ella shook her head, looking abashed. She didn't know either.

"Well then, pay attention please," Professor Hilda said. She walked to the front of the class where several metal items were sitting on the table. Picking up a broken sword, she turned and showed it to the class.

"This is steel. Most of the guardsmens' swords are made of this material as well as several other things. When it is heated, it becomes brittle and weakened. Make no doubt it will still hurt if it hits you, not just from the edge but also from the heat, but if heated enough it will not last under rough usage. It will break, as this one has done."

"Sounds like an excuse to me," Liam said with a joking tone. Richard touched his forehead and closed his eyes at his brother's comment. Liam ignored him. "I think the fellow wielding it just made a mistake."

Hilda raised her eyebrows at Liam but didn't say anything. He took the hint and smoothed his face into an expression of interest.

Putting the sword back on the table, she then picked up a metal bar and held it up for the class to see. "This is iron. It is a component of steel but behaves differently. It needs more heat to melt, much more. It is softer in general, even more so when hot. There is not much pure iron around, but you should know about it in case you run into it." She put the piece of iron back on the table and grabbed a lump of black material.

"Finally, this is coal. It combusts hotly—hotter even than melting iron—but it also needs air to burn just as wood and paper parchment do."

Ella's eyes glazed over as the recitation continued. Portia had to laugh. She might be behind in her homework, but she was not the only one who was overwhelmed. Of the entire class, only Mia seemed calm. She probably knew all this information already and no doubt could precisely heat each one of the materials mentioned. Portia tried to not feel jealous because she knew Mia's skills were honed in a childhood spent in long hours of practice and study.

Professor Hilda demonstrated heating all the elements talked about in class that day, including explosively burning the lump of coal, which clouded the room with smoke and had everyone coughing. Quick thinking Richard slammed a cup down over the smoking rock while Liam ran out the door and waved away the bits of smoke that had come out with him. The others followed.

"That smoke is going to ruin my color," Liam pronounced as he combed his fingers through his hair. It was scarlet today, with white tips. How did he do that to his hair? Ella had sworn to find out, but a year later she had discovered nothing. Liam could keep a secret.

The screech of opening windows came through the murky smoke. The air in the classroom cleared as the smoke pulled out the open windows. Hilda bustled about purposely, but she wouldn't meet any of the students' eyes. Portia wondered if she had practiced heating the coal inside before. The smoke seemed to have caught her as off guard as everyone else.

Portia's next class was history. There were many history classes during the day, and she had been unlucky enough to be assigned one that was mostly filled with students from the cryomancy house. She had not asked for a different class, not wanting to cause a fuss. It already felt unreal to be allowed in the Magic Academy. Now it was a source of pride that she could deal with those students. Most days.

Professor Aelric Terfel looked up in surprise as Portia walked through the door.

"You're back? I hadn't been notified," he said. An unspoken question and concern shone in his eyes. He glanced at the rest of the class seated in their chairs, watching them. His expression smoothed. "Well, we have covered several decades into the last millennia. I expect you will learn these lessons, in detail." He looked up at her and gave her a serious look. "They are relevant in more ways than one."

That statement more than likely had several meanings, at least one of which was for her alone as the Jack of Magic. Portia would only know when she started reading the histories. She vowed to do so as quickly as possible. There was no guarantee how much time she would have for studies before being called away yet again.

He pulled the scroll towards himself and dipped a quill in an ink pot. Writing quickly, he filled several lengths of the scroll. "Complete these readings as soon as possible. The librarian will help you find the correct sources."

Portia took the scroll from him and added it to her bag along with the other homework from Professor Hilda. All thoughts of spending free time with her friends vanished under a pile of schoolwork.

To get to her seat she had to walk past Magisend Lucy, who gave her a sickly-sweet smile. "Welcome back, Portia. We missed you so much." It was a performance for Professor Aelric. Portia hoped he was not fooled, but she herself couldn't afford to be distracted by it because there was too much else going on, things that were too important. She declined to answer.

Magisend pushed on. "You have to tell us all about your trip and how it is that you are back here already so soon. We are just *dying* to hear."

"Laying it on a bit thick, aren't you?" Portia hissed to Magisend as she walked by to her seat.

"I'm just trying to be friendly." Magisend shared her smile with Professor Aelric.

Portia shook her head. She shouldn't have responded at all. Slumping into her seat, she let her bag drop to the floor. It was going to be a long class period.

"Okay, class, time to get to work," Professor Aelric said. "We have much to cover. Who can get us up to date on yesterday's lesson?"

"I can," Magisend said, eagerly waving her hand while turning to shoot Portia a dirty look.

Portia gave her a sweet smile.

"Such enthusiasm, Magisend. It is good to see. Enlighten us. We were talking about how Lusatiana was formed," Professor Aelric said. He had an inscrutable expression on his face. Was he really happy to have her answer the question?

"Lusatiana is valuable farmland that was taken from the savage dwarves by the bravery of the good people of Haulstatt. It was those battles that formed the first noble houses, for those houses are filled with people who serve their kings and queens and protect the good people of Haulstatt. Their noble titles are recognition of their good deeds and supreme character." Magisend turned to give Portia a special smirk. "They proved their value to the kingdom."

Magisend sat back in her chair, satisfied with her recitation. Professor Aelric looked at her, one eyebrow raised, waiting for further words, but none came. The class watched both of them, a titter of laughter coming from the back.

Finally, he cleared his throat.

"That was very, ah, interesting. And it had a kernel of truth, certainly, but left out many things, did it not, Magisend?" Magisend sat up, her face twisted in indignation. "It is true that noble titles were distributed in the aftermath of the battles with the dwarves, but many would say the dwarves were not savages but indeed simply creatures trying to protect their homes. Unfortunately for them, they lost, and humans benefited greatly for it. And yes, this was all part of Haulstatt, but in the chaos of the invasion to the south and civil war nearly breaking on Haulstatt over it, Lusatiana managed to break free and form their own kingdom. They rendered moot the point whether it was acceptable to take another race's land by simply doing so with impunity and benefiting from it ever since."

This was too much for Magisend. "Haulstatt has benefited from it too. It would be no good for humans to have others too close. Now we are surrounded by human kingdoms on all sides," she said, anger in her voice. She did not like to be contradicted, even by the teacher. Portia wondered if her private tutors had ever dared tell her she was wrong. She thought not, thinking back to her own injuries from confronting Lucy.

"That's wrong," Portia blurted out the words before she could stop herself.

Magisend whirled to face Portia. "Excuse me, commoner, did you dare speak?"

"Magisend," Professor Aelric's voice warned.

"Rocabarra also meets up with Haulstatt. They are elves, mostly," Portia said quietly.

Magisend narrowed her eyes at Portia.

Portia slid down in her seat. Why hadn't she just kept her mouth shut? Provoking Magisend, no matter how much she deserved it, usually ended up with Portia falling on a patch of ice somewhere.

"Yes, yes, that maybe so, but we are mostly surrounded by human kingdoms." Professor Aelric cleared his throat. "For now." Silence settled over the room. Everyone in the Magic Academy knew of the refugees from Jukhnovo, the human kingdoms to the north, and how it had fallen to invaders. The rumors had the invaders as not human. No one had yet seen who they were, and fear of the unknown was almost as unsettling as the scores of refugees that were flooding through the kingdom.

Professor Aelric tapped his pointer to the assignment written on the chalk board. "Perhaps today would be best spent reading from our texts. Finish chapters thirty-seven and thirty-eight, and then you may go. Through chapter forty is due tomorrow. Be prepared to discuss."

The class sullenly opened their books and read. Portia did not have a copy of the book they were reading, so Professor Aelric loaned her his own.

As the students completed their work and class emptied, Portia read the book from the beginning and waited. Finally, it was only her and Professor Aelric in the room.

She shut the book slowly then placed it in her bag along with her homework.

Professor Aelric was looking at her with kind eyes. "How did it go?" he asked.

"You mean Rocabarra?"

"Of course. Did you learn the magic of the splinters?" He went right to the point.

"I learned some magic of healing them. Some. Although I fear I am not as confident with it as I should be," Portia said. The palm of her hand twitched where the scar from the exploding wood pulled. She had not stretched it recently. "I learned as much as I could."

He nodded. "That is all we can hope for. Do you need a place to practice?"

Warmth flooded her heart. He understood that she could not practice any of her new skills where another student could see. And she had no privacy, even in the pyromancy house where she shared a room with Ella.

"Yes, I very much do," she said.

"We will take care of that. I'll have something for you by tomorrow."

Portia rose to leave then hesitated. "There is one other thing I was hoping you could help me with?"

He looked at her, curious.

"I was given a sword... by the king... by King Magnus and Queen Ceola of the elves. It is an Elven sword but fits me perfectly. It is also of a strange color. Perhaps I should have asked Professor Hilda about it today. It is copper-colored, but I doubt it is of copper, for it would be far too soft—"

"It's copper-colored?" Professor Aelric asked. He sat up and leaned in towards her. His eyes glittered. "What else did it look like? Please describe it, in detail."

"The scabbard is in green leather, as is the wrapping around the hilt," Portia said, suddenly uncomfortable under Professor Aelric's intense stare. What else could she remember about the sword? "Don't laugh, but I swear it was calling to me. It felt like it belonged to me and always had. As if I had been missing something and had not realized it until I held the sword."

Professor Aelric leaned back and blew out heavily. "What is your question about this weapon?"

"Can you help me train with it?"

"That I do not know. But I must see this sword as soon as possible. Don't show it to any others. Don't act as if it is important."

A shiver ran down Portia's spine at Professor Aelric's strange admonishment.

"Bring it to class tomorrow," he said. "In a bag, covered."

"All right," Portia said, wondering why no one else should see this weapon. At least he said he might be able to train her. She'd learned her knife work long ago, but the sword was a different matter. If she was going to become as comfortable with that as with her knives, she needed a master to train her. If he could not do so, she vowed to plead with him to find someone else until he relented.

He waved her away and Portia exited, making her way back to the courtyard of portals in the middle of the Magic Academy.

The houses where the students lived were not on campus but rather hidden in locations nestled within the city and reachable only by portal doors on the campus grounds. Each door was keyed to only allow certain people admittance. The higher-ups grouped the students by magic type for each house. The school had thought it best to keep those of similar magic types living together to share their information and to help each other with homework. Unfortunately, it fostered rivalries between the houses and did nothing to tame any ill will that naturally occurred between the different branches of magic.

As a member of the pyromancy house, only the pyromancy door would open for her. She didn't know the location of her own house within the city, for any exploration from the house was forbidden. The only way to find its location would have been to exit it through a window and climb down since there were no exterior doors, at least none that were not sealed shut. Of course, she had no idea where the cryomancy and other magic houses were located.

The portal doors were located in an inner courtyard of the Academy. They stood upright in the gravel and stone garden inlaid with stones that formed a pattern of a swirl. At first glance, it looked like an art installation with decorated doors in doorframes standing alone, somehow maintaining upright status without being attached to any wall. The doors appeared to open into nothing, leading simply to the other side of the frame, but that was not the case. For if a student opened the door that was keyed to them, it would reveal the destination instead. Stepping through it would instantaneously transport them there.

Portia reached for the familiar door with a flame engraved on it, opened it, and breathed a sigh of relief when she stepped through to the pyromancy house on the other side. The din of the other students having snacks and lounging in the main room of the house was a comfort. Night practice was not for several hours, so the students were taking a chance to relax when they could. At least most were. Mia was conspicuously absent. Portia guessed she was sequestered in her room, studying hard. Mia's dedication stood out amongst the students.

Portia went directly to her room, waving at other students as she went. After her interview with Professor Aelric, she was anxious to take another look at her sword. It was doubtful she would get any clues from it, but still, it called to her. Since he forbade her from showing it to others, she could not bring it to the library and ask the librarian to research it. At least not yet. She'd have to press him for more information tomorrow when he looked at it in person.

When she reached her room, she was relieved to find it empty. Ella was not there, no doubt holding court in the kitchen. It was a miracle Ella found the time to study at all, for she spent every spare moment socializing and talking with other students.

Shutting the door behind her, Portia went directly to her

trunk, opened it, and pulled out the copper sword. It hummed a familiar greeting. What was the significance of this weapon?

———

Professor Aelric examined the sword when Portia brought it to him the next day. He seemed to recognize it, having flipped the hilt up looking for a mark and finding one there, but he stubbornly refused to tell her any more about it except that she should not share its presence with others. He had shown her a few exercises, starting with the most basic of sword work, but Portia quickly progressed even during that first practice. He frowned at the precision of her parries.

"You move as if you have trained for hours and hours with this. Have you?" he asked.

Portia shook her head.

"No, it is as if the sword knows where to go."

Aelric frowned at that. "Interesting. You might not always have that weapon. If you are to train with a sword, you need to be able to use all swords. Instinctively. That means without thinking and without relying on your weapon to move for you." He took the blade from her, and she protested as he pushed a wooden practice sword into her hands. "Again, from first position."

This time when he came at her she was slow to respond and missed her mark. He nodded at her with grim satisfaction.

"That is what I thought," he said. "You will practice with a wooden sword for two hours a day. We shall have one custom-made to match the weight and balance of that one."

He motioned with his head to the copper blade. "After that, and only for a short time, we will then practice with the real blade. We shall see what happens when it's not wasting its energy fixing your basic mistakes."

Much to Portia's surprise it was as Aelric had thought. As her skills improved with the wooden sword, they improved fourfold with the copper blade. Its speed and precision were based on her own movements, and as she was more precise it could be even more precise still. And faster. Soon she was able to disarm Professor Aelric in seconds, sometimes even with the first strike. The last time she did so, he exhaled loudly, his eyes wide. The speed of her weapon had frightened even herself.

"You need a new teacher," he said, panting. "You have reached the limit of my skill—at least with that blade. I will find someone for you to work with." With that he dismissed her.

She wiped the blade down and returned it to its sheath then walked slowly back to the portal. Her arms ached from the week of practice, her stomach queasy with both excitement and dread at her newfound sword skills. No matter what, she must improve so that even without the copper blade she could defend herself.

The next few weeks passed in a blur. Even Ella, who normally spent hours harassing her to join the other students and be social, left her to her studies. Ella had more than enough of her own work to do. With the rare exception of the hour before night practice, the house was quiet as everyone studied and practiced.

Aelric had still not found a sword master, so Portia was forced to practice on her own or with Aelric but using her wooden sword.

One night after practice, Portia reached her room and walked directly to her bed, thinking longingly of an hour of rest before more studies took her night. Ella was gone as usual.

"Hello, Portia," a voice from behind stopped her. She recognized Mark's voice instantly. Turning, she saw his grinning face. He had been standing behind the door, hidden from all those who might glance into the room.

"Mark!" she cried and ran to him and gave him a hug. He returned it enthusiastically. "What are you doing here? I thought you were in Lusatiana?"

"I was," he said, releasing her and going to sit on her desk chair. "But I had urgent need to speak to you and thought to yell at you in person for not responding to my letter that I sent months ago."

"Months ago?" Portia sat down heavily on her bed facing Mark. "It just arrived here a month past, and I'd only read it a few weeks ago." At his puzzled expression she rushed on. "I'd been gone for a while. I did send a reply immediately." She didn't know what else to say. Could she share that she'd been in Kocabarra? Hopefully he wouldn't ask.

"Maybe I passed your letter on the road to Coverack," Mark said, a wry smile on his face. "Never mind, I'm here now."

He turned to examine the books on her desk, flipping one open and paging through it. Portia noticed his clothing for the first time: a rich velvet black coat with red and blue embroidery. A thick velvet hat trimmed in shiny material and topped with a curling blue feather sat upon his head. His shoes were new soft leather, dyed a deep black. It was a far cry from the rags with holes he had worn when she had last seen him.

"You look well," she said.

He turned to face her again, noting where her eyes were roaming. He smiled. "I do, don't I? Money is a good look, I should say."

"Where did you get so much to afford such clothes? And your face—it's so much better." Only a thin white line was left of the angry and puckered red scar that had run across his left cheek.

"Coin can buy a lot, including healers." Mark smiled, showing off how well he looked. He'd not been able to smile well before with the scar pulling his cheek tight. Now he looked handsome. "It can't buy new fingers, but it can buy beautiful leather gloves with wood fingers inside them." He held up his left hand and wiggled his fingers. She couldn't tell that two of the fingers were fake.

"My new job requires I look the part of a wealthy citizen. It smooths the way to deal with city administrators. If only I had the silver in my own hands I'd be thrilled, but instead the clothes are tailored and then gifted to me. My true salary is much more modest, although they have been paying for a speech tutor, of all things."

"City administrators? Tutors? But you—"

"Are so young? Not to be the youngest son of a well-placed nobleman. No one has broken through the story just yet. Let us hope for my sake they don't. Avoiding detection is very motivating for me to work on my fancy words." A twinge of his old gang accent came through on the last statement.

Portia nodded, shocked at the change in Mark's position in such a short time.

His self-satisfied smile gave way to a dark look. "I don't think it has been worth what I've learned though."

Portia put her bag on top of her trunk and pulled Ella's desk chair close so she could sit and face Mark.

"What is going on?" she asked.

"I fear I've stumbled into a huge plot, much more than I've ever bargained for," he said, his voice low even though there were no others in the room. "The company I'm working for in Lusatiana is pushing everybody—royals, city administrators, and nobles—to cut funding to the Navy. To the nobles, it's an argument of how wastefully the Lusatianan kingdom is draining their coffers and padding their pockets at the nobles' expense. To the royals and their city administrators, it is talk of how the nobles are using the city to protect their own trades without paying back their fair share of the cost, which in turn leads to the city administrators demanding the nobles hire their own escorts from the private market. They are turning everyone upon each other. It's working too. Each side looks at the other as greedy leeches. The willingness to spend a silver on either side is gone."

"That's not good," Portia said, "but it's hardly anything new, is it? Isn't it always difficult to extract money from other people's coffers?"

"Especially when I planted false papers showing the royal treasurer pocketing the nobles' taxes and switching in false reports of what each noble house was paying." Mark nodded. "I think it is more, though. I've heard from others in the company that this was a successful tactic used in Jukhnovo. That *they* personally used in Jukhnovo."

"Jukhnovo?" Portia asked, shocked.

"Yes. It resulted in drastically less money for the Navy. Several large ships were in storage for lack of men to work them. There was no money for their pay." He gave her a serious look. "I found papers that backed this up."

"Do they know?"

"That I found the papers or read the ones I was delivering? No. I learned well from someone how to not get caught, by anyone," he said with a half smile and a wink. "Which is good, because I also found documents discussing a cult. I think the company is a front for it. I don't know for sure if it is the same cult that recruited Deyelna, but I feel that it is. How many cults could there be?"

Portia twisted her neck, rubbing her hand along the back of it. Her hunger curdled in her stomach. "That's horrible."

Her mind raced. Mark had long sleeves on, hiding any possible mark of a cult member, they having favored one of a diamond tattoo on the forearm. She shook her head at her own horrible thought. Mark could not be a member of the cult. It made no sense. For one, why would he be here alerting her to their actions if he was one of them? She didn't like how suspicious she was becoming of everything and everyone.

"But why are you coming to me with this?" she asked.

"I heard about your audience with the queen and that you protected me."

Portia looked up with a start. "You knew I spoke to the queen? You never said a word."

He blushed. "Let's just call it jealousy, shall we?" He paced the room and then faced Portia. "Haulstatt lies directly between Jukhnovo and Lusatiana. If Lusatiana is taken, as Jukhnovo already has been, and if the invaders attack from the sea as they have twice done before..." He held his hand up and made a pinching motion between his fingers and thumb. "Haulstatt will be surrounded by invaders on three sides. It will not hold."

6

Portia stared at Mark. He looked abashed at the news he brought of Haulstatt's dangerous position, but there was still a hint of the five-year-old she remembered rescuing on the street. She was so glad to see him. Then she realized with a start where he was—inside the pyromancy house where only a pyromancy student should be. The door was keyed specifically to them and only to them.

"How are you here?" Portia asked. "In this house?"

Mark chuckled. "I was surprised that wasn't your first question. Or is that just a measure of your confidence in me?"

"More a measure of my exhaustion. How did you get in past the portal?"

"Portal?"

"The entrance to this house, the one that is on the grounds of the Magic Academy."

"That magic is beyond me." He shook his head. "But I'll tell you, bribery doesn't just work on city officials. I paid one of the Upkeepers of the magic for a peek of the house rolls. I told him a long-lost brother was in one of the houses and I needed to know which. Once I knew where the rolls were stored, it was easy enough to come back at night and search for a notation of the house locations. The fools were arrogant enough to have them in the same location. It was far easier to break into their office than any warehouse in Valencia. I think they are much too confident that scoundrels will not even try."

A chill overcame Portia. Mark did have thieving skills, that was true, for she had taught him them herself, but the Magic Academy should have better security than that.

As if to reassure her, he continued. "It was difficult to find the house. Did you know there are no working doors or windows on the first floor? It looks totally normal from the street. Actually, that was weird too. The house was hard to see from the street. I knew it was there so walked up the path, and then it came into better focus. I thought my eyes were going bad. Then I remembered it was a Magic Academy house. In the end, I got in." He smiled broadly and opened his arms.

"That must be fixed," Portia said resolutely as she looked away.

Mark deflated a bit when she didn't share in his delight. "It looks like you've fully turned to the good side. No more lawbreaking for you?"

"My hope is no more danger for me. I don't think I'll get that wish."

"I'm sorry," he said.

They sat in the room in silence. Noises drifted through the shut door of other students walking through the hall and talking, the din of dishes hitting each other in the far kitchen. Mark picked at the embroidery on his jacket then stopped, smoothing it back down and looking up expectantly at Portia.

"Do you by chance know anything of these invaders in Jukhnovo?" she asked.

"Nothing except they came by sea. That, and the company thinks that they are a good idea."

"How can anyone think invaders are a good idea?"

"I don't know, but if I've learned anything from these people it's that it must have something to do with money. I do love gold myself, but I cannot bring myself to help with the scheme any longer. They will single-handedly populate a new city of orphans." He took a deep breath then spoke again. "Come back and help me deal a blow to these people. We could be a team." There was just a hint of longing in his voice, and she understood it well. They had been a team for many years in Valencia.

"I can't leave now," she said.

He rose abruptly. "Fine. Forget I asked."

Portia rose to stop him from leaving. "No, you don't understand. I can't tell you why, but I need to stay here."

"Because of the invasion?" Mark asked.

"Yes."

"Even if you have the opportunity to get more information for your queen?"

Portia stared at Mark. She had not thought of that.

Portia snuck in some dinner for Mark from the cafeteria while they bided their time.

Mark had climbed through a window on the upper story when most residents were in class and the house was quieter. Now it teemed with students, and it would be difficult to get him out of the house again, at least using the same route. They had to wait for a lull. Worse yet, Ella would be coming back any minute to demand Portia join her at dinner.

"Would it really be so bad for them to know that I got in here?" Mark asked as he shoved a slice of gravy-covered meat into his mouth. At least that had not changed about him. Perhaps they should invest in an etiquette tutor as well, Portia thought. No, they did not need any help to change him—not if it was to bend his thinking to that of a company that would invite invaders.

"It would scare a lot of them," Portia said.

"Perhaps they should be scared. Or at least wary. There are real dangers in this world. Not that I'm calling myself a danger," he said as he shoved a potato in after the meat.

"Did you not have anything to eat all day?"

"Actually, I didn't. I've been waiting here for you. Where were you? Most of the other students returned before you did. I had a vision of scrambling under your bed if your roommate came back before you."

"I think you're far too big for that now."

Mark grunted, not bothering to answer, instead focusing on the tray of food in front of him. "You get this much to eat every day?"

Portia nodded.

Mark shook his head. "I'm too cheap to spend this much coin for food. Old habits."

Finally, he finished his meal and set the plate aside. "So we're agreed; you will come with, at least for a few weeks to learn more?" he asked.

"No. I mean yes. I don't know," Portia said, flustered. Mark had a good point about getting information for the queen, but the queen had brought her back to be their champion. Leaving now, even for valuable information, felt too much like running away, nor was she sure she had the right.

He crossed his arms and stared at her.

"Fine. I will go if I get permission from Queen Lorica."

"I don't understand why you need permission. We should go right away. Waiting will not help us. I have no idea if they have advanced warning, this company of mine, but I know of at least one navy ship that is already in drydock. Lusatiana's defenses are weakening."

Portia made a decision. "We'll deal with it now, and the right way." It made no sense to wait until nightfall to sneak out of the house when most of the students were sleeping. As much as she dreaded it, they might as well brazen it with Hilda and the rest of the Magic Academy. They would demand a truth cube session anyhow to verify Mark's story, and it would all come out.

He had breached their defenses, and there was no hiding it.

HILDA DID NOT TAKE it well.

"What? This child made it into the house? *This* house?" Hilda looked at Mark with indignation. He was small for his age and looked much younger than his thirteen years. He drew himself up to speak but saw Portia shooting him a look to behave. He looked away, disgruntled.

"It was important I find her," he said under his breath.

Hilda stared at both of them from across her desk. They were in her office behind the kitchens. She tapped her fingers on the desk and finally focused her glare on Portia. "He has been here all day, and you ate dinner with him, and you are just now thinking to tell me?"

"I'm sorry." Portia cast her eyes down, blushing. "I trust him explicitly."

"I see," Hilda said, icily. "I'm not sure I have the same regard. Breaking into offices on the Magic Academy grounds is serious business. How well do you really know this young man?"

Anger flared in Portia's heart. "I trust him. He brings important information the queen and king consort should know. Information that's important to Haulstatt. He has no ulterior motive for coming here. He is trying to help."

Hilda regarded her silently then let out her breath in a sudden burst. "We shall find the truth of that. We need to pass this on immediately. I'll send word to the palace and see if we might obtain an audience tonight. At the very least, we will meet with a council from the Magic Academy. Wait outside."

Portia nodded and dragged Mark back out of the office.

The last council Portia had witnessed, the only one in fact, she had been subjected to the truth cube. They were right to not sneak Mark back out again.

Blessedly, word came back from the palace quickly and forestalled any council meeting. Mark and Portia, along with Hilda and several other Magic Academy representatives, were to go to the palace as soon as possible. Hilda keyed the portal door to Mark before pushing him through it. Portia followed quickly, not wanting Mark on the Magic Academy grounds for long without anyone else present.

From the Academy, they took a carriage to the palace. Even in his finery, Mark was in awe of the palace carriage, staring at the attendants in full livery with gold thread. He touched the lacquered carriage wall, pulling his fingers back quickly at Hilda's glare. She did not return his smile. He turned to face out the window and stare at the city lights as they made their way through the city. Portia had not thought it possible for Hilda to be so mad. She felt a little guilty at having kept the secret of Mark's presence from her that evening. Hopefully, they would get permission for their trip and obtain important information from Lusatiana, enough so that all would be forgiven.

As they walked through the palace Portia walked close to Mark. They reached the room of portraits that was just before the throne room. Portia pulled Mark to one side.

"Behave yourself," she said to him in a whisper.

"Don't I always?" Mark said, his eyebrows pulling together and one side of his mouth pulling up in a grin.

"No jokes!"

He nodded then held up his crossed fingers to her. Before she could ask him what that meant, she noticed Professor Aelric was waiting by the door, watching them with interest. He nodded curtly at Portia. She forced herself to straighten and walk away from Mark to join him.

The doors to the throne room opened. The attendant took their names.

"Portia Harris, Professor Hilda Griffiths, Professor Aelric Terfel, Mark Taylor of Lusatiana," the chamberlain announced.

Mark stared at the spectacle before him, his mouth hanging open. Portia refused to look at him, instead concentrating on walking forward with the group towards the queen and king consort.

A general stood before the monarchs. His medals shone in the dim candlelight. Bags puffed out under his eyes, and his hair was slightly askew, fine hairs escaping his hair gel. Once the announcements by the chamberlain were over, he addressed the queen and king consort. "The forts along Lusatiana are coming along as planned. There have been no delays to the south. However, the volume of refugees from Jukhnovo are interfering with our building efforts to the north. We have limited men and resources. We cannot feed everybody, at least not without more supplies. If we are to keep our schedule for the forts along the north, and I entreat you that we should, then we must increase our shipments. We also need additional soldiers and guardsmen. Looters are preying upon the refugees and spilling over to prey on our own people."

"Who are these looters?" the queen asked. "Are they of our kingdom?"

The general cleared his throat awkwardly. "I must admit some are. They think to take advantage of the chaos, for the guardsmen will be busy. But many are from Jukhnovo. It is not just the good people who are fleeing."

The queen looked to Portia, who curtsied quickly in return, followed by the curtsies and bows of those around her.

"A moment, General," Queen Lorica said.

The general nodded and backed up, clearing a path for Portia to step forward.

"Good evening, Portia. We received an interesting note that you are requesting leave to go to Lusatiana. Was it not clear that your duty lies here? I understand," she nodded at Professor Hilda, "there is much that you need to do to catch up on your studies." Her eyes focused intensely on Portia. "Please explain."

Portia shifted nervously on her feet. Steadying her gaze, she raised her eyes to the queen. "Your Majesty, I take my duty very seriously and have been working hard at it. I've learned... I've learned from a source I trust," she motioned to Mark, "that there is reason to believe there are those inside Lusatiana working to weaken that kingdom's defenses. And they're succeeding. It might be possible to go there and learn more of these inside forces, and from them more of the invaders. This information would be useful."

"That could be useful information," the queen said. She eyed Mark curiously. "This is your source, Portia?"

"Yes. I trust him," Portia said. The only time she hadn't

trusted him was when he'd been under a coercion spell cast by Deyelna, a spell Portia had broken. Deyelna was dead, and Portia felt no coercion around Mark. He would never knowingly betray her.

"He is unknown to us. We would require he submit to a truth spell."

Portia nodded and ignored Mark's pointed stare burning into her right ear.

"Even so, there is no need for you to go there personally, is there?" the queen asked. "Our champion has just returned to us. Would it not be foolish to risk her yet again?"

Mark turned to face Portia and mouthed the word 'champion' with a questioning look on his face.

"I'll explain later," Portia said under her breath to Mark. He shook his head, then looked back to the queen.

Without invitation, Mark stepped forward. "We won't get caught. No one is better than sneaking around than Portia."

The queen raised one eyebrow at this statement and looked to Portia. Portia felt her face flushing red from her neck to the tips of her ears. It was not the sort of praise she wished the queen to hear. The king consort chuckled quietly behind his hand, leaning back in his throne. Portia glanced at him and he gave her a wink. Her stomach unclenched a little.

Mark realized his mistake. "I mean, I mean she can blend into a crowd and get information without any being the wiser."

"We have spies," the queen said. "We can send those while still keeping our Jack close."

"Jack?" Mark asked.

"Our Jack," the queen said, motioning to Portia.

Portia groaned inwardly. She had told Mark nothing about this. He narrowed his eyes and gave Portia a glance but then continued his remarks to the queen.

"I'm the one with connections to learn more. I trust Portia. I don't know these spies of yours," he said, jutting his chin out stubbornly. Portia wanted to kick him but didn't dare in the middle of court.

"That is an issue," Queen Lorica said, her eyes flashing at Mark. The court quieted at her anger. Finally, Mark shifted his weight and lowered his eyes, unable to continue facing the queen's wrath.

The general standing nearby cleared his throat, catching the queen's eye.

"Yes, General?" the queen asked.

"As you are aware, Your Majesty, if Lusatiana falls, and if what this young man says is true, we will be in bad straits indeed. Forts or no, we would be hard-pressed to defend the kingdom from three sides without inviting additional forces onto our lands. Such as the elves."

"Are you telling us we would need to allow armed elves through our countryside just to defend our own kingdom?"

The general looked uncomfortable but pushed on. "It would be a risk, yes. But it would be hard to say it is less of a risk than to be unable to repel unknown invaders from the sea. We as yet do not know who these invaders are, and we have little information of their ships except that they are fast and rely not on wind or oars but some unknown force."

The queen's lips thinned.

The fine hairs on the general's head waved as he stepped back involuntarily at the queen's look. "The fact that there are no living witnesses to who the invaders are does not bode well. Not a single refugee has been able to tell us what they are like. We can only think they are deadly or intend to be so."

The queen nodded and looked again to Portia and Mark, a frown on her face. The king consort leaned in from his throne and whispered in her ear. The queen listened intently and held up one hand. The king consort leaned back in his throne.

Portia stepped forward, her need to speak warring with her fear of misstepping in court.

"Yes, Portia?" the queen asked.

"Your Majesty, if my destiny is to save the kingdom, would it not be better to do so far from the capital instead of letting the invaders come close? I am not walking away from my destiny. Never." Portia hesitated. She was loath to admit Mark was right about her skills in sneaking, but there was truth to it. "It *is* easier to be ignored if others think that one is just a child."

"We do not have any such spies," the general said helpfully, earning an angry look from the queen. The queen's hands clenched into fists and then slowly relaxed back open. She smoothed her dress.

"Do you think to know all our resources?" the queen asked the general, ice in her voice.

"No, Your Majesty. Forgive my presumption," the general said, stepping back once again.

The court was silent for a minute. Nobles held their breath, waiting for the next words.

"Fine. Very well. You may have leave for a short trip," the queen said, her voice chillingly calm. She held up a hand to stop Professor Hilda and Professor Aelric from protesting. "First, this young man will pass a truth counsel with the Magic Academy. Furthermore, you will accept all the supplies and assistance my general deems necessary."

The queen stood and her guard and attendants formed around her as she walked off, followed by the king consort and his attendants. The rest of the court melted away, whispering excitedly about what they had seen. Portia hoped none of them were spies for Lusatiana.

———

FROM THE PALACE, they went directly to the Magic Academy and a council room. Professor Aelric and Professor Hilda would not let Portia in the room while they questioned Mark, but it did not take long. Within thirty minutes they emerged again, Mark's eyes wide from the experience. He looked a little dazed, but Professor Hilda and Aelric looked more relaxed than they had at the palace. They gave Portia and Mark a sealed letter to take to the guardhouse in the morning and then escorted them to the portal doors to return to pyromancy house. Mark was to stay the night, for it was deemed safer than allowing him to go to an inn.

Most of the students were at night practice when they returned. Portia felt guilty for not going, but they were to leave early in the morning, and it would not do to start their journey sleep-deprived. Portia opened the door to her room with a sigh and flopped on the bed. Mark stood at the door and looked around. There were only Ella's and Portia's beds.

"You don't get Ella's bed. We'll flip a coin to see who has to sleep on the floor and who gets my bed," Portia said. "Unless you'd rather sleep on the couch in the common room."

"No thanks," Mark said. "I'll take the floor over being so exposed any day. Some of your students might attack me in the night thinking I was a robber, or worse." He shivered exaggeratedly. She gave a half smile, being far too tired to laugh out loud.

Throwing some blankets and extra pillows on the floor, Portia arranged the room. Mark flipped a copper coin up into the air, then caught it and slapped it on Portia's desk. "Call."

Without even looking she said, "Crests."

"Aha!" Mark exclaimed. "I get to live the life of a rich student tonight."

Portia walked to the desk to look at the coin. It was heads. Mark laughed.

"Did you really think I'd cheat?" he asked, a smirk on his face.

Portia didn't bother to answer but instead growled at him, sending him into a fit of laughter.

"Well, we shall never know because I didn't have to. Or did I?" he asked, teasing her further.

She waved away his joke.

"Who is this?" a high-pitched voice asked from the doorway.

Portia turned to see Ella standing and staring at Mark, one

hand on her hip. She looked both indignant and intrigued, her eyes looking Mark up and down. He glared back at her then pointedly walked to Portia's bed and slowly sat down, making a show of his rear end touching the bedspread.

"Portia, please explain." Ella turned her gaze to Portia, her hand still on her hip. "Who is this ruffian?"

"A friend," Portia said. She wasn't sure how much to tell Ella, for she was known for sharing secrets, not keeping them. Anything she shared tonight would be spread across the campus by noon tomorrow.

"I've never been called a ruffian before," Mark said. He pulled the ball from his pocket and threw it against the wall, catching it as it rebounded.

Portia turned to stare at Mark. She had not heard that sound in a long time. "Mark," she said, chidingly, "people might be sleeping."

He caught the ball and slipped it back in his pocket, giving Portia a shrug. "Sorry."

"Portia?" Ella said, tapping her foot now.

"Hilda knows about him. She keyed the door so he could be here. We're going to visit some of his family where he works tomorrow. We're old friends."

This got Ella's attention. "Again? You just got back a few weeks ago. Why did you bother getting into the Academy if you're never here to learn?"

"I love being a part of the Academy. I just have to take care of some other stuff. And you know how hard I work. It's not like they're making it easy for me when I'm gone." Despite her words, Portia felt a pang of guilt. It would be so much easier if she could just stay and go to classes like all the other students. And they had no idea what she was learning or doing. Did the other students really think she was just goofing off?

Tears pricked at her eyes. It had been a long day.

Ella noticed and her stance softened immediately. "Okay, you *might* have a good reason. And as long as Hilda knows. But you," she turned to Mark and waved a finger at him. "I'm watching you."

"That will be easy, since I'm staying here tonight," Mark said, flashing a smile.

"What?! Does Hilda know about that, too?" Ella asked, indignation back in her voice.

Portia nodded, too tired to explain any further.

"Fine. But I'm going to booby-trap my bed. If you try anything, *ruffian*, you're going to explode. That's what they teach us here at this school, how to make ruffians explode." Stomping into the room, Ella threw her bag on her desk then sat on her bed and glared at Mark.

Mark laughed a bit then stopped, unsure if she was joking or not. He glanced at Portia, who shook her head. He wasn't entirely reassured. His eyes were round as he looked again to Ella and she mimicked a gigantic explosion with her hands while glaring back at him.

Portia turned to the work on her desk and ignored both of them. Morning could not come soon enough.

THEY LEFT EARLY the next day, careful to not wake Ella. There was no hot breakfast in the house kitchen, it being far too early for that, but there was a note from Hilda and directions to two packed sacks of food in the cool storeroom in the back.

The guardhouse was on the edge of campus. They had been directed to go to the Academy guardhouse and not the city guardhouse since it was closer. Like the rest of campus, it was made of the blue stone that all the Magic Academy buildings were constructed of. Portia had only been to the guardhouse one time previously and it was not an especially happy memory since she had been questioned there about the death of Deyelna.

The sun was just rising as they walked through the empty campus after emerging from the portal door in the inner courtyard.

"So, what is a Jack?" Mark asked, looking at Portia. "I wanted to ask last night, but that harridan of a roommate of yours, Ella, would never leave. Does she know what a Jack is?"

"No, she doesn't. Thank you for not asking in front of her."

"I'm not a complete idiot," Mark said, shifting the heavy bag of food on his shoulder.

"I never said you were," Portia said.

"Didn't you? You sure didn't share what Jack was with me. I knew you had an audience with the king and queen... I had no idea you were something special to them."

"I'm not," Portia said, feeling defensive.

Mark stopped walking and blocked Portia's way, his legs

spread wide. He had an obstinate set to his jaw; the same look he'd had as a five-year-old.

Portia threw up her hands. "Okay, they think I'm something special. I still don't understand it. It has something to do with the different magics I can do. Apparently not a lot of people can do that."

"Well, yes, I could've told you that. I don't know about this Jack business, but it's true most people can't do much magic at all." Mark stared at her, incredulous. "How did you not realize that?"

"Most of the orphans could do some," Portia argued.

"Some, yes. But not... not what you can do. There's a big difference."

"I was too busy worrying about surviving and protecting you to keep track of it." Portia nodded in the direction of the guardhouse. They really should get going.

"Don't blame taking care of me," Mark said, resuming his walk again. He also felt the urgency of their journey.

They walked in silence for a few moments, passing several tall buildings. Once again, Portia was in the beautiful campus. Even now it didn't feel real that she was going to school here. Even with all that had happened, it still felt... so much safer than anything she'd experienced in Valencia.

"You know, if I'd made a big deal of it, Deyelna would've come down on us hard and fast. I don't know if John could have even protected us. Maybe I just didn't want to know," Portia said softly. She walked straight ahead, not looking at Mark.

He nodded at that and they kept going.

A pack of guards ran by on their way to the morning shift change.

To Portia's surprise, Captain Ross was waiting for them, leaning insolently in the front doorframe, his arms crossed. He had a wry smile on his face and tapped his toes. "So, we meet again. Impressive orders came down for you last night. Although I thought you might be here earlier."

Captain Ross was a slight man she'd met only one time before. He thought it amusing that a thief such as she could do so well in the Academy. Her heart warmed at seeing him.

"Good morning, Captain. Are we late?" Portia asked.

"Oh, not that late, but our good man here is glad to see you I'm sure. Now he can stop keeping your horses warm." The captain motioned to two beautiful horses being led around by an Academy guard. She sucked in her breath at the high sheen on the horses' coats and their rippling muscles. These were no ordinary horses. She nodded apologetically at the guard who didn't seem as mad as Captain Ross implied.

"The Academy has good taste," Mark said, clucking appreciatively while appraising the animals.

"Oh no, we do not normally rate such fine animals," Captain Ross said. "Those were sent down by the general, along with a letter for exchanges of horses along the way. Riches I've never heard of any student getting, except for those who purchase such benefits with their noble house coffers, of which I know you have none, Portia." He pushed off the doorframe and came closer to Portia. "What have you done this time?"

"Nothing bad," Portia said, her face turning red.

Captain Ross stared at Portia but then finally waved her and Mark into the guardhouse. "I should hope nothing bad, for it would be a bad example indeed to reward bad behavior with such fine mounts. Come, I'll show you what else is waiting for you."

Inside the guardhouse there was a bundle of papers addressed to Portia, as well as saddlebags full of supplies and a coin purse with silver. The papers were letters authorizing the exchange of horses on the journey, at least as far as the border to Lusatiana.

Mark pulled at Portia's sleeve as she was examining the letters. He nodded for her to step aside so they could speak in private.

"These horses are a problem. We will stand out too much. Just having horses alone will attract attention," Mark said.

Portia noticed for the first time what Mark was wearing. Gone was the rich embroidered jacket, changed out for one of dull brown linen, clean and serviceable but unremarkable. She had worn her own green traveling outfit: breeches, linen shirt doublet, and jacket. They were well-made but from afar did not look luxurious, having no decorative stitching or other fancy embellishments. She nodded at Mark but didn't know what else to do. These horses were from the general, under direct orders from the queen.

"Is there an issue?" Captain Ross asked. He stood by the desk containing their traveling goods. He must be assigned with seeing them off.

"The finery of the horses might be too much for some to

resist. We do not wish to attract too much attention," Portia said.

"Ah, that could be a problem. Many would want those horses. However, we have been authorized to send a few guards with you. The last exchange is for plainer rides to use inside Lusatiana."

Portia chewed her lip while thinking on that solution.

Captain Ross held up the orders. "I don't think any of us want to go against these."

Nodding, Portia agreed. This plan did get them to the border quickly. They would worry about fading into the crowd when they got closer. There was too much chaos with the refugees, as well as the roving bandits within the kingdom, to ride on alone, no matter what the horses looked like.

Mark grunted. "At least this will be a faster journey than my journey here," he said, grabbing one of the saddlebags and shoving his own pack of clothing and one of the packs of food inside.

Captain Ross looked Mark up and down. "Where are you two going exactly, anyway?"

"Rodaine," Mark said. He turned and stared at the captain. "Is asking that question in your pack of orders as well?"

"Mark," Portia said, warningly, while touching his arm.

Mark shrugged off Portia's hand but turned away from the captain who had raised his eyebrows at Mark's retort.

Portia grabbed her own pack and walked out.

The journey took four days, riding hard. They were able to stop at several guardhouses to change horses where they were also given simple but solid meals. The two guards escorting them to the border left them to ride together, mostly following from behind and sometimes scouting ahead. They did not lend themselves to small talk.

When they were close to the border with Lusatiana, they stopped at one last guardhouse and were given two nondescript horses whose manes and tails had been allowed to grow out and become shaggy. Despite their rough appearance, they were young healthy animals. They traded out the new saddlebags for older ones, patched and well-worn, and they put on their oldest clothes. They stashed most of their money in hidden spots on their person and in second purses hidden under their clothes.

"I thought your reputation," Portia whispered, not wanting to give away too much to the guards standing nearby, "was that of a young rich man. I don't know many who dress like that."

"They dress like that if they want to survive when they don't have their guards or their carriages with them," Mark said. "I'll change once we're safely inside the city walls."

It took two days from the border to reach Rodaine. There were fewer people on the road. They were able to find a quiet spot in the woods to rest overnight rather than risk going to an inn.

Mark had told Portia nothing about the capital city of Lusatiana, so when they crested a hill and viewed it for the first time, Portia gasped. There was an enormous wall built out into the sea and stretching out to meet the coastline past either side of the city. It rose, dark and towering, a hundred lengths into the air. The structure dwarfed the tiny ships below passing through a small opening that led from the harbor out into the open sea. Looking more closely, Portia realized the ships were three-masted warships. They were not tiny, but still, the wall dwarfed them. How could such a thing be built out in the ocean?

"You worry about this city being invaded from the sea?" Portia asked.

He looked back and gave her a lopsided smile. "A wall, no matter how high, is worthless when the door is left open."

Portia nodded, understanding. Treachery could undo any city.

It could undo anything.

7

They rode down the hill and approached the city. The seawall dominated the harbor and the city itself, casting a long shadow. Movement flashed on the far side of the central opening as something passed across it. Ships. It was hard to tell how many since the wall hid the ones closest to it, as well as the ships themselves having no sails, making them hard to pick out from the dark sea. But even so, Portia counted five formations further out at sea.

Her horse stumbled on the path, pulling her attention back. Patting the horse on the neck, she vowed to be more alert.

"Are those the invaders?" Portia pointed out to sea.

Mark squinted at the formations. He swore softly but didn't answer her. He kicked his horse into a trot and raced down the path to the gate. Portia followed. She guessed that meant they were invaders.

The city gates were closed despite it being the middle of the day. Mark's eyebrows knit together, and he would not meet Portia's concerned look. They stood in the gravel pad in front of the shut gates.

Mark yelled up to the guard on the arch overhead. "We wish to enter."

The guard laughed and motioned for them to leave back the way they had come. "The gates are shut, can't you see that? Go away."

Mark's horse danced backwards as the bit pulled tightly in his mouth. Mark loosened the reins, then dug in his saddlebag and pulled out a folded piece of parchment. "We have business here."

"Are you daft?" the guard asked, no longer smiling. "There's probably a hundred naval ships outside our wall. We're under siege. I'm not opening the gate for anyone, no matter how much of a runt ye may look like."

Mark did not waiver and held the guard's eyes. "Understood about the siege, sir. All the same, I'm going to insist that you open the gate for us. I beg some understanding of the anger of my employers were I not to return to work." Mark waved the paper up at the guard. "I would not be the only one to feel their wrath."

The guard stared the paper for a moment, then swore and came down the inner stairs to emerge at a small door next to the main gate. He grabbed the document from Mark's hand and opened it, his eyes widening just a bit as he read it.

Folding it quickly again, he shoved it back into Mark's

hand. "In you go—and hurry—we're not to leave the gate open for long."

One of the main doors swung open just wide enough for the horses to pass, nearly shutting on the tail of Portia's mount when they passed through.

Once they were some distance from the gate, Portia turned to Mark. "What was that parchment?"

"A work pass. From my company."

"A company that scares the guard?" Portia asked, her stomach tight. What had Mark gotten into by working for a company that held sway over the city guards?

But Mark only shrugged his shoulders and wouldn't look at her. Portia gritted her teeth. It didn't feel like much of a team when Mark was holding back so much from her.

"Are the ships new? Those on the far side of the wall," Portia pressed.

"There being that many is new but not unexpected. When I left there was but one or two. Things are happening faster than I feared they would." Mark's face was white.

"Invaders?"

"Probably. My company will be pleased." A frown pulled at his mouth.

The city was strangely quiet. They passed through a market on the way to Mark's home, but rather than a boisterous affair, it was one of subdued talk and whispers. Citizens snuck glances to the harbor even as business was conducted over sacks of grain and measures of cheese.

Mark's home was a small stone structure nestled between two large warehouses. At one time it might have been a luxurious house of a wealthy merchant next to his place of business. There was even a stable for the two horses behind the house. Fashion had long ago taken the wealthy to a new neighborhood, but even in disrepair, the quality of the home was clear.

They settled the horses in the back and then walked around to the front door.

"How can you afford this?" Portia asked, gazing at the building Mark had all to himself. "Several people could live here."

"But most wouldn't want to live in this neighborhood, so I've gotten it cheaply. Even with having to spend money on clothes, I can still save something here and there," Mark said, as he shut the door behind them in the living room.

Portia flopped down on the couch along the far wall. A cloud of dust puffed up around her and she coughed. "Don't you ever clean?"

"You're cleaning it for me. Sit in the far end now. I'll open the windows and we can wave the dust out."

"That's not how it works," Portia said.

"Are you sure?" He smirked at her, arms crossed.

"Never mind." Portia leaned back and sighed. She was not going to clean Mark's place, so she'd better not talk about it anymore and keep giving him ideas.

"Lunch?" Mark asked as he passed through to the kitchen. It was a small room with a single hearth and pot on an arm that could swing over a lit fire. He pulled two plates from a cupboard and brought them into the living room. They shared the provisions they had bought at the market. The cheese was exquisite, better than she'd ever had in Haulstatt. The purchases included nuts, fruit and bread, although everything had been frightfully expensive. Mark poured two glasses of mead.

"Tell me again why you think your company is involved with the cult?" Portia said around a mouthful of bread and cheese.

"Well, they're rich as Croesus, and the money just seems to appear." Mark took a swallow of his mead.

"So? There are lots of rich folks."

"Yeah, true. But these folks are different. They talk differently. It's almost as if they're talking in a code. And some of them have these odd expressions on their faces. Their eyes glow with something creepy. I don't know what to call it. Obsession, perhaps." He gave a small shiver. "They don't trust me fully, not with everything, but I've snuck in and seen some papers. I didn't dare take any, being here by myself, but perhaps that caution was a mistake. Maybe it would have been better to have those papers with me back in Haulstatt. I had no idea you could get us an audience with Queen Lorica."

Portia threw an olive pit onto her plate. She hadn't really known she could either. Hilda had made that happen.

Mark leaned back. "So, what exactly have you been learning? And where were you? What was your roommate complaining about—you always being gone?"

"What is this, an inquisition?" Portia stalled, filling up her plate a second time. Mark knew about her Jack designation now but didn't know what it really meant, or its history.

"I spent the last couple months in Rocabarra," she finally said.

Mark looked at her quizzically.

"It's an Elven kingdom to the northwest."

"No kidding," he said, putting his glass down and staring at her. "Did the queen send you there too?"

Portia's face reddened.

"Who are you?" Mark looked at her as if seeing her for the first time.

"You know who I am!" Fear and irritation and fear crept into her voice. "I'm the same person I've always been."

Marked stared at her from underneath hooded eyes. "Perhaps."

"I am," Portia insisted. She went to the kitchen and retrieved a pitcher of water for them, filling their glasses.

"Okay, same Portia, what did you learn in Rocabarra?"

"I learned some better healing spells. A lot of them, actually. But they have to be sung and take some time."

"I thought you were pretty good with the healing before," Mark said. Portia had healed many of their bruises and cuts earned from gang assignments in Valencia.

"Pretty good. But I'm much better now," Portia said.

Mark whistled under his breath. "I see you've also acquired a fine new sword. Was that a *gift?*"

Portia glanced at her pack. He must have peeked inside. "Actually, it was a gift. I'm learning to use it. Slowly."

"Fast would be better considering where we are."

"I'm trying. You could have stayed and learned too."

Mark scowled and looked away. "You know I couldn't have. Is this the thanks I get for coming and getting you when I learned of danger? I could have just taken the money and run. Like some people."

"I didn't run!"

"No, you just magically appeared in a different city," Mark fingered the scar on his face then got up and went into the kitchen and dug in the cupboards for another bottle of mead. He had that scar because of her. She'd left him behind in Valencia at Deyelna's mercy, or lack of mercy.

Portia couldn't meet his eyes when he came back and refilled her glass. The mead mixed with the water still in her cup. She glanced up at him as he sat down heavily again, sipping on his full glass.

Silence hung over the room.

"What about you? Have you learned anything new with your magic?" Portia asked, picking at her food.

"Actually, I have." Mark pulled the coin from his bag sitting nearby. Holding it up, he made it glow with his light magic, shimmering dots of light covering its surface and making it hard to look at directly. He dropped the coin into the clear glass pitcher of water, and it sank to the bottom, the lights still covering it. Rainbows danced on the wall from the prisms coming through the water.

"That's impressive. How did you learn that?" Portia asked, determined to learn it herself.

"It's called boredom. And hours alone thinking about what would happen in a sea battle. What could be more useful than seeing underwater?"

"Not being underwater?" she retorted.

"Well, there is that." Mark rose and gathered the dishes, taking them into the kitchen. "We should get some rest. It might be a long night."

He grabbed two blankets from a pile in the corner and tossed one to Portia. They both lay down, one on each couch, and pulled the blankets over themselves. Napping on demand was a skill they had both learned as orphans.

A QUARTER MOON hung low in the sky. It gave some light but not too much. Fortunately, they didn't have to go far for their first target—a nearby warehouse. Mark had outfitted them with rope and caltrops. It felt like old times when Portia and Mark ventured into Serpent's territory in Valencia. It was as if she had never left that old life, except now Mark was at least a foot taller, and she was probably taller too. She felt much older.

As in Valencia, long metal ladders were fastened to the side of the warehouses and led to the roofs. They climbed one close to Mark's house and then ran from rooftop to rooftop, easily making the three foot or so jump between them. They could have traveled the entire distance at street level, but it was safer to do so on the rooftops where fewer people could spy them. It was one of her old thieving rules: go in at the highest point in the building.

"What gangs do we have to watch for here?" Portia asked.

"None," Mark said, huffing slightly from his last jump.

Surprised pricked at Portia's scalp. "What do you mean, none? Are the guards that good at keeping them off the street?"

"Ha! No, that's not it." Mark shook his head and gave a rueful laugh. "There are no orphans here. At least not many that I could see, or at least notice."

She stared at him. "No orphans! How can that be? There were so many in Valencia."

"I know." Mark stopped walking along the rooftop edge and looked to Portia. "Makes one think it might not be a natural situation, no?"

Not natural. Then why would Valencia have so many children without parents? Even Coverack, the capital of her kingdom, had more than a few orphans. Many of those in Coverack were from the plagues, but that still didn't explain the large numbers in Valencia. She'd never heard of the plagues reaching that far—at least not in her lifetime.

"Maybe it's this city. Something about it is not quite right."

Portia snorted. "Why, because parents take care of their kids?"

"You mean the parents live?" Mark's voice had an edge.

Portia remembered the scene of his mother's accident. "Sorry. That's not what I meant."

Mark stopped at the edge of one building, squatting low to not be seen from below. Portia joined him.

"In all the time I've been here, I haven't found out who made that giant wall out in the harbor. No one seems to know." He motioned to the surrounding city. "They act as if it's always been there and asking them about it only makes them uncomfortable."

"Why uncomfortable?" Portia's brows knit together.

"I don't know. It's odd. This city is odd." Mark rose to move on.

Finally, they reached the warehouse at the end of a long line of warehouses. It was newer than the rest. Less debris littered its rooftop. They found an access hatch tucked in the far corner of the roof. Mark pulled a crowbar from the bag slung across his back. The hatch was constructed of ironwood, and a newer style, which was more difficult to open than the simple soft-wood hatches of the older warehouses. It took both Mark and Portia leaning on the crowbar to pop the covering up. When the hatch finally released from its hinges, it skittered across the rooftop making an enormous amount of noise. They both froze, listening for any reaction to what they had done. There was none.

"That's not good," Mark said quietly, retrieving the hatch and fingering where the hinges had been broken. They would have to put it back on top and affix it the best they could, but a close inspection would reveal the damage.

The hatch opened up into a small room that overlooked

the rest of the warehouse. Using tiny magical lights sent into the warehouse, they scoped out the layout. There were no exterior windows to leak light to the outside. They only had to worry about someone being inside and seeing them, but blessedly, there was no one there. Climbing down into the small room, Mark pulled the hatch back over the opening to keep the light from escaping upwards.

It was quiet inside the warehouse. No guards roamed the halls.

The warehouse was split into many large rooms. They came to the first door. It was locked.

"Here," Mark whispered. He held out a small leather pouch.

Unwrapping it, Portia found a small pick set. She'd lost her last one in Valencia.

"Yours. A gift. I thought we might need it." Mark winked at her.

Portia made quick work of picking the lock. The first room held nothing but junk, as did the rest of the rooms down the hall. Moldy cloth, broken bits of furniture, some cheap pottery in wooden crates. It hardly seemed worth locking the doors for.

"Why do you think this warehouse is important?" Portia asked after the third such room, shaking her head in disgust. She wiped her hands on her pants.

"This warehouse was mentioned in some of the most secretive papers I found," Mark said, perplexed. "Could it have been a misdirection?"

A twinge of fear gripped Portia's heart. A misdirection

might mean they knew someone was reading their papers. They could be onto Mark. Hopefully, that was not the case. They must be missing something. She shrugged her shoulders while turning away so any anxiety on her face would not be apparent to Mark.

She looked into the room one last time as she was about to pull the door shut and noticed a mismatch on the depth of the far wall. There was an unevenness to it, a shadow from floor to ceiling in one section. If not for the flickering lights they used, she would not have seen it. Instead of shutting the door, she walked back into the room and tried to get to the shadowed area. A stack of crates blocked the way.

"There's something here," Portia said. "Is it possible this isn't an exterior wall?"

Mark followed her, his face scrunched. "I'm not sure. It seems like it should be bigger inside than it is."

There was only one corridor down the warehouse, one they had walked as they explored each room. If there was anything beyond the wall, it was not possible to reach from the corridor.

Trying to be quiet and move quickly, they pulled the crates away from the wall and felt with their fingers where the wall did not line up exactly. There was another shadow an arms' width further down the wall. The distance between the two shadows was the width of a large door. On impulse Portia pushed the wall between the shadows as hard as she could and then stepped back. The wall swung slowly inward. It was a door. The hairs on her arms rose with the ease of finding how to open it.

"How did you know how to do that?" Mark asked.

"I didn't. Lucky guess." She didn't mention the slight tingling she felt from the magic around the door. She had willed it to open as she had pushed but could not clearly explain what that meant to anyone else. She did not really even understand herself.

An enormous metal object dominated the room, filling the center and extending to the far wall. A wide-open gullet faced them, as if a gigantic stew pot was placed on its side and waited to be filled. It hung over a grated hearth and was topped with a flue and venting that extended up to the ceiling and the outer wall. Lumps of melted metal, including what looked like a drop of gold, lay scattered on the floor. A bin of wood sat next to it, along with a set of bellows so large it could only be operated by two people.

"What is that, do you think?" Mark asked. He kicked through the debris on the floor, stopping when something caught his eye. He bent down to pick it up. It was a small disc. Portia came over to examine it.

"That looks like gold," she said, trying to remember the melting point of gold from Hilda's class but couldn't quite. She really needed to make an effort to be a better student.

Mark flipped the disc and then rolled it between his fingers. "It feels like a gold coin, except it's smooth. This is strange."

"True," Portia said, looking around. "They are using this to make something but don't want anyone to know."

Mark flipped the gold disc one last time then slipped it into his pocket.

They went back and checked the other rooms again, but none had a hidden door in them, at least none that they could find.

They exited the warehouse the same way they entered and ran over the roof to the next warehouse over. Despite its older appearance, it was nicer on the inside and not full of junk. Instead, it had neat rows of crates and a workroom off to the side that was swept and well-cared for.

Portia went to a crate and pried it open using Mark's crowbar. Pushing the straw aside revealed hundreds of gold disks that looked just like the one Mark found earlier.

He gave a low whistle. "Could all that really be gold?"

"Does it need to be real if we can't tell the difference?" Portia asked.

Searching the room, she found a hidden compartment in a trunk beneath the workbench which yielded a tray of small metal blocks. Pulling two of the blocks out triumphantly, she laid them on the workbench.

"Give me the disc," she said to Mark, holding out her hand.

"Get your own, this one's mine," he said, a touch of a whine in his voice.

"I'll give it back! Just hand it over."

Mark huffed but withdrew the disc from his pocket and handed it to Portia. Putting one of the metal blocks on the stone floor, she placed the gold disc on top and covered it with the second block. Portia pulled a large hammer off the work room shelf then used it to strike the top block as hard as she could. The noise bounced around the warehouse and rang in their ears.

"Hey, we're going to get caught!" Mark whispered urgently, looking around as if guards were going to instantly appear. "And what are you doing to my gold?"

"Sorry." It had been louder than she thought it would be.

They waited for a moment, listening, but there was no other noise. Portia quietly placed the hammer back on the workbench then lifted the top metal block from the stack on the floor. Pulling out the golden disc she grinned then placed it, now a gold coin of Haulstatt, into Mark's hand.

"Holy Blessings, they are making money!" Mark said.

"Is that what they pay you with?" Portia asked, a glint in her eye. "Do you really think it's real gold?"

"They pay me in silver," Mark said, thrusting out his chin.

"Wanna bet we can find a crate of silver discs around here?" Portia asked, rubbing it in.

Mark scowled at her. "It's probably real," he said, pouting. "They must be mining it from somewhere. Though I don't understand why they don't just sell the raw gold for coins."

"That would attract a lot of attention, I'm guessing, but so does being a rich company. There is something we're not getting here."

The company had a lot of power in the city, that much alone was evident from the guard's reaction to Mark's work pass. Was it based in bribes, or something more deadly? The guard had acted not just cowed but *terrified*.

Checking one of the crates, Portia found a name stamped

on the outside; *The Luminance.* "Do you think this is the name of a ship?" she asked Mark, pointing to the stamp.

"It could be. I don't know all the ships, but that sounds like a likely name for one. There's no company by that name, at least none that I know."

They looked at each other. Portia guessed he was thinking the same thing she was. They had to go and investigate the pier.

REACHING the pier was not a fun exercise in the middle of the night. The city was even quieter than it had been during the day, with most residents sleeping or at least safely inside their homes. The silence felt oppressive. Any noise they made would stand out. Anyone out on the streets would attract attention.

The warehouses ended far from the harbor which was at least one neighborhood over, so walking along their flat rooftops was not an option.

"Act like my date," Portia said.

"What?" Mark asked, surprised.

"Don't people have dates here? Besides, if we act drunk, we can get away with being idiots out and about. Surely there are some drinking idiots in this city too."

"Oh, that there are. Fine," Mark said, then made a slight gagging motion in Portia's direction. He stuck out an arm for her to place her own in. "You are too much like my sister for this."

"We're *pretending*, remember?"

"I'm a drunk, remember? Just take my arm and stop complaining." Mark held out his arm, faking a stagger, so she had to grab it before he fell over.

They only encountered one man on their walk to the pier. He was dressed like a soldier and laughed at Mark's stumbling down the street. "Take that idiot home, miss, there's a curfew!"

"Will do sir, sorry sir," Portia said, bobbing her head and not making eye contact with the soldier.

Things got more complicated as they got closer to the pier. Unlike the mostly empty streets they'd found so far, the pier was well lit and heavily guarded.

Mark pulled Portia insistently along, trying to bluff their way onto the pier. He waved at the nearest guard and smiled. "G' night fancy guard peoples..." Mark's speech was convincingly slurred.

The guard chuckled a bit but then moved firmly in Mark and Portia's path, blocking access to the pier. He stood with his feet apart and one hand out. "No fun here tonight. Go home before I lock you up for violating curfew."

"Oh, come on, you know how 'tis. I want to show my girl the shimmering water and how romantical it is," Mark said, slinging an arm over Portia shoulders and dragging her close. "Just for a few minutes. You remember what it's like, you know." Mark tried to wink at the guard; instead his entire face scrunched up on one side. He was surprisingly adept at imitating a drunk.

"Not tonight, kid. You can thank me for the favor later."

The guard grabbed Mark by his shoulders and turned him around, dragging Portia along too, and pushed both of them back the way they had come. They stumbled away with the guard's laughter ringing out behind them.

When Mark and Portia had gone far enough to be out of the light they stopped behind the edge of a building.

"Is that new?" Portia asked, straightening and stretching her cramped back, glad Mark was no longer hanging off her.

Mark rolled his head and stretched his neck. "The guards? Yeah, I think that is, although I can't be sure. I've never been down here at night. There were no guards, at least none that I noticed the one time I was here during the day."

"I mean the curfew."

"Yeah, that too," Mark said, scowling and looking around. "This explains why it's so quiet around here."

"They make me want to go on the dock even more. Something valuable is out there." Portia peered around the corner of the building back towards where the guards were. The guards were laughing and joking standing in front of a stack of crates. It should be possible to sneak around behind them, especially if they kept to the light. Portia motioned to Mark and explained what she was thinking.

He nodded, considering. "The worst that could happen, I suppose, is we fall off the back into the water."

They walked around the block and came back through a tiny alley to get a different vantage point of the pier. Rats scurried away from their steps. The mouth of the alley opened up to the back side of the stacked boxes on the pier. Crouching low, they ran behind the boxes and the guards. Just as they were passing the guards, Mark grabbed Portia's sleeve and pulled her to a stop so they could listen.

"Stupid kids. Not that I wouldn't give much for an ale right now," one of the guards muttered.

"Quit your complaining, mate, you can buy a keg of ale what they're paying us for these extra shifts," a second voice said.

"I suppose. Still rather be home with the woman or tossing back a pint," the first guard said. "How long you think this will go on for?"

"I dunno. For as long as possible, I hope. More money's always a good idea."

"Maybe," the first guard said, sounding like he didn't believe it. "Do you think it's true about there being a mine out there?"

"Hush! You heard the warning about gossip. I'm not giving up my share of tonight's pay because of your big mouth," the second voice said, with both a warning and a threat.

"And who's going to tell them? Besides, if they're mining out there what's going to happen to our wall? Where ya gonna spend your money if that wall falls?" the first guard said with anger.

"You're so ridiculous; ain't nothing to touch that wall. Now shut up, ya idiot."

Neither guard spoke after that. Mark and Portia looked at each other and then moved on.

Stacks of boxes ran out just before the edge of the pool of light around the guards. Portia peeked around the corner of the boxes and waited until the guards were facing the other way then motioned to Mark. They ran down the dock as quietly as possible. Running on missions as orphans had given them lots of practice muffling their footfalls, and they made barely a sound as they made their way down the dock and out towards the ocean. There were only a few ships in the slips. It felt dark and dangerous so far out on the water, even while standing on the safety of the pier.

Salt water made the wood of the pier slippery. Portia slowed, followed by Mark. They stood in the dark, feeling the spray wash over them and looking back to the lights on shore. Further out on the ocean, the seawall was a dark shadow where no stars showed. A thin edging of moonlight lit the top. Chains and ship rigging clanked and echoed over the water.

A single building sat on the pier ahead of them, lit by a tiny lantern.

"What's that?" Portia whispered to Mark.

He shrugged his shoulders. "That light's not bright enough for a warning for the location of the pier," he said, looking out to sea.

"True. It's only bright enough for those on the pier. Do big ships come in at night?"

"Some must."

"There must be another light for them." Goosebumps rose on Portia's arm.

"It's not lit now."

They crouched low and ran to the small building, stopping underneath the single window. No light shone out from it. Not a sound came from within. Mark rose slowly and peeked through the pane. He shook his head at Portia; there was no one inside.

Portia grabbed the door handle and slowly turned it. It was unlocked. Pushing the door open, they went inside and shut it closed again. It was a single room with only a table and two chairs within, along with a jug of water in the corner.

"This must be a watch point for the harbor, but why is it empty?" Portia asked, looking around then picking up the water jug and shaking it. It was half empty.

"Maybe they think no one will come with the blockade. I don't know if I'd take that risk and lose my first warning by not having someone here all the time," Mark said. He looked out the window to the seawall. It dominated the harbor.

"I agree. This doesn't feel right." A shiver ran down Portia's back. Suddenly, she felt light on her feet, as if the ocean didn't exist and they were hanging in open air high above the ground below. A slight nausea tickled at the back of her throat. They needed to leave this spot. Immediately. They needed to get back to shore.

Portia grabbed Mark and then went to the door, pulling it open. No light fell into the shack, at first confusing Portia until she realized a huge figure stood in the doorway blocking most of the light from the lantern outside. It was clothed head to foot in dark loose material. Only its eyes shone from beneath the hood which shadowed most of its face. It was so tall and large, it blocked the doorway from left to right and would have to duck to get inside the room.

The thing stared right at Portia. It knew she was there. Portia tried to slam the door shut on it, but it extended one hand and stopped the door with a shuddering bang. Her hand stung. It was as if she had slammed the door into a boulder.

Portia backed up towards the window, glancing to see if it had a latch to open it. Mark gave her a subtle shake of his head. The only way out was through the door, or to jump through the panes of glass in the window. The creature ducked and stepped inside, its head brushing the ceiling as it straightened. The air seemed to go out of the room. Mark and Portia retreated further.

A foul smell reached Portia's nose, the scent of leather mixed with rotting garbage. It roiled her stomach.

Portia raised her hand to throw a light spell at it, but before she could, the creature reached into its cloak and pulled out a huge knife. She and Mark yelled, each trying to draw its attention and perhaps rattle it. Just as Portia threw her light spell, Mark did one as well and a burst of combined light hit the creature's eyes. Portia shut her eyes just in time and hoped that Mark did too. They ran around the creature, one to each side, and through the door and down the dock, their footsteps pounding down the pier, the fear of being heard less than the fear of being caught by the thing. A roar of pain from behind them let them know they had injured it.

They were almost to shore when a whistling sound overtook them from behind. Portia flattened onto the dock, skittering forward on her front, but Mark was not fast enough. He let out a cry of pain as something hit him, then he went down, tumbling into a ball. Portia swore under her breath and then scrabbled back towards him.

"Are you all right?" she asked, grabbing at his body and

looking for an injury. He cried when she touched his shoulder but everything else seemed fine.

Mark scrambled to his feet. "Go! Go go go." He ran down the pier, dragging Portia. The wooden pier shook as the huge creature ran after them, but luckily it couldn't keep pace and had no more knives, at least none that it threw. Its heavy steps faded into the background.

They slowed and quieted, easily making their way past the guards by running behind the crates. The guards were too preoccupied bickering to even notice. Going back through the alley they had come and then down several more streets, they finally stopped and huddled inside a doorway, panting.

"Do you know what that was?" Portia asked.

Mark shook his head and winced in pain. He tried to touch his shoulder, but it hurt too much to reach around with his left hand, so he gave up. Portia turned him around and looked. The wound was a several-inch gash that was open and bleeding heavily from their exertions. Putting a hand over it, Portia concentrated on an Elven healing spell, softly singing under her breath and tapping her foot quietly. Mark's shoulder loosened under her hands and relaxed as she continued singing the spell. He let out a soft sigh of relief.

Seeing a rain barrel down the street, Portia went to it and pried the top open. She scooped water and poured it over Mark's back, rinsing the blood out of his clothing and trying to clean him up. Once done, it only looked like he had torn his jacket.

"Are you okay to go on?" she asked, breathless from the spell.

"Yes. Things have changed disturbingly fast... and we need to know what that thing was."

Portia agreed. A pain in her gut told her what she didn't want to know—the creature was something from her nightmares, and her nightmares were coming true.

8

Portia breathed in deeply. "I don't know if we'll find out what the thing was, but at least we have the name of the ship that we're looking for... and for gold or silver. Some sort of mining."

"I told you, the silver is real."

"They're probably both real. Besides, we didn't see any silver discs," Portia said, exasperated.

"That's because my silver coins are real," Mark said as he tested the motion of his arm. "You have gotten better at healing. I approve."

Portia made a face at him. "Okay, smarty, where to now? We have to be careful if there really is a curfew."

"I wager nothing will stop the folks here from going out on the town. We just have to look more closely."

They walked back to the downtown district, staying in the shadows as much as possible. Only the sound of an occasional rat scurrying across the cobblestone streets cut the silence of the night until the footfalls of a man echoed down the street. Portia pulled Mark back into the shadows. They watched the man until he knocked on the door of a darkened tavern. It appeared closed, but when the door was answered, a sliver of light fell into the street and noise leaked out. It was packed with people. The windows must be covered and muffled. Once the door shut and the street returned to silence, Mark pulled Portia back out of the shadows.

"Here we go. You ready?" he asked.

Portia nodded. They presented themselves in front of the same door and Mark knocked sharply. The door swung open just a few inches and Mark held up a silver coin in the opening. A hand plucked the coin then snaked out and grabbed Mark and Portia and pulled them inside. The door slammed shut.

People filled the tavern. Boisterous voices and the thumps of mugs on the wooden tables made a sharp contrast to the quiet night outside.

"I told you," Mark said, a smug look on his face. "Nothing keeps these folks in."

"Let's hope they are the gossiping type."

"There are ways to make sure of it." He held up another silver coin as he walked to the bar, drawing the other patrons' eyes to his ostentatious show of money.

"You're going to get us robbed," Portia whispered in his ear as she grabbed his arm.

Mark gave her a grin, looking around the tavern and waving at someone at the far corner. "We'll worry about that later. I'm trying to make friends now," he said under his breath, shrugging Portia off.

Portia backed off but subtly checked all her knives. She might need them now. There was some advantage to them over a sword, which would be too obvious in a place like this.

The bartender eyed the coin as he walked over to them and slapped his rag down on the counter. He gave Mark a sickly smile. "How can I help you spend that, young man?"

"A fine dinner for my girl and I, and some mead and a good table. There's more where that came from," Mark said, slapping the coin down on the counter and pushing it towards the man.

The bartender picked up the coin and gave a bite then nodded at a quiet table in the far corner. Mark nodded back and then walked to the table, grabbing Portia's hand on the way and bringing her with him.

"Quit with the manhandling," Portia said.

"Relax, it's all part of my persona."

"Your persona is gonna earn a kick," Portia said as she sat down across the table.

No sooner had they been served two glasses of mead than an old man appeared by the table. Mark looked at the old man and then at Portia with a smarmy look.

"What can we do for you, fine sir?" Mark asked the man solicitously.

"I was hoping for a wee bit of food, seeing as how you yourself is so well-off, and for such a young man too. A rich thing like you could spare a few coppers for an old man like me for bread, or perhaps even some meat," the old man said, giving Mark a smile and then looking at Portia for reassurance. She smiled back at him.

"That's all you want? Bread?" Mark asked.

The old man hesitated, then went on. "Meat would be nice too." Mark smiled at him but said nothing. The man clutched his hat in his hands and shifted on his feet. "And maybe even a glass of ale."

"Now we're talking," Mark said, thumping on the table with his hand. "But in return, perhaps you could tell us some tales." Mark leaned in conspiratorially. "You wouldn't perhaps happen to know any mining stories would you?"

The old man's eyes widened at that. He looked around the room and then back at Mark.

Mark waved over a server while holding out another coin. "Bring this man the largest glass of ale that you have and make sure it's never empty. Also food. Whatever we're having."

The old man's eyes widened even further, and finally he nodded. Portia pushed out an empty chair at their table and the old man sat. When the ale arrived, he grabbed the mug with both hands and drank, finishing off a third in just a few swallows.

Mark leaned in to the old man and gave him a grin. The old man leaned back and smiled hesitantly.

Portia kicked Mark under the table. "Could you please see about our food? I'm so hungry," she said sweetly.

Mark started to talk, then hesitated and finally said, "Anything for m'lady." He rose and left Portia alone with the old man.

"I'm sorry about that, sir. My friend doesn't like mining.

He's trying to convince me to talk my brother out of it. My poor brother's heard there's good money in it, and he's determined to do it," Portia said apologetically to the old man.

He nodded at her. "There is money to be had in it, but it's dangerous work. Especially in these times."

Portia feigned surprise. "It's dangerous? Don't tell me that. I would hate anything to happen to my brother. He just wants some money to help support our poor mama. You know how it is."

"I wish I had a son who would think that way about me. Mine just ran off with the ships. Ungrateful lot." The old man drank another third of his ale and was already looking around for a server for more. Portia saw Mark at the bar, serendipitously looking at them while chatting with the bartender.

Portia tapped on the table to get the old man's attention and leaned in. "Tell me about the mining. Tell me what my brother needs to know to stay safe."

The old man looked at Portia's eager face and leaned back. He took a deep breath, relaxing into the storytelling. "How could I not help ye, wee one? I know alls about the mining. But this is just between you and me, young thing, you and me. The best money, the place where your brother should go, is the one by the seawall. Not too many know about it. And I should say you owe me a tip for giving you this information. At least a silver, but I know you might not have the money of your friend so even some coppers would do."

"Oh, anything." Portia made a show of digging around in her purse and pulling out a few coppers and handing them to the old man. "I'm sorry it's not more. We just don't have—"

The man patted her on the arm patronizingly. "It's all right, lass. You can give me more once your brother starts making money, eh?"

Portia nodded eagerly at him. Her skin crawled where he had touched her. *As if I would give you anything.*

"Where exactly by the seawall? It's so long. You know you're so much more helpful than those city guards, knowing all this. All the guards do is yell at him," Portia said, helpless sadness in her voice.

"Ack, those stupid guards. Stay away from them." The old man shook his head then leaned in. "He needs to go to the south side. That's all I know. The south side, and don't let the guards know what he's doing. There's work there, but it's supposed to be a secret." He tapped his cheek. "Lucky for you nothing escapes this old eye."

Portia nodded. "Is there anything else he needs to know?"

"Nope," the old man said and then finished off his ale and waved the tankard around for the server to come and refill it.

Portia touched his arm to get his attention, but his eyes only slid to her once a server came over with a fresh mug of ale. After the server left again Portia leaned in. "Were there any especially large people working at the mine?"

The old man squinted at Portia. "Well they ain't going to be's little skinny misses like you." He gulped down more ale. "Everyone's big'en compared to you."

Portia leaned back and kicked out her legs, giving Mark a subtle nod. He returned, followed by a server holding three dinners. Mark and Portia didn't say anything further and the old man was too preoccupied with eating his meal and trying to drink the second glass of ale quickly enough to get a third before the food was gone.

"Thanks, old man, your company was grand," Mark said as he slipped a few more coins towards the old man and then slapped him on the back as he rose. Portia followed him to the front door. The bouncer opened the heavy wood door and peeked out to make sure the coast was clear before shoving them out into the street.

Mark and Portia pulled their jackets tight against the cold night air and walked down the street towards the warehouse district.

"So?" Mark asked.

"South side of the seawall. Either he didn't know or wouldn't share any more than that," Portia said. "He said to not let the guards know. This probably ties in with the warehouse secret room, don't you think?"

Mark nodded. The wind coming in off the water picked up and blew through their hair. Salt stung Portia's eyes. "Did you learn anything from the bartender?"

"Not about gold, no. But he did mention some unlikely folk now having coin to come in. He suggested mining based on how dirty some of them were and their talk, and he made mention of a rumor of unusually large overseers. He chalked it up to drunks exaggerating about their woes."

Portia thought back to the huge size of the person who had chased them. There was no need to exaggerate how large they had been. The reality was terrifying.

The city fell away, and soon they were trudging through sandy dirt and low brush. The last rickety house grew small behind them as they approached the hills on the south side of the city. Climbing one of the gentle slopes, they had a better view of the towering seawall that rose out of the vast darkness of the sea and reached to the shore beyond the city.

There were no large buildings anywhere near them. Nor were there docks or ships. It looked utterly deserted. Maybe they had been fed a lie and the old man had taken them for suckers. Portia kicked at the ground and looked around at the desolation.

A movement further down the shore caught Portia's attention. Two men ran to the water. There was a dark smudge where the land met the beach and the men were running directly towards it. From the distance, she couldn't tell what it was. She nudged Mark and pointed. He saw them as well.

"Perhaps they know something we don't," Mark said.

"Or they're looking to rob us. You and all that money flashing," Portia whispered back, the hairs on her neck standing up.

"You could take them."

Portia growled back.

They watched the men, but when they reached the dark spot they disappeared. No one ran past it. Mark and Portia exchanged glances. Waiting several minutes, they then scrambled down the hill towards it. Where had the men gone?

"A trap," Portia whispered to Mark, pulling him back to approach more slowly.

"Possibly. Possibly not," he whispered back.

When they got closer, the dark spot resolved into a tiny shack standing alone on the beach. There were no windows on it anywhere. One full circle of the structure showed no one hiding behind it. The shack was made of bleached driftwood and from afar almost looked like a pile of rubble. Several rocks stacked next to it added to the camouflage.

They crept up on it as quietly as they could. There was no sign of the two men. Portia grabbed the door and pulled on it slowly to peek inside, finally swinging it wide, but the shack was empty. There was a hole in the center and the rungs of a ladder stuck out.

"Mine entrance?" Portia asked, whispering.

Mark shrugged. He looked around the beach and saw no one. He motioned for Portia to enter and followed, stepping inside the shack and letting the door shut. They stood still for a moment at the edge of the pit and listened. The only noise was the sound of the waves breaking on the beach outside the shack. Mark made a small magical light mote and held it over the hole in the ground. They peered into the darkness, but all they could see was the rungs of the ladder fading into blackness. The bottom of the ladder was out of reach of Mark's light.

Portia exhaled, her heart pounding in her chest. They would have to go down into that blackness. Her hands shook as she reached for the ladder to go first. Mark tried to push her away, but she held on to the ladder firmly and put a foot on a rung, concentrating on keeping her breathing calm as she lowered herself down. Mark swore softly above her then dropped a light down the pit. Portia watched it fall into the blackness until finally it winked out several seconds below her. Nothing cried out. No alarm sounded. There was nothing to prove the two men they had seen earlier were anywhere close or had passed this way. If they had, they must be further inside now. Portia increased her pace down the ladder, willing herself to reach the bottom before she fainted. Her hands felt tingly and weak. Mark scrambled after her. They reached the bottom and stood in the loose sand at the bottom, listening once again. Not even the sounds of the waves reached where they were standing.

"What were you doing?" Mark whispered furiously.

"Exploring. Isn't that what we're here to do?" Portia whispered back.

Mark slapped his hands on his legs in frustration. "Yes, fine. Just don't rush forward like that."

Portia shivered. She didn't want to admit that if they had stayed too long at the top of the ladder her fear would have overcome her. Mark did not need to know that. Something about going underground unnerved her nearly completely. She turned away from Mark.

Unnoticing, Mark put a hand on the wall around them and left a glowing handprint when he pulled it away again. The light from the handprint illuminated the small area they were standing as well as a tunnel that led away from the ladder in the direction of the ocean.

The tunnel went under the ocean.

Portia's dizziness returned. They would be under the weight of that enormous mass of water. She ran her fingers through her hair. Blood roared in her ears with each heartbeat as she looked at the gaping black tunnel, but there was no other option. It was either go down the tunnel or go back up to the surface and admit defeat.

Squaring her shoulders, Portia entered the tunnel and walked quickly, her jaw clenched.

"Hey!" Mark called after her, trying to be quiet but also get her attention. He ran up and grabbed her arm. "What about not running off?" An edge of fear ran through his hissed question.

"I'm not running."

"Fine." Mark slapped an angry hand on the wall, leaving another glowing hand mark.

"Quietly," Portia hissed.

They walked on in silence, Mark having to trot occasionally to keep up with Portia. The tunnel seemed to go on forever, but Portia guessed they had only been walking for a quarter candle. Mark left an occasional glowing spot on the wall. Turning around, Portia thought she could see them going off into the distance, but it could also have been a trick of her eyes. It was so dark down there.

The tunnel sloped downwards slightly. As they went in further, the air grew thick with moisture. Portia reached out and touched a wall. It was wet. When Mark put a glowing spot on the wall, it reflected a sheen on the walls and roof of the tunnel.

Finally, they reached a wider section of the tunnel. The sounds of their footsteps changed and brought more of an echo with each footfall. The tunnel branched out in several directions. Picking one at random, Portia walked to the right and down the furthest tunnel. Mark held up a glowing light.

After a few minutes, it became harder to walk through an increasingly deeper layer of sand. The tunnel didn't shine as much as the wet earlier ones.

"Stop for a second," Portia said, then squatted to look at the ground.

It was covered in a fine black dirt. Clumps of the dirt lay here and there, as if they had fallen off someone's shovel. Portia picked up a pinch, sniffed it, and then pulled back. It smelled like rotten eggs. The whole tunnel smelled of it, and it was getting worse the further in they went.

"Is that what's stinking?" Mark asked, scrunching up his nose.

Portia nodded. She stopped and brushed off her hands. She wished she could wash the powder off her fingers. Residue was visible even in the dim light.

They continued down the tunnel until the powder underfoot grew thicker and ended with a large pile of the dusty, black dirt blocking off the tunnel. If they wanted to go further, they would have to wade into it or else climb on top. Portia's stomach roiled at the thought of getting it all over herself, and the hairs on the back of her neck were already up. She didn't know what the black powder was, but something told her wading hip deep in it was not a good idea.

"We should turn back," Mark said, his brash persona gone.

"Where did those men go?" Portia said, frustrated. "Is it possible they didn't come down here?"

"They didn't just vanish into the ocean."

Or did they?

Suddenly coming down here felt like a huge mistake. The fear that she'd been holding back at being down in the tunnel and under the immense ocean surged back at Portia. She wanted to yell at Mark but didn't dare, biting back a retort. If anyone was down here, she didn't want to alert them with her voice echoing down the passageways.

"How long do your glowing marks last?" she finally asked, her words coming out reasonably calm and quiet.

"Only a few minutes. The ones on the long tunnels were set for a bit longer."

"That's good for other people to not find them." Portia turned suddenly to face Mark. "But how are we to find our way out again?" Blood raced in her ears, the sound suddenly so loud that it made it hard to breathe.

"We were going down a straight path. How lost could we get?" He didn't sound so sure.

That was true at first, but now they had taken a branch. They had to be careful to remember how to get out again.

They went back the way they had come until they reached the place where the tunnels widened. There were two other tunnels they hadn't explored yet. Mark went to the first of them and would have gone down it except Portia grabbed his sleeve and made him stop. She then went to the tunnel she knew led back to the hut on the shore and used the hilt of her long knife to scratch a mark on the tunnel entrance at head level. Even if they got turned around, they would know how to get out. She nodded at Mark and they went down the passageway he had selected.

The tunnel looked more recently used than the first one

they had explored. There were fresh, crisp footprints in the dust ahead. Someone had been this way recently. There was also more of the black putrid earth. A warning shivered up Portia's spine.

Grabbing Mark's arm, she pulled him close. "Don't use your magic if we find anyone," she whispered. "At least not the most powerful stuff. The glowing lights seem okay."

"Why?"

"I don't know. Just don't." Portia didn't know how to explain her hunch, but she'd been right enough times in the past that Mark just nodded and pulled out his knife. They turned back to the depths of the tunnel.

After moving through the dark tunnel for several minutes, a scratching sound came from ahead. It was lit only by the dimmest glow of a light mote in Mark's hand, which revealed nothing that could be making that sound. As they continued forward, the sound grew louder, soon drowning their footfalls. After several more minutes, a glow came from around a curve in the tunnel, blocking the view ahead. Portia grabbed Mark's arm again and nodded at his light. He snuffed it out and they stood in the tunnel now only lit from ahead. It was enough to see around them. Portia pulled out her long knife and crouched lower, ready for anything that might attack.

The sound grew overwhelmingly loud as they walked forward, bouncing off the walls and reverberating down the tunnel. As they turned the corner, they saw two men dragging long pickaxes against the wall and then pulling back and swinging them again. Fortunately, the men were facing away and didn't see Mark or Portia. Even so, they hung back, staying close to the tunnel walls. These must be the men they saw above. If not, they had others to worry about as well.

Mark and Portia nodded at each other and then rushed forward and attacked, each trying to hit one of the men on the back of the head with the hilt of their knives. Mark managed to get his man, but Portia's target, somehow sensing her approach, had turned at the last minute and evaded her swing by ducking to the side. Portia flew forward with unchecked momentum. She tried to kick the man's lowered pickax as she passed him, but he pulled it neatly away before she could. He whirled to face her and raised the ax. Portia scrambled back.

"Hey!" Mark yelled, getting the man's attention before he could attack Portia.

The man was trapped between Mark and Portia. He swung the large ax around him indecisively, trying to keep an eye on them both. The erratic movements made it difficult for either to get to him. Their knives—even Portia's long one— didn't have nearly enough reach to make contact with the man without coming within reach of that ax. She reached for the short knife that she kept by her ankle, but the man saw her motion and lunged at her, sending her scrambling back. She tripped over a pile of rubble and landed on her back. The man ran in to strike, raising the weapon over his head. Mark's eyes bulged.

"Hey, dirt grubber!" Mark yelled as he threw his knife at the man's neck. It missed, whizzing by the man's head and flying towards Portia. She yelped and threw herself to the side just in time. Luckily, it had been enough to distract the attacker, and the pickax hit the floor of the tunnel inches from

Portia's stomach. He was so close she could smell the acrid smell of his sweat and the stench of old ale.

The man recovered his footing and swung the ax at floor level towards Portia, not even taking the time to lift it. Portia panicked and sent a shooting of ice towards the ax, fixing it to the tunnel floor. The man's eyes opened wide.

"No magic!" he said with a thick accent, his voice rising into a screech.

Was that a warning?

Portia flipped her knife and ran to the man while dodging his grasping hands and knocked him on the head as hard as she could with the hilt. He crumpled unconscious to the ground.

Breathing heavily, Portia looked around. The tunnel continued on further, but there were no other sounds nor lights showing from further down the passage. Mark ran down, holding a dim light just to be sure, but came back shaking his head.

"I saw no one else," Mark said.

"They could be hiding. We made a racket." Portia dusted herself off.

"Not any more than those two with their axes."

Portia looked at the two men crumpled on the floor. They were out for now. She dug into the pockets of the one nearest to her.

"Stealing now? Isn't that a little low?"

Portia gave Mark a sharp look but kept digging around. There was a wad of paper stuck in a pouch the man had under his jacket. She pulled the bunch out and held it up for

Mark to see. He nodded understanding and went to search the second man.

In the same pocket the papers had been, Portia found a few gold coins as well. There was something wrong with one of them. Portia held it up to be sure. The crest on the back of the coin was off center and didn't line up with the face. It was a defective coin, possibly one of the disks made in the warehouse. A tingle of warning on her neck greeted the thought of putting it in her own pocket so she quickly stuffed the coins back into the man's bag. He could keep them.

Opening the papers, Portia's heart dropped when she saw the diamond symbol of the tattoo. It was a flier for the common man, advertising money for labor as well as a place of honor at the coming change. It had the last part in capital letters and embellished: The Coming Change. What change? The splinter?

Mark looked over her shoulder. "Propaganda." He threw down papers from the other man on the ground next to Portia. "I've seen men from that company visit where I work. They throw around money even more freely than my bosses."

A cold wave went down Portia's back and she whirled to face Mark. "These men come to your company? Do they work together?" The world was spinning. Did Mark work for those with the diamond tattoos? Unable to stop herself she glanced down at his arms to see if he had any tattoos. His eyes followed her look, and he slowly pulled back his sleeves to reveal his arms.

His untattooed arms.

She looked up at him, eyes wide.

"How did I know?" Mark asked. "I've seen the tattoos on some of them. I didn't think it meant anything."

"Those people tried to kill me," Portia said quietly. If Mark was one of them, he would know this already. And he could have killed her several times over already.

Mark sucked in his breath and looked away. He hadn't known. "I've just seen them a few times. They had some business with my company, but I haven't figured out what yet." At Portia's stare, he kept going, unable to stop talking. "I just started working for them. And they pay really well. Really well." He paced a few minutes then came back to face Portia, his eyes apologetic. "I had no idea. None. I came all the way to Coverack to let you know, for crying out loud."

To let her know or lure her into a trap?

Portia nodded numbly, staring at the man below her unseeingly.

"It's not a trap." His voice followed over her shoulder. Portia shuddered at the way he had answered her unspoken thoughts.

One of the men moaned. Portia went to him. "Sorry," she said and struck him again with the hilt of her knife. She pushed back her doubts and fears about Mark. They'd known each other for so long. He would never intentionally hurt her. "Let's get out of here before we have to kill one of them."

"Should we check the other two tunnels?" Mark asked.

"If we can quickly. We should get out of here. The answers we need are probably at your company anyhow." Portia's voice shook. Now that they were no longer fighting, the thought of the oppressive ocean above them came back unbidden. "It would be good to get out of here," she said more quietly.

There was nothing in the other two tunnels except for more of the black dirt, some of it in sacks spilling over. There had been holes cut in the side of the tunnels where the bags of the stuff had been pushed in with ropes coming out of the sacks and leading down the tunnels. They had been intentionally placed that way but to what purpose was unclear.

Anxiety pressed upon Portia, and she motioned to Mark for them to return before they had fully explored either of the other passageways. He didn't argue, instead picking up his pace as they returned to the exit tunnel and almost raced down the end of it, going as fast as they dared in the near darkness. Only the dim light he held up kept them from tripping over the rocks scattered on the wet tunnel floor.

When they emerged from the driftwood shack, the moon was still up, but it was much closer to the horizon. Pink tinged the sky to the east. Portia breathed in the sea air deeply, grateful to be above ground. The sensation of timelessness she had felt within the dark tunnel faded along with her anxiety.

They made their way back to Mark's house without incident. Farmers and merchants were already on the streets preparing for their day. The feeling of a normal city day was reassuring. They were even able to buy some rolls from a passing baker's wagon, still hot from the oven.

"I have to go back to work today anyway. Maybe we could pass you off as someone who needs a job," Mark said around a mouthful of roll.

"Work?"

"I'm sure those jerks of the guards sent notice to my company. The guards don't like being bossed around by anyone." He gave Portia an apologetic glance. "It was hard enough getting time off. They think my poor mother died."

"Well, that's true," Portia said.

"Yes, but not last week."

Portia nodded and grabbed another roll from the bag. She wished they had some eggs to go with it but was too tired to stay up for the opening of the market. "It was a long night, but we learned someone is making gold coins and that the cult is in the town. Are those two things related, you think?"

"Perhaps. All I know is the people I work for have a lot of money, and some cult members visit them. There is a records room in my company. There might be more information there."

Portia stopped and stared at Mark. "A records room! Why didn't you say that first? We should have gone there before all else. You should have gone there."

Mark wouldn't look at Portia, staring down as his feet as he walked instead.

"Mark?"

"Those guys scare me." His faced turned red. "Besides, now that you're here, we could pass you off as another worker and distract them from the inside and sneak in. Or something."

They scare Mark as well as the city guards. "Why do they scare you?"

"They have some brutal methods. I've seen them kill people for not much."

Portia absorbed that as they walked on in silence. The cult had already proven deadly and widespread. Now, this company was dangerous too. It was bad enough there was some overhanging doom coming from strangers coming through a splinter, but the people already here were mortal threats. What was going on?

"Is it normal to have tunnels under the seawall?" Portia asked. "Is it for maintenance or something?"

Mark shrugged. "Doubt it. Those guys were working at night, after curfew."

Once they were back at the house, Portia lit a candle in the kitchen, for the sun had not yet reached the windows since the house was so deeply nestled between two tall ware-houses. The candle flame passed close to her dirt-smudged hand and suddenly the dirt residue burst into a blue ball of flame and then went out. Portia yelped in surprise. The hair on the back of that hand was gone and her skin was red and tingly. All that was left of the black residue was a wisp of smoke.

9

Portia stared at her red hand while Mark came running into the kitchen.

"What was that?" he asked.

"That black dust. It burst into flame."

"How?"

"The candle," Portia said, pointing. "I can't believe they were using pickaxes down there with that stuff all over the place. They throw off sparks. We could have been blown to bits. No wonder that miner was so panicked about magic." She put her hand in a basin of water to cool the stinging pain. Mark kicked at one of the chairs behind her.

"Those tunnels are underneath the seawall."

Portia's eyes widened. "With the invader ships on the far side."

"Yes. We should have asked more questions at the tavern."

Portia nodded. "Collapsing in the seawall would be a lot faster than destroying the city's defenses one ship at a time.

There were so many ships out there past the wall that the city wouldn't stand a chance if they got into the harbor. We should tell someone."

"Who?" Mark asked, skeptical.

"The city guard?" Portia asked.

"And how do we know they're not in on it?" Mark crossed his arms. "I don't trust anybody in this city. From what I've seen, my company seems to own it. If we tell anyone, we run the risk of being grabbed and thrown into prison—or worse. What has happened to you in Coverack? We always took care of our own problems."

Portia sat down heavily in a kitchen chair. "There are some people that are trustworthy. We have to find some here, or at the very least get more information we can bring back to Coverack."

Mark shook his head at the word trust. "We won't be going back to Coverack if we're grabbed by the wrong people. I'm not going to trust anybody."

Portia looked up at him, tilting her head.

"Except you."

Portia nodded.

Judging by the amount of black powder in those tunnels, they didn't have much time.

⸻

THEY ONLY ALLOWED themselves a few hours to nap. They had to get back to Mark's workplace before his company became suspicious. Portia reluctantly got up, sleep still heavy in her eyes and her brain foggy. She would have given ten silver to sleep the whole day through, but it wasn't worth the risk.

Chewing leftover bread and cheese, she watched Mark get ready for work. He had on the ostentatious clothes again with the thick velvet and the brilliant blue and red top stitching.

Turning, he looked at her clothing. "Don't you have anything else? Something a bit fancier?"

"What for?" Portia asked.

"You have to look the part if you want a job. I got away with cheap clothing at first, but if you're going to be my sister, they will expect you to know better. Or they'll think less of me. Much less. They can't be sending street urchins to the most important houses of the city."

Portia dug through her bag, but she didn't have anything comparable to Mark's finery. She pulled out her best green outfit.

He spied the sword. "Put that on. They'll think it's ornamental, especially on you. It looks expensive, and it matches your clothes."

Portia snorted at the arrogance of thinking she couldn't use her sword. Even so, she felt better having it with her. It was too valuable to leave behind in the empty house.

"Here." Mark put a jaunty black hat on Portia. The hat probably cost more than her entire outfit. Pulling a thick black ribbon from a shelf he tied it around the hilt of her sword.

"That's ridiculous. Take that off," she said, protesting.

"Nope. It matches the hat, and it looks great. Even more

importantly, it makes the sword look like an ornament. It's a fine balancing act. You have to look put together, but not dangerous."

Portia looked down at the ribbon around the hilt of her sword. She felt silly.

Morning light shone down on the city. The streets, so quiet at night, were now filled with people, although there was none of the boisterous yelling and happy calls of Coverack or Valencia. The subdued whispering and looking in the direction of the port was a constant reminder that the city was under siege even if normal day-to-day business continued.

They reached Mark's employers. The building was located close to the pier where they had been the previous night. It was an ostentatious building with a sign rimmed in gold paint. *'Couriers and Pages for hire.'* Outside, a heavily armed guard held a crossbow, and another matching guard on the far corner of the building was armed with knives and a sword. Passersby in the street gave the guards a wide berth.

"Why the thugs?" Portia asked Mark under her breath as they approached.

"I don't know. Image, maybe? They weren't there when I left." Mark thrust his chin up and took on a cocky swagger as he approached the door.

One of the guards stepped in front of him, blocking access to the building. "Halt."

"Clearly you're new. I work here. Step aside," Mark said, puffing out his chest. Portia marveled at his bravado.

"I've never seen you here. Scram," the guard said, waving Mark away.

Mark lifted his chin with a huff. He slowly pulled out a piece of paper from the pouch strung around his shoulder and handed it over to the guard. The guard read it and gave Mark a scowl. "You're just a page."

Mark was unfazed. "I do my job extremely well. My clients are very happy with me, and so is my boss. Might I hazard she's also your boss as well?"

The guard snorted then nodded in Portia's direction. "There's no mention of her. Who's she?"

It took all of Portia's will to not shrink back under the guard's gaze. Instead, she lifted her chin in an imitation of Mark and willed her heart to stop pounding so loudly.

"She's my sister. Dear Mama has passed, and it's time she found a profession. She would do well here taking messages for the ladies and others who would be reluctant to let a courier into their domain. *Now* may we enter?" Mark said imperiously to the guard.

The guard handed back the paper then stepped out of the way, glaring at Portia and Mark. Making enemies did not seem like the best idea to Portia, but she had to trust that Mark knew what he was doing with this company. He'd been here for months.

The inside of the building was just as ostentatious as the exterior. The front door opened into an open waiting area ringed with padded chairs, all embroidered with gold thread. An attendant sat behind a gold painted desk trimmed with intricate carvings. The desk was absolutely clear. The attendant looked as much an ornament as the rest of the furniture.

"Welcome back, Marcus," the attendant said to Mark. "Janrelle is not here yet. Your assignment isn't set for the day."

"Excellent, a day off. But I was hoping to talk to another courier about the west side," Mark said, clapping his hands and then vaguely waving to the west of the city.

The attendant looked surprised. "What?"

Portia quickly stood in front of the man and pulled his attention away from Mark. "I've never seen a doublet like that. Did you have it custom-made?"

The attendant looked down at his shirt with pride. The gaudy maroon and puce striped shirt was horrific, but the attendant puffed out his chest with pride. "It was custom-made. No other in the city has this color of green."

"Oh, it matches your eyes perfectly," Portia gushed, leaning into the courier while behind him Mark snuck back into the corridors of the main building. "Where do you go? I need a tailor now that I'm in town. A good one."

The attendant looked Portia up and down, a slight sneer momentarily on his lips which he quickly smoothed away again. He raised his eyebrows when he saw her sword. "Yes, dear, I can see that you do. Let me help you."

Portia ignored the slight, instead speaking conspiratorially. "Oh please, do. I feared this town would be nothing but cow patties and dirt, but seeing you gives me hope. Marcus has good taste, but you," Portia clicked her tongue, "you take it to a whole new level."

"That I do. That I do." The attendant leaned back in his

chair and pulled open a small drawer in the desk and withdrew a piece of paper, a long quill, and a pot of ink. Carefully opening the ink, he used it to write a list of shops for Portia. "Now these wonder workers will cost you, but they are worth it. Well worth it."

The attendant was nearly done with the list, but Mark was nowhere in sight. "But before I go there can you tell me, please, what would impress the ladies here? The high styles are not the same in this town, and I must fit in. It is my goal to become a ladies' courier. One of their most trusted messengers in fact. Marcus has done so well. I want to be like him."

"Yes, Marcus is a beauty," the attendant said, staring off into space and then catching himself. "We do have ladies that want female couriers, but for what reason I do not understand, for they are not as able to take care of themselves or their messages."

Portia bristled at the insinuation she could not defend herself but schooled her expression to hide it. What this man didn't know might help her in the future. Instead, she forced her eyes open wide and exclaimed, "It's dangerous here? Marcus said that no one dared touch the employees of this company, not in this town. Is that not true?"

"Oh, it's true," the attendant said, chuckling. "But still, women running around with this work is not seemly in my eye."

"Maybe it's only because so many of them have such poor taste in fashion." Portia dared to nudge him on the arm.

The attendant burst out laughing at her jest and gave her the first smile that reached his eyes. "If you are related to

Marcus, I'm sure you'll do us credit. I can already see the resemblance," the attendant said, mirth still in his voice. "You are looking to work here, are you not?" He looked more closely at Portia.

"That would be my dream," Portia said. Was she pouring it on too thick? He didn't seem to think so. She felt an impulse to gag and pushed it back.

"Well, if that is so, then visit these shops and waste no time. They are worth the coin. The only thing I would keep is that sword and maybe the hat. The rest is no good." He clucked disapprovingly at her attire then pushed the paper listing the shops to Portia.

Portia slowly drew the paper close, trying to buy some more time, but blessedly Mark came back just then.

"They're all gone on assignment. When will Janrelle be back?" Mark asked. "I want to be working this city again. My people need me."

"Not today. You're to come back tomorrow. She's expecting you."

Mark nodded at that and put an arm around Portia to steer her towards the door. She waved at the attendant and gave him a smile. He tilted his head slightly in acknowledgment as they exited out the front door and went past the guards.

Once they were outside the door and halfway down the block, Portia shook Mark off. "That man was—"

"Is very powerful. And has ears everywhere," Mark said under his breath, smiling as he looked around.

Portia glanced around as well. None of the people on the

street seemed to be paying special attention to them, but just in case she modified her words. "He was quite knowledgeable about shops. I'm lucky to have his advice," she said, holding up the paper he had given her.

"Excellent. You've done well. I too am the lucky owner of some advice that I'll share with you after lunch."

Pushing aside her curiosity, Portia steered Mark towards the city market. She wanted something more substantial than rolls and cheese. If he couldn't talk now, at least he could buy her some decent food.

PORTIA RUBBED her full belly with happiness. There could never be too much stew in the world.

"Are you sure you don't want a third serving?" Mark asked sarcastically.

"Perhaps. I'm making room now."

"No, no, no. We're getting out of here." Mark pulled some coins from his bag and handed them to the server.

Portia made a face at him but got up anyway. The tavern they were in was exceedingly fine and filled with well-dressed citizens. Her clothing felt grungy by comparison. Mark's insistence on wearing finery was becoming more understandable.

They left the well-to-do area that was near Mark's work and headed back to the warehouse district, passing through the open market on the way home and obtaining more foodstuffs for the house and a section of rope at Mark's insistence. They also picked up more supplies for the horses. The animals needed exercise if they were to stay in town much longer. As it was, it was dirty work taking care of them without a groom.

Once back at the house, Portia took off her sword and flopped down on the couch. "Okay, share. What is the advice you got?"

Mark looked serious as he pulled several papers from within his shirt where he'd hidden them. Sitting down heavily on a chair by Portia, he slid them on the low table towards her. "I stole these from the records room. I could only scan them quickly; what I read was not good."

Portia raised her eyebrows. "You took them? I thought you didn't want to risk them knowing that you've been snooping?"

Mark's face turned red right up to his ears. "No, I don't want them to know. But this was too much. I couldn't memorize the addresses. And they're proof."

"Proof?" Puzzled, Portia picked up the papers and read. "This says slave pens. *Slaves.* Here?"

Mark swallowed, then nodded. "Apparently so."

"That is horrific."

"Agreed."

"Does this mean your company owns slaves?" Portia asked, confused.

"I don't think so. I've never seen or heard anything of the like. It does say they were engaged to carry messages between this location and another. I couldn't find any details on the other location. There also seems to be something else important at the location, but they wrote in code, that much I recognize, but I don't know the codes. Only those much higher in the company know them."

Portia look through the sheaf of papers. Much of it she didn't understand, but one page was a map, and several locations were marked for slaves. "Slavery has been outlawed in Haulstatt forever. Is this something that is allowed in Lusatiana?"

Mark shook his head. "Not that I know of, but my company does not seem much concerned with what is allowed, only with what pays the most. I thought that was fine until this. No silver is worth being a part of such misery." He pulled his purse from his person and threw it down on the low table forcefully, sending it skittering off the surface and spilling pieces of silver onto the dirty floor. "I cannot work there again."

"No one should work there again," Portia muttered under her breath, trying to take in the meaning of what the papers said. She looked up at Mark. "Did you see anything about the docked ships? Or the mines?"

"No, and nothing about the cult either. I don't understand. All the papers I found before about the cult were gone. Vanished. And the company isn't paying for dry-docking ships anymore. It looked like the payments just stopped." Mark rubbed his eyes. "Why would they stop doing that when they were crowing about it taking Jukhnovo down and making them all rich?"

Portia was still confused about that. "How did that make them rich?"

Mark shrugged his shoulders. "Somehow it did. Maybe

that's what's written in the books in code."

Portia frowned. *Code.* Would that spell cast by the old elf librarian allow her to read the coded text, or would it just work on Elvish? "Can we go back and look at those books? Maybe I could read the code."

"How? It's not easy. I've stared at documents in it for months and still don't have a clue." Portia stared at Mark. He huffed. "Fine. We can try, but that's really risky."

That was true. It was risky. Portia looked down at the map marked with locations for slaves. "We could do that tomorrow, I guess, when you go back. We're both supposed to be there anyhow."

"Good idea." Mark didn't look happy.

"Let's go find out more information about these locations tonight. Maybe we can figure out what's there without the code and do something about the slaves."

Mark sighed. "Yes. After a nap. I'm exhausted. We hit the mystery secret location first, while we're freshest."

"Agreed." Portia rubbed her belly. They had a long night ahead of them. She should have insisted on that third bowl of stew.

THEY WAITED until the sun went down to go out again and passed through town, sticking to the shadows since the curfew was still in effect. The mystery location was on the north-western edge of Rodaine, just inside the outer gates but away from the main road, lying on the far side of some rolling hills from the city. Portia gasped when they crested a hill and saw four sprawling buildings with a clear view of the sea.

Guards patrolled outside the buildings. More guards were visible on the rooftops, their helmets glinting under the moonlight. They were not taking care to be hidden, nor were they making any pains to be quiet; laughter and calls amongst the men floated up to where Portia and Mark lay in the grass above them.

"That's a fortress," Mark whispered.

"You knew nothing about this?" Portia asked.

He shook his head. "Wonder who does? Those are not city guards. It's hard to tell in the dim light, but the insignia doesn't look right."

A chill ran down Portia's back. Funding that many guardsmen would be formidable for a private company or person. Whoever was running this was very wealthy and very powerful.

"Shall we?" Portia asked, pushing aside any misgivings. They had to find out what was so important there.

Mark motioned for Portia to go first. They climbed down the hill. They had not gone far when Portia's heel slipped on some gravel and she skittered down the slope, sending rocks clattering down the hill towards the compound. Grasping wildly, she found a bush and was able to stop falling by clinging to the tough branches growing from the hillside. Two guards ran towards the sound and partially up the hill while scanning for intruders. Portia turned her face away so they wouldn't see her eyes and held her breath. Mark was somewhere behind her but there were no sounds from that direction. Finally, after what seemed an eternity, the guards went back down the hill.

"Stupid dog. I told you to stop feeding it scraps," a male voice said, the sound drifting up to the hill to Portia.

"Shut up, you heartless cur..." another male voice answered in irritation.

The guards walked away, the sounds of clinking armor and their fading voices marking the retreat.

Portia exhaled in relief. Slowly she released the bush and found her footing. Her hands were bloody from thorns on the bush. Mark climbed down to where she was.

"What happened to your sneaking skills?" he asked jokingly, but there was concern in his eyes.

Portia looked away and muttered. "I slipped. It was an accident."

Mark pursed his lips then sidled around Portia, taking the lead.

At the bottom they found a tall wall surrounding the buildings. It had been difficult to see from the hill, being dark and partially in the shadow of an overhang. Mark winked at Portia as he pulled out the rope they had purchased earlier and attached a hook to one end. The hook was partially wrapped in cloth, but it still made a noise upon impact as Mark swung the rope and hook and neatly landed it on top of the wall. He pulled on the rope, and the hook dragged for a few seconds before catching on the lip of the wall. Testing the rope firmly, Mark turned and nodded at Portia. It would hold their weight.

Portia grabbed the rope and took a running start. She

scrambled up the wall, using her arms to pull up the rope while her feet ran up. Her arms ached with the strain, but she reached the top just as her muscles were starting to give out. The rope stung her wounded hands. Mark easily made the climb and caught up behind her, pushing her the last bit up onto the wall.

The top of the wall was several feet wide, allowing them to lay flat and rest. Most of the inner courtyard was visible from their perch. Mark pulled the rope behind them and stashed it and the hook back in his bag. They didn't have enough rope to leave it here, and they might not be exiting the same way they came.

"Any idea what these buildings are?" Portia asked quietly.

Mark shook his head. "We'll have to check each one. Follow me."

Waiting until two guards passed through the courtyard below and around one of the buildings, Mark slipped his legs over the edge of the wall and leapt down, landing noiselessly on the ground below. Portia followed. The impact stung her ankles but didn't inflict real damage. The voices of guards on the roof grew louder as they came closer. Mark and Portia ran to the nearest building and slipped around the corner, finding a wooden door inset into the wall. It was unlocked.

Mark gripped the handle and pressed slowly on the latch, releasing the door and pushing it inward with one outstretched hand. Blessedly, it was well oiled, and the hinges made no sound as the door swung. Mark peered into the room then quickly entered and motioned for Portia to follow.

It was a barracks. Rows of bunk beds were set along each

wall. All had blankets on them. If these were for the guards, there were a great many of them indeed. A light came from a room further in the building, along with the sounds of splashing. There must be a bath attached to the guardhouse. There were no papers nor anything else of value in the barracks, so Mark and Portia quickly exited again before they were caught.

The next building over was also unlocked. This time Portia pushed open the door while Mark kept watch around them. She sucked in her breath and gasped when she saw the inside of the simple square building. It was full of weapons of all sorts: swords, maces, bows and arrows, and even a few spears. It wasn't as fine as the armory in the Elven kingdom, but it had nearly the number of weapons. Enough for an army. These arms were in addition to what the guards were already wearing. Instinctively, Portia felt for her own knives and sword. Mark did as well.

"That's not good," Mark said, under his breath.

"Not for us." A tingle on Portia's neck warned her of danger. Rather than just leave the room, she raised her hands and motioned at all the weapons. A coat of frost and then ice covered them and then grew thicker until all the weapons were embedded in sheets of ice. Finally, Portia stopped and leaned against the wall, panting heavily. She felt dizzy and put a hand on the wall, willing the blood to go back to her head.

"Wow," Mark said quietly. "You've gotten better."

Portia grimaced at him. Perhaps she should keep some of her skills secret. "It should slow them down a bit. With these weapons anyhow."

After a moment she felt better and nodded at Mark. They exited the armory to check another building.

The third building was squat and long. They found a door facing away from the courtyard and out of the light of the torches burning there. Mark jiggled the handle and then looked at Portia. Nudging him away from the door, she pulled the small metal tools she had from within her pouch.

"At least you remembered the picks," Mark said from behind her.

Portia growled under her breath but didn't bother to respond. All her concentration was on the tiny lock. It resisted all attempts at first, the metal pick uselessly sliding on the mechanism inside, until finally she understood the lock and forced it open with a quiet click. Breathing a sigh of relief, she stashed the pick in her bag before glancing back at Mark and then slowly opening the door. There were desks and cabinets in the darkened room. The room was much smaller than the building. A door on the far side must lead to the rest of the structure. Portia crept into the room, followed by Mark, and they quietly pulled the door shut behind them.

The far door was not locked. Opening it slowly, Portia appeared around the corner and saw another darkened room, this one even smaller.

After several more such rooms, Portia moved more quickly. The fifth door she opened was also into a darkened room. When she stepped into it, she realized her mistake—a large figure sat behind the desk on the far wall staring right at her. She halted. Mark nearly pushed her over from behind, not expecting her to stop.

"What the—" Mark said, then looked into the room and saw the figure. He leapt around Portia and pulled out his knife. Portia pulled the throwing knife from her ankle hostler and threw it at the figure's head before he even stood. But the figure was quick and turned his head to send the knife glancing across his face rather than burying itself in his throat as she had intended. Portia grabbed her long knife and held it out defensively, crouching low.

Portia's knife throw also had another unexpected effect. The flying blade pulled back the creature's hood. Large scales covered its face and head, for it had no hair. A broad, flat nose took up the nearly the entire width of its face under black eyes with no irises. It looked more like the face of a snake than a man. The knife had flicked up several scales, leave a nasty gash that seeped blood.

Mark and Portia circled the creature, ready for an attack, but to their surprise, it grabbed the desk and threw it towards them. It must be immensely powerful because the gigantic desk lofted through the air and hit them both, knocking them to the ground and nearly crushing their legs with its weight. Biting back a scream of pain, Portia lifted it just a fraction and managed to pull her legs back, feeling Mark do the same on the other side. They had to get to their feet. It was terrifying being under the desk, for she could not see what it was doing on the far side.

The room was empty. The creature had fled through a door that was now open behind it. Ignoring the pain in her legs, Portia ran after it through the door, heedless of what might be there. It was another empty room, but one with a door that opened to the night air outside. Portia pulled Mark back as he came into the room behind her.

"What was that?" Mark asked.

"I have no idea, but it was scary. Did you see how big it was?"

Mark nodded, his Adam's apple bobbing in his throat.

"We have to get outta here, back the way we came." Portia dragged Mark back into the room around the desk and through the building towards the far exit. They had to get out before the alarm was raised.

They made it to the far exit and out the building, checking first for any guards nearby and then closing the door quietly behind them. Portia twisted the lock before shutting the door so that it would set and hopefully slow anyone who might be searching for them.

"Dare we keep looking?" Mark asked.

"We have to. But fast."

They ran to the fourth building. Blessed fates had the door unlocked. They pushed open the door and quietly crept in just as guards ran by on the gravel paths and swarmed to the third building. The guards knew about them now. Banging on the wooden door they had left by gave away that the guards did not have a key, but the other door had been left open, so they wouldn't be delayed for long.

The room was long and dark with boxes everywhere. There were lights and voices coming from the door off the main room, including a low, oddly deep burbling mumble. Portia and Mark exchanged glances and crept along the side of the room to get closer to the open door so they could hear better. The deep voice continued. Portia risked looking around the corner, crouching low first so her face would be at eye level. It was the creature they had just run into. He towered over several guards and barked commands at them. One guard ran off towards the open door, and Portia pulled back, quickly pressing herself against the wall. The guard ran past and out the front door, not even noticing Portia and Mark. The commands from inside the room continued.

Portia motioned for Mark to follow her as she snuck away from the open door, going deeper into the building but out of sight of the open doorway, hiding behind boxes as they went. They only found more crates and boxes in the rest of the building. Portia rose on her tiptoes and peered inside one tall crate that had been left open. It was full of coins. Gold coins. She reached in and grabbed a couple and gasped quietly. Instead of the normal faces and crests of a Haulstatt coin, this one had the face of the creature emblazoned on one side and a ship on the other. She passed the coins to Mark, who blanched when he saw them.

"We have to go," he whispered, slipping the coins into his pouch.

Portia nodded. They'd learned a great deal there, probably more than they wanted to know.

10

With most of the guards swarming into and around the third building, it was easy to sneak back over the wall and out of the compound, scrambling up and over the hill and away towards the city. They ran as fast as they could, but Portia was already out of breath and weakened from using magic to ice all the weapons. She struggled to keep up with Mark.

They had just entered the woods that stood between the hill and the city when a large cracking sound reverberated across the land and bounced off the trees, sending the noise echoing over the countryside. Pain shot through Portia's ears. She pressed her hands to them then looked around wildly, but there was nothing close by that would have made that noise.

Mark stopped, and Portia nearly ran him over. He stood, listening, but the booming noise did not return, so they ran on, exiting the trees to see the city and the seawall. Or what was left of the seawall. White foam frothed around one section of where the seawall had once stood. On the other side lay its remains, half collapsed and fallen into the sea.

A dark bobbing mass appeared in the gap where the seawall had been. Suddenly a blast of fire erupted from it. Moments later, the sound of breaking wood and the screams of men drifted over the harbor waters. A cannonball had landed precisely on one of the defending ships in the harbor, ripping through it.

Another dark ship appeared behind the first, and it too shot a cannonball towards the defenders. The cannonball blasted a second defending ship, but instead of just putting a hole in the target, the missile burst into flames when it hit. Flames curled over the struck vessel as wood caught fire faster than Portia thought possible. The bright flames illuminated the remains of the seawall and the rapidly increasing number of invading ships pushing through into the harbor.

"No, no, no," Portia said under her breath.

The assault did not stop. One of the invaders' ships powered away from the rest and made a dash for the inner harbor. No defenders were fast enough to intercept it as it raced towards shore. It let loose a massive cannonball that tore into a building on the harbor front. The structure leaned precariously to the side and collapsed in slow motion as the flames licked around it.

"That was the harbor garrison," Mark said under his breath.

Portia turned to look at him, eyes wide. "They know exactly where they're shooting, don't they?"

"Apparently."

Another blast caught her attention. A second building on the harbor shattered, bits of wood flying in the air and black smoking rising from it.

"And their armory," Mark said, fear edging his voice.

"They have a source for this intelligence. Someone gave them a map."

"Or worse."

Portia looked at Mark questioningly.

"They could have traitors on board."

Portia paled even further. "The city will never survive."

Mark shook his head, dazed. "No, it won't. We have to go."

Portia stared at the battle raging in the harbor. The city's ships were hopelessly outnumbered. The only chance for the populace was to flee—except some couldn't because they were trapped as slaves. Portia's fist balled and her chest burned. She wouldn't leave them there. Leaving Mark back in Valencia was the worst thing she'd even done in her life. That regret haunted her often. This time she had to try harder to help.

"After we get the slaves."

"Are you crazy? We have to go!" Mark yelled. Portia clenched her jaw and stared at Mark. He pointed at the harbor. "You see that, right? Your eyes are working?"

"I'm not leaving without at least trying to help them! You of all people know I've made that mistake before. Not again." She motioned to this city. "This chaos might actually help us."

Mark glared at the battle at the harbor, the flames reflected in his eyes, his jaw set.

"The slaves might have additional information we need if

we're going to win against these invaders. Somehow this is all connected," Portia said, a touch of pleading in her voice.

Mark growled for a second under his breath and then nodded. "If we're going to do a suicide mission, then let's at least get our horses. The slave location is far away. We have a better chance if we can go faster."

Portia looked at him doubtfully.

"The horses are on the way. We need the speed. This battle looks to be over quickly."

Portia scanned the harbor. Another building burst into wood bits from a ship's attack. "Right, let's get them."

They ran towards the city.

———

THE BATTLE in the harbor raged on as they approached. People were already pouring out of the inner walls, and Mark and Portia had to push against the crowd to get inside. Cannonballs whizzed towards the pier and the closest buildings. The warehouse district was several miles inland and nothing had struck that area. Yet.

When they got to the house, Portia ran inside to get her bag and another bag which she stuffed with food from the kitchen while Mark went to the back and saddled the horses. She brought the bags out and met him in the backyard.

"Get your stuff. I didn't know what you wanted," Portia said. He nodded and raced inside while she strapped her bags to her horse.

The mounts were skittish and jumpy from the loud

noises. Portia held on to the reins tightly, smoothing down the neck of the nearest horse.

"It's okay. We're going to get out of here."

The horse's ears swiveled back and forth, but it stopped trying to pull at the reins. Portia did the same for the other horse and, blessedly, it calmed down as well.

Mark ran out of the house and threw his bag over the back of the saddle of his horse, strapping it on. They mounted and rode away from the house.

Booms and flashes from the harbor continued, lighting the city in bursts. People crowded the streets, rushing west and inland, away from the waters. Some children cried, but most were quiet, fear etched on their faces as they were pulled along by their grim-faced guardians. Few had horses, and only the occasional cart clogged the streets. A panic-stricken wagon driver plowed his horses through the crowd, nearly running several people over. The street smelled of fear.

Mark and Portia cut across the crowds, using the horses to force a path and making their way south to the location marked on the map as a slave hold.

When they passed the last of the buildings on the southern edge, they rode into an open field leading to a dark copse.

"Another field is just past those trees, I think," Mark said.

Portia nodded. "Let's hide the horses in the woods."

They were far enough away from the harbor that the light splashes no longer reached them, but the distant booms carried to where they were, reverberating through the trees. The horses were calm enough to be tied to a tree, but the whites of their eyes still showed with the loudest booms. Portia smoothed their manes and sang a song of calming. Mark watched, wide-eyed, as both horses quieted and put their heads down to graze.

"Nice skill to have," he said, staring at the horses.

Pushing through the woods, they came to a field on the far side just as Mark had thought. Keeping back within the tree line, they scoped out the setup. On the far side of the field lay another large complex also surrounded by a fence. Helpfully, the fence here was not as high as the one they had scaled earlier, nor was it of stone. Wooden slats were tied together between tall posts. It surrounded a dirt area with no grass where several rundown-looking shacks stood scattered here and there. Some structures didn't even have walls and were only being rough roof shelters. Motion from inside gave away that the compound was full, perhaps overfull, with people. It was difficult to make out more details from that distance.

A few guards patrolled the perimeter of the fence on the field's side. Most were distracted and looking towards the harbor.

The wooden fence and dirt compound reminded Portia of how farm animals lived. Except those inside the wooden fence were humans—men, women, and children. The back of her neck tensed along with her fists. She wanted to pummel those guards. How dare they keep people trapped inside this fence? Who did they think they were?

"We don't have time to sneak around. Let's just defeat these guards and go," Portia said, keeping her voice low with effort.

"Agreed," Mark said, anger in his voice matching Portia's. "Can you work more of that ice magic?"

"I've got something better, just for them."

Mark nodded. "I'll protect your back. Crush them."

Portia considered for a moment. There were not that many guards, but even so, it would be better to get them all together so they didn't have to worry about being surprised from behind. This meant attracting their attention. That would be even harder with the noise from the harbor. She had to order things in exactly the right way.

Finally, she nodded at Mark and stepped forward. She cast a series of brilliant white lights towards the guards, most landing about two thirds of the way towards the compound. The guards' eyes pulled away from the harbor and stared at the lights, then looked around, holding up their weapons but otherwise freezing. Some were dazed and just stared. Portia cursed to herself. She needed them to come together and not just stand there.

She stepped forward towards the complex, exposing herself in the middle of the field. "Hey, idiots! You big bullies! Come pick on someone your own size." Waving her hands wildly, she got their attention. The few stuck in place moved when they saw the source of the lights was a small girl. One guard even laughed, although it had a tinge of hysteria to it.

"It's just a girl! Catch her," another called out. Several of the guards ran towards Portia. When they had closed half the distance, Portia jogged to the side and threw several more flashes towards the men. The bursts were showy but did little damage. Let them think she was harmless.

"Is that all you've got? Don't you want to come and play with me?" Portia asked, taunting them. Mark chuckled from the tree line. *Please, Mark, stay there. Let them be lured out.* Dancing forward once again, Portia crooked a finger at the nearest guard, beckoning him to come closer. Turning her attention to the others on the far side, she did the same.

One of the guards laughed unpleasantly. "I'll come play with you, but you might not like it." He rushed towards Portia, tossing aside his spear to grab at her. Steeling herself, Portia stood her ground and then, at the last minute, she doused the guards with water. One minute they were dry and then suddenly their clothes were soaking wet. Angry yells burst out. The guard about to grab her scowled. "You're going to regret that, *girl*."

Dancing back, Portia lifted her hands and sent bolts of white-hot light to all the guards. They sparked brightly. Several of the guards shook uncontrollably as the power coursed through them, the water giving it an easy path. When the bolts dispersed, they were followed up with freezing ice encasing each guard and leaving them affixed to the ground, most moaning in pain. Several others were quiet. Portia hoped they were just passed out.

Portia turned to Mark to give him a wink, but his eyes were focused beyond her and he was running across the field. Portia whirled to see a guard launching a spear right at her. At least one of the guards had not been pulled into her trap. She yelped as the spear launched. It flew through the air and would have hit her if she hadn't seen it in time and ducked out of the way. Mark reached the man and tackled him just after the spear left his hands, knocking him over. Wrestling furiously with the guard, Mark finally got the top position and pummeled the man with a fist, knocking him out with the first strike.

Silence followed. Even the noises in the harbor had stopped. Mark and Portia looked around, but there were no more guards coming to attack.

"Let's find out who's in there," Portia said.

They approached the wood fence. No guards ran up from the far side. A single lock secured the gate. Portia easily picked it and they were inside. The wooden structures they had seen from the outside were lined with steel bars, even the open-air ones. The bars kept in crowds of people, all of them filthy and thin. They stared at Mark and Portia. The hairs rose on Portia's arms as she stared at the faces all around her.

"Hello?" she said quietly.

Suddenly the compound exploded with noise as people yelled at her to come open their enclosure. They banged on the bars with their hands, making the metal ring. Picking one enclosure at random, Portia ran over and opened the lock. No sooner had she done that than the door pushed open from the inside and the inhabitants of the pen rushed out, most of them running away and out through the gate of the wooden fence. A few people lingered. Most of them were older or looked especially weak.

Once all the pens were open and most of the inhabitants gone, Portia looked around at those left.

"Follow me if you want to be safe," Portia said.

One of the men, especially thin, looked her up and down.

"How old are you, miss?"

"Fourteen."

One woman laughed harshly. "My goodness, you're a child. But I thank ye all the same. That pit is no place for any person."

"You'll be safe no matter how old I am."

A few chuckles met that pronouncement but no one else left.

"Ay, child, we saw that battle. You're an impressive one, even for being so wee and small," another man said.

Portia blushed with the praise and nodded awkwardly at the man. Looking around the complex, she saw no other guards. There hadn't been that many on the outside. "How could they keep you here? Don't any of you have magic?"

The men and women shook their heads sadly. One stepped forward and spoke. "Not us. I heard the guard speaking. They chose us because we can't do magic. Most of us owe money and were taken in when we couldn't pay."

"That's a lie!" said the woman who had laughed earlier. "They made that up so they could grab us. Bunch of liars is what they are."

"Who are they?" Portia asked. Mark stepped forward to hear the answer.

Silence met them. Finally, the man standing in front muttered, "We don't know. We only saw the guards, and they would never tell us what was going on, except to say we were worthless, magicless, and poor. But I'll tell you, even they seemed afraid of *them*, those bosses, whoever they were. They never would say their names."

A massive explosion rang out in the air from the direction of the harbor.

"We have to go," Portia said. "Follow me."

"Are we going back to the city?"

They didn't know.

"No. We are going to Haulstatt," Portia said.

Mutterings greeted that news.

"The city has fallen," Mark said sternly.

One of the women moaned softly.

"What's your name, child?" the man who was acting as spokesman asked.

"That doesn't matter. We have to go."

"We didn't know their names either," a voice from the back called out.

"I'm not them! My name is Portia, if that matters at all," Portia said, more sharply than she had intended. She rubbed her eyes and pulled her hair back, turning to leave the compound. She held her breath as she walked, listening to hear if they were following. Mark fell in beside her, and she could hear the shuffling sounds of those behind walking on.

To her consternation, the group behind could not keep up with even a moderate pace. They picked their way slowly through the field. It would take them forever to get anywhere, even to the trees where the horses were tethered.

She went back to the group to see why they were going so slowly. All the prisoners were limping or moving slowly. "Are you injured?"

"Ay. We're all hungry too."

"We have some food, and we'll get more. But we have to

get out of here first." Portia waited for them to pass by as she started singing. Her voice cracked with exhaustion, but she pushed through anyway, sending the magic over each one of the ragged people as they walked by her. Their pace increased, and one even skipped a step or two, as Portia sang her song to heal them so they could continue onward.

They reached the copse and retrieved the horses. Mark found the eldest in the group and put them on the horses, two on each, while Portia distributed bread and cheese to everybody. They ate while they walked and rode through the trees.

When they passed out of the copse again, they could see the city and the destruction visited upon it. All that was left of the buildings edging the harbor was rubble and smoke. More of the seawall had fallen, leaving only a few piles of rubble above the foamy waters. Not a single masted city ship remained above water. They were all sunk or fled.

The harbor itself was full of the strange dark vessels that just hours before had been kept back outside the seawall.

Chills ran over Portia as she stared at the immense destruction. Some women looked on with tears running down their faces while the men muttered angrily. Mark looked livid. He would not meet Portia's eyes.

Portia shook herself and looked to the road to the west and the throngs of people on it. "Come on, we have to go." She walked to the front to lead the way.

Mark joined her and spoke softly. "Which border are you heading for?"

"Haulstatt."

"The dwarf kingdom in the mountains is closer. If we could gain entry, we would be safe."

"The kingdom to the west?"

Mark nodded. "Morgani."

"Have you ever been there?"

Mark shook his head.

Portia bit her lips and looked back at the people following her and, beyond them, at the destruction of the city. She was sent here by Queen Lorica, or at least allowed to come in hopes of helping Haulstatt. If they fled to Morgani, they would be turning their backs on the kingdom.

"What about Haulstatt?"

"We can't help them if we're dead."

Portia looked sharply at Mark. "We're not going to die. That kingdom is so far out of the way, it would take us forever to get back to Coverack."

"Well, what about them?" Mark gestured at the people following.

"We'll take care of them. At least until we reach the border. There will be guards there to help with them. We have to go back and tell the queen what we know. I could never forgive myself if Haulstatt falls. There isn't even a seawall there. Jukhnovo is gone, and Lusatiana cannot help now."

Mark nodded.

Portia hoped she was making the right decision. Haulstatt was depending on her. And so were the people behind her. They would just have to be faster than the attackers behind them.

11

They kept walking for several hours. The road grew emptier and emptier. The farther they went from the city, the more difficult it was to see in the night. Only a few guards watched the people flee through the city gates. Portia wondered where the rest of the city's force was. There had been so many watching the gate when they had entered just a few days ago. The guards did not hassle Portia's group as they joined the others leaving city.

The help of Portia's spell only lasted for a few hours. The people they'd rescued once again walked slowly, exhaustion taking over them. The day's heat had long ago shimmered away into the sky, leaving only the icy stars above and the cold night air below. Soon, the moon would set and rob them of most of the remaining light.

"Let's rest here," Portia said.

Muttered agreement and moans met this. One man sat right in the road, not taking a single step further.

"Any more food in that bag, miss?"

Portia pulled out a bag of dried nuts and fruit. She had packed enough for Mark and her to make it to the border, but it was not nearly enough for all of them, with them having picked up nearly a dozen more people. But it was all they had for now, so she handed the bag to the man. "Please pass this around."

He nodded eagerly and grabbed a large handful before passing on the food. Blessedly, the bag made the rounds of all of them before it was finally empty.

Another man, the youngest of those with them, with only a few strands of gray in his beard, approached Portia. "If you can loan me a knife, I could hunt for us. There must be some animals in these woods. We could wait until the sun comes up to cook. Less chance anyone seein' the smoke."

Portia nodded. They needed to rest anyhow. A few hours of sleep would do them all good. She handed him one of her short knives, hilt first. Anxiety pricked at her mind, but she shoved it away. It was possible that he would take the weapon and leave them all, but there was no choice but to risk it. She could not hunt as well as defend them and do everything else.

Mark came up just as Portia was giving the knife to the man. He raised one eyebrow. "That's a good idea. We need to eat. I'll help you."

The man nodded curtly, and he and Mark went down to the ditch next to the roadside and up again into the field leading to the dark woods beyond it.

Portia scanned the area. They only had two blankets with them. Untying the damp wool rolls from the saddles, she took them to the small clearing beside the woods and laid them out. She assisted the four oldest amongst them to the blankets, and then wrapped the edges of the wool around their frail shoulders. They would have to huddle close to stay warm. The rest of the group followed and found space between the eldest on the blankets, packing in like fish at market.

Once the group was settled, Portia led the two horses towards the trees. There was a good spot to tie them there, having both access to water from a small stream and grass. Unbuckling the saddles, Portia pulled them off and checked Mark's bag for what supplies he might have packed in town while she was busy in the house. There was a feed bag and a sack of oats for horses. Portia gave silent thanks for his foresight and filled the feedbag, putting it on one of the horses. The other horse huffed a whinny.

Portia went to him and patted his neck. "No worries, you'll have your turn too." She brushed him down while he grazed to keep him happy until it was his turn for the feed. It didn't take long to get both horses settled for the night.

Once Portia was done, she went back to the quietly talking people. They were huddled even more closely on the two blankets, some even laying across the legs of others. To Portia's surprise, one of the women patted an open spot next to her and beckoned Portia to come sit.

Gratefully, Portia picked her way to the spot in the center of the blanket. The heat from those around her was a welcome change from the crisp night air.

"Thank you, child, for coming to get us," the woman said, wrapping Portia tightly in her arms and squeezing.

"You're welcome," Portia said, patting the woman's arms and pulling back. She looked down, away from the expectant faces around her. Exhaustion poured over her, and suddenly it was hard to keep her eyes open.

"Were you looking for your mother?" another woman asked.

It took a moment for the question to reach Portia's brain, now foggy with the need for sleep.

"My mother?" Portia asked. *Her mother.* That was not something she said often.

"Your mother. When we were taken, there was another woman with us who looked just like you. Spittin' image, girl. Right down to the chin. She was in the jail with us but was taken to some other location, me thinks."

"My mother's dead." Portia shook her head.

"Then your sister, perhaps? The resemblance 'tis striking. She looked old enough to be your mama."

"Are you sure?" Portia asked again, scratching at her cheek.

The woman laughed. "I might not have magic, girl, but my eyes work just fine. You and that person, whoever she is, must be somehow related. People don't just resemble each other in'un that way—not so strongly. You be relations. I'd place a crest on it."

Portia stared at the woman, frowning. *A relation.* Her stomach fluttered. That woman couldn't be her mother, it just wasn't possible, but perhaps, she was someone else... someone related.

Looking down, Portia grimaced and opened her mouth to

say something, then shut it again. The possibility of meeting someone she was related to had been forgotten long ago. Then what the woman said sank in, pricking at Portia's neck.

"There are other locations? You mean there are more of you prisoners? More slaves." Bile rose at even having to say the word.

The group nodded as one in response.

"Many times us," one of the men said heavily.

"One of the guards mentioned being stationed at a camp to the north. He hated the commander there. Said he worked them too hard," the woman next to Portia said, then chuckled bitterly. "Horrible guards, only thinking of themselves and not what they be doing to us!"

Portia's stomach sank. She had left so many of them behind. And one of whom might be related to her. No, that wasn't possible. It just wasn't. Her family had died a long time ago, leaving her abandoned in Valencia as an orphan. Surely one of her relations would have come to get her if anyone had been alive to do so.

Still, a small part of her wanted to see this woman for herself.

A noise in the nearby woods caught her attention. Mark and the man emerged from between the trees. They both held their shirts out by the hem, cradling something within them. At the sight of Mark, Portia's face heated. *He* was her family. So why then was she so excited about the possibility of meeting this woman? No. She shook her head. It was not possible.

"All the critters are now sleeping safe in their holes, this being the depth of night and all, so we'll have to make do with some berries," Mark said as he reached the people huddled on the blankets.

The other man sat down on the edge of the group and leaned in with his hoard of berries, offering them to those closest, juice from the berries making dark streaks on the white linen. The spoils were quickly passed around. Mark sat at the edge of the blanket closest to Portia and offered her some berries as well as to those around her. The berries were sweet, but it was still difficult for Portia to swallow. Her throat felt thick. She gave Mark an awkward smile.

He looked at her and tilted his head. "What's happened?"

"There is at least one other camp," Portia said. "Possibly many more. We left so many behind. Perhaps most of them."

"And one of them is this girl's mother, or sister, or something," the woman next to Portia said. Portia's face turned red as Mark stared at her and then the woman, then tilted his head and looked at Portia again.

"I'm sure it's not my mother," Portia said, rushing in. "You know my family's dead."

"Are you sure?" Mark asked.

"How can you ask that? How can you even?"

Mark popped a berry in his mouth and shook his head. "Didn't you tell me you never saw what happened? You only heard the cries and yells, and someone told you that they'd been killed. You don't even know what town that happened in."

A shiver ran over Portia. This was true. It was surprising that Mark remembered, for even she had forgotten it. She had *wanted* to forget it. The day she had lost her family was the worst day of her life. Portia ate more berries, not even tasting them.

"Aren't you even curious?" Mark asked, his eyes kind.

Of course I'm curious. The others were listening to their conversation. Portia raised her voice to ask the group, "How many others do you think there were?"

"Many. Maybe hundreds. Our camp was just a small group of them," a woman next to Portia said softly. Nods from the others confirmed this.

Hundreds. Hundreds of prisoners trapped helplessly with whomever was coming on those awful ships in the harbor. It was bad enough to be slaves, a horrible fate, but who knew what worse fate was coming for them with the unknown beings in the strange ships. She doubted the invaders who had so ruthlessly destroyed so much of the city would show any kindness to those they encountered. It was possible they would just kill everybody. Portia thought of the book she had found in the special library and its bloodthirsty descriptions of murder and carnage everywhere. The person who had written that book had no empathy for anyone they had met and took glee in the more brutal battles, counting it an accomplishment to make them as bloody as possible.

If these invaders were anything like the author of that book, Portia could not leave these people behind. She just could not.

"I'll go back and get them," Portia said to Mark, her voice suddenly sure.

Mark stared at her and stopped chewing. He glanced

around at the watching people and then back to Portia. Finally, he nodded. "I will get everyone here to Haulstatt and then get the message to Queen Lorica of what has happened here."

Portia blinked back surprise at his response. For some reason, she had expected him to argue or try to come with. But his plan was a good one, for it would get the information back to Coverack, keeping Portia's word in that regard, while allowing her to go back for the others.

Mark leaned in and touched Portia gently on the knee. "If someone told me my mother might be back in that city, nothing could keep me away," he said softly. "Rest here for a few hours then go."

Tears stung Portia's eyes, and she had to look away. If only it would be her mother.

THEY SLEPT for a few hours huddled there together on the blankets. Portia had wanted to leave immediately, but even the adrenaline of knowing there were others stranded back in town was not enough to keep her eyes open. Her body demanded rest. And truly, it would help no one if she fell off her horse and broke her neck because she was exhausted.

"Please follow Mark. I trust him fully, and so should you." Portia looked around at the group. She felt attached to them already even though she'd known them for less than a day. The women came and hugged her, and the men patted her roughly on the back. They would stay for several more hours to sleep, but they had all gotten up to say goodbye to Portia, some even waking others despite Portia trying to stop them. 'They will want to say goodbye to you and thank you,' was all they would say before shaking the others to wake them.

"Take care, Portia. We'll be waiting for you, or at least I'll be. If you don't make the border within a day of me, I'm heading straight to Coverack. This news cannot wait," Mark said.

"Right, I'll see you there at the latest. Be safe." Portia hugged Mark then mounted her horse. Despite her misgivings about leaving two of the most infirm to walk, they had all insisted she needed a horse to get back quickly to rescue the others. It had already been hours with the invaders in the city. Portia's stomach clenched at what she might find. Anxiety nudged at her, making her fingers fumble as she tightened the saddle and readied her mount.

Riding down the road, she turned and waved back at the others who stood as a group, waving back at her, their faces lit by the pink and orange-tinged eastern sky behind her. At least she would have some light to see, although that did not help her sneak up on anybody. She'd have to be very careful.

Patting the pouch that held a rough drawn map of the city and the surrounding area, she turned her horse back to the city and rode on. One of the men had been a former merchant and knew the roads well and where secret compounds could be out of sight of eyes in the city. Compounds that could hold hundreds of prisoners.

Getting closer to Rodaine revealed the source of the smoke in the air: fires burned by the harbor, sending plumes of dirty brown smoke into the sky. The smell of burnt wood hung thick in the air as well as a sour, more unpleasant smell that made the horse's nostrils flare and his eyes show white.

Portia leaned forward and patted him on the neck, giving him a rub. "It's okay. Nothing's going to happen to you. I don't like the way it smells either."

She turned off the main road and headed north of town, following the directions on the map. One possible compound area was close to the first area she and Mark had visited last night—the fenced complex with the armory and guards and strange gold. She had forgotten about the gold. Mark had it, and hopefully he would show it to Queen Lorica. It was irrefutable proof of the strangeness of what was going on here.

The map directed her to turn off the smaller road she was on and go even further north, helpfully skirting around that first compound. Portia exhaled a sigh of relief, not even realizing she'd been holding her breath. The thought of encountering that huge creature again filled her with dread. Let her face one hundred guards before she had to face that thing again. Somehow, she didn't think she'd have much choice in the matter.

Once again, there was a copse of trees surrounding the area where a compound could be. Portia quietly tied the horse on the far side. It was partially shielded by the woods, but the trees were not so thick as to conceal it completely. Pursing her lips, Portia turned back and stared at the horse and then cast the darkness spell she knew over it. The horse wouldn't be completely invisible, but unless someone was directly looking for it, they would only see a shadow out of the corner of their eye and ignore that area. It would work if the horse remained quiet.

Cautiously, Portia stepped into the trees and stood and listened. The crack of dried undergrowth reverberated in the trees, startling Portia. Holding her breath, she tried to place where the noise had come from. For a long minute there was nothing, then a twig snapped off to her left. Making way in that direction, she silently ran from tree to tree until one peek around a tree revealed a guard in the woods. He was crouched down, looking around wild-eyed and holding out his sword in front of him, its tip wavering as he swiped it back and forth.

Pulling back around the tree out of his sight, Portia dug around in the dirt until she found a rock. Quickly, she lobbed it around the tree and overhead to land on the far side of the man. At its crash in the undergrowth he yelped and whirled to face the sound. The tip of his sword was shaking. She almost felt sorry for him.

Almost.

Shooting a stream of ice at him, she quickly froze him over from top to bottom, covering his mouth before he could scream, leaving only the top of his head clear. His eyes bulged as she ran to him and knocked him out with the hilt of her knife before breaking the ice away from his face. He did not have to die; he just had to be out of her way. Preferably quiet.

A tingle on her arm alerted her to danger nearby. There were other guards close. Those at the compound had probably seen the seawall fall and forced some of their compatriots out into the woods to be an advanced guard. It was a measure of their enormous fear of their employer that they had not run back to protect their families or else just fled entirely. It was a marvel that any were still there at all.

They had to be dealt with, but Portia didn't dare draw too much attention since Mark wasn't there to guard for surprise attacks. This forced her to sneak up on each guard one by one and disable them without using light magic or any other sort of pyromancy for fear others would see it. Instead, she had to use the more draining ice magic. The muscles in her arms burned by the tenth guard. The amount of them seemed endless. Finally, there seemed to be no more in the woods.

Creeping to the edge of the field in front of the compound, she saw one last guard stationed just outside the gate. He paced nervously and looked quickly from side to side, no doubt looking for his vanished brethren. No other guards were visible inside the compound. There was no easy way to approach the guard or sneak up on him. She'd have to draw him out but do so in a way as to not raise the alarm just in case there were others out of sight.

"Little help here, I twisted my ankle," she said in a low guttural voice, trying to imitate one of the older guards.

The guard at the gate looked around wildly, trying to pinpoint the sound of the voice.

"In the woods, you idiot," Portia said, imitating the rough way that guards talked to each other.

The guard by the fence still hesitated, unsure.

"Get your butt down here and help me before I report your insolence to your captain and have you thrashed!" Portia yelled in her deepened voice and followed it with some curses.

That did it. The guard's face turned white and then he ran down the slope through the fields and towards the wood.

"No, no, no. No need for that. Where are you, sir?" the guard cried wildly.

"Right here," Portia muttered under her breath as she struck him on the forehead as he ran past. He fell with a clatter of armor to the ground, out cold. Portia encased him in ice just to be sure.

After dragging him deeper into the woods next to the rest, she ran over the field to the fence and peered in between the wooden slats. There were pens on the inside just as with the other compound, except far more of them. At the distant end of the compound stood an enclosed building that looked more solidly constructed than anything else. One guard stood on the outside of it. No other guards were visible.

A young child in one of the pens noticed Portia staring in through the fence. He opened his mouth to cry out when a woman clapped a hand over it, cutting off the noise. The guard outside the door of the building didn't move or look their way. Portia nodded at the wide-eyed woman clutching the child.

Running to a wide gate further down the fence, Portia made quick work of picking the lock and gaining entrance. Shutting it carefully behind her, Portia set the gate so it touched the fence post but did not latch. If anyone glanced at it, they would think it secured.

People in the pens stared at Portia. They were dirty and bedraggled. A crowd gathered in the pens, watching her. Portia held up a finger for silence then waved them away, wanting them to act nonchalant. Any strange behavior would get the attention of the solitary guard that she saw. There were probably more inside the building, and the last thing she wanted was for them to come rushing out knowing she was there.

At first it worked. The people in the pen stopped moving and watched her silently. She crept towards the enclosed building.

Suddenly a voice cried out, "Hey, over here. Unlock this door!"

A dirty man held the iron bars of the pen he was in and shook it, the noise of metal clanking echoing through the compound. His compatriots grabbed him, pulling him down and putting hands over his mouth, but the damage was done. The guard in front of the building noticed and was scanning the compound wide-eyed. It took him only a second to see Portia, but she was already running towards him, shooting out ice with her right hand.

The ice covered the guard's mouth before he could yell a warning. His hands flew up to his face to grab the offending substance, his eyes growing wider. From the way he scrambled in panic Portia knew she had overshot, and the ice must be up his nose, cutting off his air. Pulling out her knife, she hit him on the head with the hilt and knocked him out. Then she warmed his nostrils with pyromancy. Water tricked from his nose. He breathed but was still unconscious. Cutting strips of his clothing to use as rope, Portia tied him up securely then dragged him to the side of the building and around the corner.

Mutters reached her from the pen. Holding a finger up to

her mouth, she turned to stare at the prisoners, hoping they would understand she would return for them. They quieted down, at least for the moment.

She pulled the door handle. It was unlocked and unlatched, opening easily. Peering around it, she looked into the dim interior. There were two guards dozing in chairs. Sending in more ice, she repeated what she had done with the outer guard, leaving two more tied-up bundles.

Once done with that, she looked around the room. There was a large desk in the middle surrounded by chairs and a small filing cabinet, or what looked like a filing cabinet. When opened, it only revealed stashes of food and some foul-smelling dirty clothes. Portia gagged a bit and shut the drawer. The desk had more revealing contents. Sheets of parchment were shoved inside. Rifling through the papers quickly, Portia saw many of them had the markings of the company Mark worked for. It didn't prove they knew about the slaves, but somehow his company and this compound were connected. Portia hissed. What had Mark gotten into?

Rolling the papers, she shoved them into the inside pocket of her jacket. They could be examined in more detail later. There was nothing else in the drawers except for some broken quills and a set of gambling dice.

One of the guards moaned. Portia hit him again, feeling slightly bad at the welt swelling up on his head. But a second later, a child's cry reached her ears, reminding her of those trapped outside and banished any further guilt.

Exiting the building, she looked around. There were no other guards in sight. Running to the nearest pen, she picked the simple lock and pulled the gate open while holding a finger up to her mouth. Those inside filed out quietly. One man reached out and squeezed her shoulder as he passed by and nodded at her before quickly walking away and following the others to the outside gate.

She was at the second such pen, working at the lock, when someone from the back of the pen yelped. Looking up at the sound, her heart thundered. A squad of a dozen or so huge creatures raced in through the second exterior entrance in the rear of the compound. The slaves from the first pen were gone, leaving her and those in the pen to face them.

The creatures were enormous, towering over the pens and the humans inside them. They were covered in brown, draping clothes with deep hoods. Only cold eyes set in faces with huge overlapping scale showed, but that was frightening enough. A chill ran down Portia as she turned to face them. Pushing away thoughts of fleeing, Portia ran towards them to distract them from the humans and shot out ice to encase the creatures. Her ice was not as effective in stopping them as it had been with the human guards. These creatures were far too strong and broke most of the surrounding ice immediately. What they couldn't shatter, they hacked at with their weapons.

The ice barely slowed them. The muscles in Portia's back tensed as her stomach drew into a cold ball. There were a dozen or more of them.

One of the creatures, one hidden in the back behind the others, stepped out from behind his compatriots and pulled out a small stick and waved it in Portia's direction. A ball of flame shot from it right for Portia's head. The fireball snapped her out of her shock. Fire she knew. If he was going to shoot fire at her, he'd better be prepared to get it right back.

Easily ducking the fireball, Portia sent back a huge ball of flames to the creature with the wand. Fire magic was much easier than ice, and working it felt like breathing, not like the sensation of struggling through a thick swamp like when she used cryomancy. She'd avoided fire before to not draw attention, but now was not the time for such niceties, not when survival was at stake.

The creature with the wand had fallen to his knees after shooting the small ball of fire at her. He leaned forward, panting, and barely reacted when her giant ball of fire enveloped him and set his clothes ablaze. He howled, the dissident sound sending a chill down Portia's spine. He flopped over in the dirt, burning alive. His compatriots beat at his clothes and rolled him in the dirt, Portia temporarily forgotten.

It would've been the perfect time to shoot more fire at them, but something about his howl of pain stopped Portia. She couldn't just kill them in cold blood, no matter what they were. Steeling herself, she drew from her last reserves of strength and cast thick sheets of ice upon the creatures, thicker than she'd ever done before. Her feet tingled with the effort, and her head felt woozy. Hopefully, it was not a mistake to show them compassion, but it wasn't within her to just kill them.

The ice worked this time. She was able to make it thick enough to immobilize their arms. Remembering her overshoot of the guard, she avoided their mouths. They yelled ferociously in a strange language she'd never heard before. Its growls and spits and guttural tones were horrific to hear.

The ice had the added benefit of finishing their work in putting out the fire burning on the one creature with the wand. It lay encompassed in ice, still panting heavily, staring off into the distance.

Portia walked closer. One of the creatures stood out from the others with a large purple mark around one eye. Portia grabbed its head. It looked up at her, eyes wide. Touching it was worse than she thought it would be. Its skin was rough and contained tiny barbs that dug into Portia's hands. The purple mark was deformed, curled scales. The rest of them looked like gigantic snake scales. Portia hated snakes.

Holding tight despite her urge to get far away, Portia concentrated on what she could remember of the spell from the librarian in Rocabarra, the spell that allowed her to understand the Elven language. She sang the words into the creature's face. She had to know their language.

At first, she felt nothing. No tingling, none of the vibrations in the air that told her the magic was working, but then, faintly, she felt a tingle. Modifying the song a bit, the tingle grew stronger. Portia continued to sing, adjusting as she went. The creature fought her, twisting its head from side to side and growing more agitated as she fumbled her way through the spell, correcting her mistakes and getting closer to casting it correctly. Finally, she could feel the magic vibrating through her chest and up through her neck and around her ears. She imagined she could see the magic reaching out to the creature and wrapping its head within it. The creature growled intensely at Portia and spit out words at her, words that suddenly clarified into something she could understand.

"Let go of me, you filthy thing! You unclean creature."

The creature's lips were moving, and Portia realized she understood what it was yelling at her. She sat back and stopped singing. Her jaw hung down as the creature continued to berate her. A retort welled in her mind and she realized it was in the creature's language. Could she speak it?

After several attempts which resulted in a sore throat and an unpleasant vibration in her nose, Portia managed to get out a few words in its language. *"Stop! Enough. What are you doing here? This is not your place."*

The creature shut its mouth and stared at Portia, pulling its head back to get some distance. Heavy silence settled in the compound as the other creatures stopped yelling and the humans in the pen stared in shock.

Anxiety gripped Portia. She yelled again, louder than she intended. *"What are you doing here?"* The last syllable tore her throat. Speaking their language was uncomfortable, if not damaging, and she could not do it for long.

The creature shook its head and answered back quietly. *"We are here for the slavesss. We have paid for them, and they are oursss. If you do not like it, you ssshould talk to thossse of your ugly kind that sssold them."*

Portia hissed in displeasure. Paid. They'd paid for these humans. Her hands tightened into fists.

"They are not yours. No human is for sale."

The creature laughed at Portia. It took all her willpower not to strike it in the face. She stood and leaned over it and yelled, "You are to leave here! Do you understand? When this ice wears off leave this place and never come back."

The creature stopped laughing but stared at her with what Portia could have sworn was a sneer. She walked back before she lost control. Circling the group of creatures, she found the one that had been burned. Its wand lay on the ground beside it. Portia picked it up. It looked like nothing more than a smooth stick with symbols burned into it.

On impulse, she gripped the stick in both hands and broke it in half. When it cracked apart the creature on the ground stiffened and howled. It slowly focused its eyes on Portia and the broken wand. Portia threw the wand to the center of the compound, but the creature's eyes never left Portia. Being the focus of its stare was uncomfortable, so she moved once again to the other side of the group to the one she'd cast the spell on.

Now would be the perfect time to have a truth cube. She needed information from these creatures. Going back to one she'd cast the spell on, she tried again.

"How many are there of you?"

The creature looked away and growled.

Frustrated, Portia stepped into his eyeline and crouched down close to his face. *"Answer me!"* The language burned her throat. *"How many? Are there more ships than those in the harbor?"*

Once again, the creature growled. Portia pushed her face even closer, forcing it to look at her.

"You ssstink! Ssstep back," it spat at her.

"Who are you to order me about?" Portia asked, losing her patience. *"I'm not the one wrapped in ice."*

"You'll regret thisss. There are more of us than ssstars in the ssky. This place is oursss. We claim it." Somehow, even sitting below her, the creature managed to look down its nose at her, its scales glinting in the sunlight. Its breath was foul, reminding Portia of the garbage dumps they had sometimes raided in Valencia.

Stepping back once again, she looked around. The sun was beating down on the compound, and the day was drawing on. There had been a huge number of boats in the harbor last night. If the city had fallen, it would not be long before the invaders went exploring further than its walls, especially if they thought there were slaves waiting for them. They had to escape while there was still time. She clenched her fists. Of all the magic she had ever wished for, she never thought she would wish for Deyelna's power of coercion, but she wished for it now, for no other reason than to make this creature talk.

The invaders were huge. If they had been smaller, perhaps they could have captured one and taken it with them, but the humans in the pen looked thin and hungry. Even the smallest of the creatures wrapped in ice looked too large for her horse. Portia kicked the ground and blew out heavily. At least she knew what they look like now and some of what they wanted.

Dusting off her breeches, Portia focused on the pens. Some humans inside made eye contact with her and yelled. A sturdy man in the nearest pen called to Portia. "Hurry let us out. Before more of them come."

Nodding at the wisdom of this, Portia trotted to that pen

and picked the lock quickly before walking on to the next pen. There were five more in all.

When she finished opening the last pen, she looked up into eyes that looked just like hers. A woman covered in dirt stared, recognizable as a mirror image of Portia. This was the person they must have been talking about, the one who could be a relative. Portia's hands trembled, and she shoved them into her pockets before standing in front of the woman and blocking her escape.

"You have to come with me," Portia said. "Please."

The woman nodded mutely. Her hand reached out to touch Portia, but she retracted it again quickly. People poured around them towards the exit, but several stayed around Portia.

"Child, we thank you. How did you do that?" an elderly woman said, clutching at Portia's forearm.

"Magic—and luck," Portia muttered, then looked around to find more staring faces.

"Aye, if we had magic, none of us would have been stuck here," a voice muttered from the group gathering around her.

"Or a sharp sword," a tall gangly man said, eyeing the weapon on Portia's back.

Portia nodded at him, not quite sure of his intentions, then looked around at the rest. "I'm heading to Haulstatt and any who wish may join me."

"What about our homes? What about Rodaine?" a woman said softly.

"I wanna go home," a young boy clutching the woman's

arm said, his face serious. Portia's heart hurt when she looked at him.

"Rodaine fell last night. Your homes are most likely gone," Portia said heavily. "You can go look for yourselves if you wish, but I recommend you don't. Strange ships fill the harbor and probably have more of these within them." Portia waved to the creatures still encased in ice and glaring at them.

Some moaned, and a few others cursed angrily, but no one argued with her. One or two would probably sneak back to look for themselves, unable or unwilling to listen to the truth, but Portia couldn't worry about them. She had to get back to Haulstatt with the information she'd learned here. And bring back the woman who looked just like her.

Several of the former prisoners moved closer and nodded to Portia.

The gangly man waved dismissively. "The dwarf kingdom is much closer. All those who wish to be free follow me to Morgani." His words rang out over the crowd, and many rushed to join him. Portia felt a rush of relief when they walked off. He had made her uncomfortable. She was glad to have him gone.

The group headed for Morgani left first, followed by Portia and her group. As they passed by the creatures in the compound on the way to the main gate, the one she had grabbed turned to her and hissed. "We will find you in Haulssstatt, ugly thing, and make you payyy."

Portia turned to it, her eyes wide. It had spoken in the common tongue. It knew their language.

12

Portia stared, her mouth open. The creature glared back at her. "Ugly thing, you will be my ssslave. Plaaan on it."

"How do you know common? How do you know it!" The words caught in Portia's dry throat.

"Ugly and ssstupid you are. You ssshoved this ssstinking language in my brain. I will make you paaaay for violating me."

Portia backed up, shaking. She had given this creature the common tongue by casting a spell she had never done before. Maybe for the safety of all, she should kill it now before it shared this knowledge, but she couldn't do it. Not in cold blood. There had to be a way to take the language back, but she didn't dare try now, having no idea how to even start. It would take too much time to figure it out, and the delay in doing so would only increase the chances of more creatures coming.

Drawing herself up to project a bravery she didn't feel, Portia yelled back, "You will do nothing of the sort. Stay away if you know what is good for you."

She shot a stream of ice at the creature's mouth just for good measure. Her right hand was shaking, and she pulled it back quickly as soon as she was done so the others would not see it, but the woman who looked just like her saw her trembling fingers and gave Portia a gentle look. Portia acknowledged the woman's gaze with a brisk nod and then turned, leading her group away while willing herself to stop trembling.

"Wait, I know where they keep the food," the woman with her arm around the young boy called out. She pointed to a small shack with a locked cellar to one side. They had several days' journey to the border and more to Coverack. Food would be needed since the countryside would most likely be picked clean by the refugees who had already left the city. And none of the prisoners looked like they were in much shape to hunt any wily game smart enough to escape the most obvious traps.

They took the time to raid the supply shed, stuffing the food in shirts, pockets, and spare clothing used as packages, having few bags with them. One or two of the stronger men carried sacks of nuts, and even the children helped in carrying what they could, sneaking a bite here or there. None of the adults had the heart to chide them, and they let the children snack as they walked.

They exited through the field to the woods, and Portia was grateful to find her horse still there, tied where she had left it.

None of the others had found it, for she couldn't believe any would leave a horse if they had seen it. Portia loaded the horse with some heavier foodstuffs and walked along with the others. No one looked like they were in need of a ride... yet.

They walked along the road in silence, both out of exhaustion and a consciousness of invaders being in the land. It would be good to not invite too much attention. That, and they were apparently paid-for goods and someone might come looking for them. One young man volunteered to be lookout from the rear, and Portia kept an eye out ahead. But they encountered no one. Only a dropped scarf or other household item alongside the road was evidence of those who had passed ahead of them. It was eerily quiet. The skin tightened on the back of Portia's neck and scalp. The silence was almost worse than the cries of battle. At least the birds were still singing. That much at least was a comfort.

The sun rose to noon and then continued past, but no one was inclined to stop, instead eating while walking and taking quick rest stops in groups of two or three and then running to catch up to the rest of the group. They would have to sleep sometime, but Portia wanted as much space between them and the city as possible before then.

Sweat was dripping down her neck and under the makeshift hat she had constructed out of one of her old shirts when the woman who looked like her came up and walked next to her, sneaking glances. Only exhaustion kept Portia from staring back at the woman as well. Instead, Portia focused on the road ahead and waited for the woman to speak, for obviously she wanted to. Finally, the sound of the woman clearing her throat interrupted Portia's thoughts.

"My name is Cecilia. Your name is Portia, you said?" the woman asked hesitantly.

Portia nodded. She wanted to ask questions, but her mind was fuzzy with exhaustion. All the ice magic she had done that morning had drained her, and that was hours ago, before they had been walking on the road all morning. Portia's right hand and arm, that side being closest to the woman, tingled in an odd sensation, as if the proximity was tickling her magic. It should have been alarming, or possibly exciting, but the blanket of weariness pressing down on Portia tamped down that feeling. Mustering her energy, she turned to face the woman and yet again was surprised by how similar they looked. Only a few wrinkles and a slightly different tilt of the woman's nose differentiated them. A funny feeling tumbled in her stomach, flopping and churning until Portia realized with chagrin that the feeling was hope.

No. She couldn't afford such a luxury. Portia turned away and stared at the road again.

Still...

As if she could read Portia's mind, Cecilia spoke. "Where are your parents from?"

"Of that, I have no idea," Portia said, shaking her head.

"They never told you?"

"I never knew them."

Silence met that response. A few paces later the woman ventured again. "Where did you grow up?"

"Valencia," Portia said, memories of her orphan childhood

flooding her. Shoving the thoughts away, she forced herself to focus on the gravel on the road and the crunch of everyone's footsteps around her.

"Oh, I do not know that town," Cecilia said, her voice falling.

Portia snuck a glance at her. Cecilia's eyes were focused on the road. "Do you have family? Are there others that look like you?"

Cecilia gave a bitter laugh. "You mean besides you?"

"It's rather uncanny, is it not?" Portia retorted.

"That it is." Cecilia sighed. "I had a daughter, but I didn't keep her."

Portia narrowed her eyes at the woman.

"Oh no, it's not like that. It was not my choice. The child was stolen from me, and no one in the city would listen to me. They thought I was babbling and hysterical, and who would not be if their child had been taken. It was only later that I realized the city guards were probably bribed by some traffickers. At the time, I only thought I was losing my mind because my precious little one had been taken and no one would listen. Now I know they listened, but they didn't care. Someone gave them enough coin to not care, I'm sure. They were corrupt... evil, horrible... I cannot even think of it; it upsets me too much. All by the guards who were supposed to protect us."

"That's dreadful," Portia said, trying to imagine the betrayal. It was frightening that this could happen in the adult realm, and not just in the land of orphan gangs and childhood tactics. Would there never be a safe time? Apparently not.

Dangers were always there, just in different forms. "Where was that? Whose guards did this to you?"

"The village of Coray."

Portia shook her head. It was not a name she was familiar with.

"It's on the border to Srubna. We lived in the western portion of Haulstatt, and I looked for that child all over but didn't dare venture to Srubna. I figured that's where they took the child, but I wasn't brave enough to go into a strange kingdom. The guilt haunts me still. How could I have been so cowardly?" Cecilia said sadly.

Portia wanted to hug her and say it was all right, and at the same time yell at her for being so craven. Instead she settled on giving Cecilia a sympathetic look. The mixed feelings confused Portia, so she tried to shove them away and walked away from the woman. Her head hurt.

Looking back over the group straggling behind, Portia called for a stop. There were a few trees and a stream nearby. It was the same spot she had stopped at earlier with the first group of freed prisoners. It was hard to believe that was just earlier that same day. Exhaustion wore upon her. So much had happened since then.

They rested there through the heat of the afternoon and then started on again. Portia remembered there were some thicker woods on the road back to the border. They would make for a good resting place for a longer stop. Cecilia hovered near Portia once or twice, but Portia was not ready to talk. Her chest felt jittery around the woman. She both wanted her close and wished she'd never met her. It was all so confusing.

———

Night finally settled on the long summer day. They walked until the sky was fully dark and the stars appeared. They reached the woods and its comforting darkness, a darkness that would hide them from any invaders that might be following. They'd seen none that day, but that did not signify anything. They had such strange fast ships, who was to say they did not have even stranger vehicles for the land.

Several of the travelers handed out nuts and cheese. What little bread they had was long gone. Several trampled into the woods to look for game, but Portia doubted they would find anything.

That night her sleep was interrupted by yet another nightmare. This time, the figure reaching down the sky was the creature she'd talked to. Instead of the usual dream silence, his hissed threat of capture and enslavement rang out across the land. Portia awoke with a start.

Pink sky peeked through the spaces between the trees. Only the person assigned watch was awake. Portia gave him a nod and then rose, stretching. She gathered her knives and sword and went to the edge of the woods near the road. There were no vehicles upon it nor any noise from others approaching. The world was silent except for the cry of birds.

Pulling out the sword from the sheath across her back, Portia stared at it. It gave her a tingling sensation as always—

the same tingling she had also felt around Cecilia. Daily practice had been neglected on this mission, nor had she used it in any conflict. If she was ever to get better, she needed to put the time in.

Running through the basics—first position, second position, start defense—loosened her limbs and sent heat to her face. The sword hummed in approval and thanks. It felt so good to use it, Portia wondered that she never thought to while in the heat of battle. The pleasure of swinging the blade was so intense and so addicting that the sensation edged on terrifying. What if she never wanted to stop?

Finishing the last of the basic forms, she stood up, panting, and shook out her shoulders. All felt right with the world. Just moving with the weapon banished the anxiety and confusion she felt yesterday, at least until she looked up and saw Cecilia staring at her and the sword.

"That is a stunning blade. I swear I've never seen it before but yet, it seems... familiar." Cecilia's eyes never left the weapon.

Portia gave a small laugh. "You too?"

Cecilia raised her eyebrow.

"It called to me from the wall of a castle armory, and here it is now with me two kingdoms over," Portia said.

"You give it a lot of power."

"Do I?"

Cecilia came closer and looked at the weapon and then at Portia. "Perhaps not. Why didn't you use that yesterday?"

Portia shook her head and stepped back, sheathing the sword. "Would you believe me if I said I feared it was more bloodthirsty than I? Truth be, I don't know how to disable with the sword, only kill. Perhaps if I'd been a prisoner for as long as you, I'd be more willing to do so."

"There are many ways to disable with the sword," Cecilia said with confidence.

Turning, Portia squinted at Cecilia, who shrugged back under the scrutiny, breaking eye contact. "Or so I've heard." She waved back towards the camp. "They're looking for you so we can leave. They're anxious." Cecilia's eyes shifted down the road towards Rodaine.

"As am I."

The group was packed and ready to go when Portia reached them. Someone had thought to take care of her horse, and she nodded gratefully.

That day passed in a blur of walking and eating until the food was gone and then it was just walking. A few of the children cried, and Portia distracted them by giving them short rides on the horse which was no longer burdened with food sacks. The next day was even more of a blur, and no one spoke, the growl of their empty stomachs lowering spirits. The forest was long left behind them. More and more debris was by the side of the road from travelers who had passed before them. Soon the border was once again visible, even from a distance, due to an encampment of refugees around the keep at the border. Most of those from Rodaine must have passed through, but those lingering were enough to crowd the fenced structure that marked the border between the kingdom of Lusatiana and the kingdom of Haulstatt.

Two guards rode out from the keep, scanning the group.

"Hail. Who are you and where do you come from?" one of the guards said, not unkindly.

Portia stepped forward and spoke wearily, "We are traveling from Rodaine. These are Lusatianans, mostly. I'm from Coverack and need to get back as quickly as possible. I would like transport."

The guard who spoke raised his eyebrows then leapt off his horse while the other guard watched warily from behind him.

"If you're refugees, we can help, but we need to make sure that is all you are."

"We're not hiding any of those gigantic creatures, if that's what you're getting at," Portia said. Dizziness from lack of food pulled at her vision, and her tone was sharper than she intended.

The guard looked at her curiously. "Creatures?"

"Invaders," Portia said.

Now that they were no longer walking, an overwhelming urge to sit down washed over her. She noticed a canteen at the guard's hip and stared at it, licking her lips. He followed the path of her gaze and wordlessly detached the canteen and handed it to her.

"Thank you," Portia said gratefully.

Aware of those around her, she took only a small swallow and asked permission with her eyes to the guard before handing the canteen to one of the refugees standing next to her. The second guard also detached his canteen and tossed it to a man in the back.

The first guard quickly walked through the crowd of

people, checking each one individually then turning to the one still mounted, and nodded permission for them to continue. The crowd wearily started walking again towards the keep. A man pushed the two empty canteens into the hands of the guard on his mount as he passed by.

"You'll have to talk to our commander about any transport to Coverack. We've permission from the royal house to help all refugees but beyond that... he'll decide. Anyway, he'll want to know about these creatures." The guard stared at her curiously, his own desire to know more apparent, but he was considerate enough of her weakened state to not press her at the moment. "Come. There is food and drink inside."

Portia couldn't summon the energy to respond, instead walking in the direction he indicated, followed closely by Cecilia.

Inside the walls of the keep, people sat on benches and straw spread over the dirt, eating from wooden bowls and talking quietly. Portia looked around for any of those from the first group she freed but didn't recognize any of the people. Perhaps they had all moved on already.

"You lucked out," the guard said. "They're still running the dinner shift, and your meal will be hot."

Portia looked longingly at the food but turned to the guard instead. "First, we need to speak to the commander."

"Eat," he said gently. "The commander will be by soon."

The commander found them a short time later. He was a harried man with white hair stuck up on one side as if he had been pulling it constantly. Despite his frazzled appearance, he gave a slow, gentle smile to Portia and Cecilia, who were sitting on the ground eating bowls of stew.

"So, Portia, tell me, what of these creatures?"

"You know my name?" Portia asked, surprised.

"That I do. Your young friend Mark passed through here a day ago. But you have news that he doesn't?"

Portia finished chewing and swallowing the last of the potato and handed the bowl to Cecilia. "I do."

Telling the commander everything she knew about the creatures, Portia hurried over the part where the creature learned common from her. Her face turned red during the admission, but she knew she could not omit it—leaving it out would endanger too many others. He sucked his breath in and pulled his hair when she spoke of it. The danger was readily apparent to him.

"You'll have your transport. We've some urgent messages for Coverack, so they'll go by carriage with you instead of by horse. You'll leave as soon as they are ready."

"Sir, I need room for one more." Portia motioned to Cecilia. "She must come with me."

"Why?" The commander peered curiously at Cecilia.

Why? With all that was happening Portia felt foolish for demanding this woman be with her, but something within her said it was important. Very important.

"She just has to. I can't explain why. Please trust me," Portia said, the ridiculousness of that request coming over her. He didn't know her at all. Why should he trust her? But luck was on her side, or else he saw something else, for after a moment of staring at both of them he nodded.

"All right then. Both of you. Just be ready. The rest will have to stay here for now or else walk on their own. Horses are in short supply." He gave a stressed sigh. "We can't keep all these folks for much longer. We're running out of food and room."

"Have there been a lot?" Portia said, looking around again. "Of people coming through I mean."

"Too many, child, too many. This is not good."

Portia was too disturbed by those words to be offended by being called a child yet again. She had just found her place in the Magic Academy when it seemed the whole world was crashing down.

The transport was a rickety but serviceable carriage just barely large enough for Portia and Cecilia and two guards. With Portia's permission they had loaded up her horse with items to go to the capital and tied it to the back. It would help their speed if the two horses pulling the carriage were not taxed too heavily.

Cecilia looked around the interior of the carriage with wonder. Portia suppressed a smile, remembering her own reaction to the royal carriage. While this one was not nearly so fine, it was obviously much better than Cecilia had ever experienced before.

"How is it that you merit this ride?" Cecilia finally asked Portia, her eyes wide. "I've never heard of the guards getting a carriage for someone. Who are you?"

"I'm no one. I have information to bring back, that's all," Portia said, trying to keep her voice light.

"I don't understand. Can't they just send a letter on a fast horse along with the other messages?"

Selfishly, Portia was glad the commander had not tried to insist on that. The urgent need to get back to Coverack pulled at her. "Some of it's information I'm not sure who I can share with." At Cecilia's curious look she rushed on. "I'm on a mission for the royal house."

"The royal house! You? I mean, you're so young." Cecilia leaned in and whispered to her, "Is it because you have so much magic?"

"Sort of. Mostly because I'm good at sneaking around," Portia said, not wanting to mention anything about being a Jack of Magic.

Cecilia laughed at that. "You didn't do any sneaking that I saw. Or not much. Not too many I know would fight so many others."

"They surprised me," Portia said, feeling uncomfortably defensive. "I *tried* to sneak in to free you."

"And for that I'm grateful. We're all grateful," Cecilia said, her voice becoming serious.

They rode on in silence after that. Portia stared at the countryside passing by and the occasional group of refugees on the road, thinking of what they could do to stop the invaders. Their ships were so strange and fast, and large. Everything about the invaders was large. The only good news she had to share was that they seemed to have little magic.

"You never knew your parents?" Cecilia asked. Her question startled Portia, who turned to face her, once again struck by how much they looked alike.

"No. They're dead. At least I think so."

"You don't know?"

"I didn't see them killed, but something bad happened. I could hear it, and they never came back."

Mark's admonishment that she had never seen them killed came back. Their deaths had been a certainty in her mind all her life. It was disorientating to think that they might not be dead after all. The worst part was, if they weren't killed, why had they never come back for her?

"Who took care of you?" Cecilia asked. The concerned look in her eye made Portia squirm in her seat. She looked out the window again to not have to see it.

"I don't know. I have some vague memory of a yelling man and a soft woman who whispered in my ear. Then all I remember after that is the dirty streets of Valencia... until I met John. He took me in."

"He raised you?"

Now it was Portia's turn to laugh. "If you call it that. He was the age I am now, I think, when I met him. He let me be in his gang. I learned to steal from him."

"And survive," Cecilia said softly.

"And survive," Portia acknowledged.

"I wish I could have raised my little girl."

"To steal?" Portia couldn't help teasing a bit. It kept the seriousness at bay.

"No! Well, maybe if that's what she wanted."

Portia stared at Cecilia.

"Of course not to steal. But, really, I would have taken her in any form just to have her back. You can't understand what it's like to not have your little girl."

Portia pursed her lips and looked away.

"I'm sorry... maybe you do understand a little about missing your family," Cecilia said, apology in her tone.

Portia nodded but refused to look at Cecilia again.

"How old are you?" Cecilia asked softly.

"Fourteen... I think."

"Oh my!"

Portia looked back at Cecilia's exclamation. Cecilia's hand covered her mouth and her eyes were wide as she stared at Portia.

"What?" Portia asked defensively.

"It's just that... that is how old my daughter would have been. Would be. Is. I must believe she is still alive." She stared at Portia.

The carriage bounced along in silence.

The resemblance is remarkable, Portia thought, but she didn't know Cecilia at all, and Cecilia knew that Portia had some influence in the royal house, something that anyone would want for themselves. Even so, a guarded sense of hope snuck into Portia's heart against her better judgment.

"I understand." Portia understood the wish for things such as loved ones still being alive. Even so, Cecilia's intensity was unnerving. "My age could be a coincidence."

Cecilia nodded but did not look way.

Portia shifted in her seat. "Let's not talk of it further." Between the odd sensation in her stomach, the tingling she felt from sitting so close to Cecilia, and the bouncing of the carriage on the road, she didn't feel quite well. She closed her eyes and pretended to sleep.

The journey to Coverack took nearly a week. Portia had money to pay for inns for her and Cecilia, while the guards took care of the horse and carriage, as well as themselves, at the tiny towns' guardhouses.

When they arrived at Coverack, the gate was just as crowded with people as it had been prior, and many were still being sent away and told to go away from the sea and travel inland. The guards driving the horse had a few words with the gatekeeper and the carriage was ushered in and driven directly to the palace, much to Portia's surprise. At the palace, Portia stepped out to see Mark standing directly in front of her, waiting outside the palace entrance. With a glad cry she ran to him and gave him a hug.

"Who is this?" Cecilia asked, staring at Mark.

Mark turned to Cecilia at the sound of her voice, and his jaw fell. He stared back and forth between Portia and Cecilia. "You found her."

"I found someone," Portia said. "Let's not get our hopes up." Mark turned to her, the expression on his face asking *why not?* Shaking her head, Portia mentally willed him not to say it.

"Who is this?" Cecilia asked, jumping into the awkward silence.

"This is Mark. My brother. My adopted brother... he was in the same gang. I found him," Portia said awkwardly. Mark was the only family she'd known, along with John and a few others from the gang, and all too briefly Elyas, but she couldn't bring herself to say that to Cecilia.

"She saved me. And I've repaid her by being a typical younger brother." Mark laughed. "Luckily, she stuck by me."

Mostly. Guilt racked Portia, but she shoved it away as she ducked her face and hoped the burning heat of her shame was not visible. Mark had forgiven her after she left him behind in Valencia, but she had never forgiven herself. *I'm the lucky one*, Portia thought.

"We saved each other," she finally said.

Cecilia tilted her head while staring at Portia. Curiosity burned in her eyes.

The steward standing by the door, alongside several footmen, cleared his throat.

"They're waiting for us," Mark said quickly. "Somehow there's been word of your progress beyond what I brought. Since you were so close behind, they wanted to wait so I could share my information in front of you." Mark shrugged his shoulders. "Or perhaps they just don't trust me."

Portia frowned. Things were too urgent to wait. Why did they not just use the truth cube on him? But she was not a royal. Perhaps there were things the rulers knew that she did not.

Queen Lorica and King Consort Aldis were waiting along with the full court. When Portia stepped in, followed closely by Cecilia, the court gave a collective gasp. People stared and pushed to get a better look at Cecilia and Mark following closely behind. The queen waited without expression for Portia to approach the throne.

"What has happened in Lusatiana?" the queen asked.

"Once again our borders are flooded. This was not the outcome we had hoped for."

Portia shuddered, not just at disappointing the queen, but the danger their kingdom was in. "My apologies, Your Majesty." She didn't know what else to say. They couldn't have stopped the invaders, not just with her and Mark.

The queen waved away Portia's apology. "You are not personally responsible," Queen Lorica said. "Are you?"

Portia shook her head quickly, looking up in shock. Only the brief flicker of a smile on the queen's countenance gave way that she was teasing Portia. It quickly vanished, and Queen Lorica spoke on more seriously. "If it was known how desperate things were, the discussion would have been of sending an army, not a single girl."

Mark bristled at not being included in the quest, but he returned the tiny smile Portia gave him and lowered his shoulders again before turning again to the queen. "There was a betrayal from inside Lusatiana," Mark said. Queen Lorica tilted her head at his speaking without invitation but did not stop him from continuing. "They blew up their own defenses."

The entire court silenced to hear more.

"Please explain," Queen Lorica said to Portia, turning away from Mark, who bit his lip at being pushed aside but said nothing. Portia exhaled gratefully for his restraint, not daring to look at him again.

"Your Majesty, their gigantic seawall was blown up. From the inside. There were tunnels. We explored it the night it blew up. The explosion resounded even in town... The sight of that huge wall falling... It was awful."

"Luckily for us, you were not inside when it happened," King Consort Aldis said, his gentle brown eyes smiling at Portia, who only dared nod in response.

"The wall fell because of tunnels. Was there magic involved?" the queen asked.

"I don't think so. There was some strange black powder all over the inside of them, sometimes in big piles. I got some on my skin and it burned off in a flash when exposed to a candle." Portia grimaced at the memory of the sharp pain from the fire exploding on her skin.

"But it wasn't magic?" the queen asked, confused.

"I... I don't think so. But I'm not sure. Perhaps Professor Aelric or your advisors would know more than I. It was a foul scented and clung to everything."

The queen looked to her advisors, and as one they shook their heads. The substance was unknown to them.

"We have an unpleasant and dangerous mystery on our hands."

Portia nodded. "There were also strange ships without sails."

"Those ships have been there for a while, before I had even come to Coverack, but they were so far away it was unclear exactly what they were," Mark said, jumping in. "When they came into the harbor, it was easier to see. They moved in some unknown way, like ducks in the water. They're fast too."

The queen tapped her cheek. "How rich these visitors

must be to have ships of metal. And their mysterious black powder. Did you see any of them?"

Cecilia grabbed Portia's arm at the mention of the invaders.

"Yes, they are huge. And covered with scales, as if snakes had been turned into men."

Whispers in the court broke out at that.

"Then we do have invaders." The Queen's face betrayed no emotion.

Portia nodded.

"Well then, we will need to be briefed in more detail. Our scribes will meet with you immediately after this and you will answer their questions until they are satisfied," the queen said briskly.

"Your Majesty," Portia said to get her attention.

"Yes, dear one."

"I have some information about the betrayers and what they have further done to the people of Lusatiana. They sold them to the invaders as slaves." Gasps came from the audience. "They also had something to do with the wall falling. Some of those people, those of that group, might be in our city now," Portia said in a rush.

Mutterings rose from the court and people looked at each other, as if they might find the betrayers in their midst in the audience hall.

The queen held her hand up for silence. "You have proof." It was more of a statement than a question.

Nodding, Portia reached into her jacket and pulled out the papers she had stolen from the last compound. She handed them to the guard at the foot of the queen's throne who then passed them to the queen after inspecting them.

"It was as Mark thought. His company had something to do with this. The mark of his company is all over these parchments. These were from a large compound filled with hundreds of slaves. It looked as if they targeted those without magic, most likely because they are easier to control."

Mark shifted from foot to foot as the queen examined the papers. Portia looked to reassure him, but he would not meet her eye. He had warned the court. This information was not something he had tried to hide.

She turned back to the queen. "The papers show the mark of the cult, the diamond shaped tattoos just as in Rocabarra and on the attackers in the road. Somehow, they are all connected. They are working with the invaders, for one of them spoke of it, of buying slaves from them. If the cult is in Coverack, then they are working to enslave our people for their own profit."

Queen Lorica's lips thinned. Her eyes blazed as she looked up again at Portia. "That will not happen." She turned to the advisor standing next to her. "Get Commander Korja here, as well as Captain Ross. Now."

The advisor nodded once and scurried away, his long robes swishing behind him as he went.

The queen took a large breath and exhaled it slowly, carefully. The court was silent. No one dared speak in the face of her rage. The expression on her face rapidly changed as her eyebrows knit and she turned to Portia once again. "You *spoke* to an invader? It spoke common?"

Red burned Portia's face all the way down her neck. Willing her voice to be steady, she said, "Yes. I had used an Elven spell on it to learn its language. Apparently, it learned mine at the same time."

"That is unfortunate," the queen said dryly. "Did it get away?"

"No," Portia said, in a voice barely louder than a whisper. "I don't think so." They left it tied up, but had it been freed since then?

"Did you kill it?" the queen asked.

"No," Portia said, even more quietly. "I couldn't do it."

The queen stared at Portia. The king consort leaned forward to look at the queen's face, but after a moment's consideration he leaned back again and said nothing. Portia wanted nothing more than to shrink to the size of a crawler and disappear between the cracks in the floor tiles.

Finally, the queen turned to stare at Cecilia. "Who is this? Her name is not familiar, although her face is, is it not, Portia?"

"When we were freeing slaves, they spoke of one who looked just like me, so I found her," Portia said, glad of the topic change.

"Is she a relation of yours?" the queen asked. Her advisors leaned in around her to hear the answer. They must be wondering if she also had Jack powers, Portia guessed.

"I don't know. Most likely not."

"Portia is the same age as my stolen daughter, Your Majesty," Cecilia offered, giving a quick curtsy and looking down after having spoken.

Queen Lorica examined Portia's face and then Cecilia's. "That cannot be ignored when your faces are the mirrors of each other."

King Consort Aldis leaned forward but this time put a hand on Queen Lorica's arm. She turned to him with a start. They communicated something silently between them and Queen Lorica nodded. The king consort looked uncomfortable but withdrew his hand and leaned back, leaving the queen to face the court once again.

"Where are you from originally, Cecilia?" the queen asked imperiously.

"Haulstatt, Your Majesty."

"We will verify this. Bring the red mage," the queen said.

Another attendant ran off. The court waited in silence. Portia's legs throbbed from the days of walking and then the long days cooped up in the carriage. It took all her willpower to stay still and attentive and to not shift from foot to foot. No one but the queen and king consort had chairs.

The attendant returned with a woman dressed in deep red robes in tow. The woman came to stand before the queen and bowed. "Your Majesty."

"We will determine where this one is from and who she is." Queen Lorica motioned to Cecilia.

The mage turned and considered Cecilia, her eyes narrowing. "I see. This is a task for the spirit." Portia leaned forward to hear the woman's quiet words, drawing the attention of her dark eyes. "You are curious about the spirit? It knows the truth of who everyone is and can follow their life lines down the paths of history. There is no fighting it."

Portia's mouth made a small circle. There was a way to find out where orphans had come from? She had to learn this magic. Not just for now but for Mark and those other orphans.

The woman in red gave a low chuckle but said nothing further to Portia. She took a small black box she'd been carrying with her and set it down on the dais in front of the queen. Opening it, she stepped back and bowed. Portia peered inside but the box appeared to be empty.

"Gracious spirit, we have questions. Please bless us with your answers," the mage intoned.

Portia felt nothing, not the usual tingle she sensed from magic nearby. Despite that, a voice answered from above the mage. "Yes, yes, what do you want?" Portia, Mark, and Cecilia jumped. No one else seemed surprised.

"Thank you so much, generous spirit," the mage said.

"Speak your questions," the voice said, its tone impatient.

A faint red form materialized, hovering over the black box. It was dressed in red robes just like the mage's, but it was a much tinier version of the woman, only standing about half a length high or so. Despite floating in the air, the figure was no higher than eye level. It scanned the room until it stopped at Portia and stared.

"Where is this one from and who is she?" the queen asked, gesturing to Cecilia. The tiny figure turned to the queen and gave a small curtsey, then turned to look where the queen was pointing.

It stared at Cecilia until finally saying, "The blood of Callac is always a part of Haulstatt."

An uproar came from the surrounding nobles, a bold few yelling while others asked frantic questions. Some knew what that meant, while others did not. A chill ran down Portia's arms at the strength of the reactions. Anger boiled in the crowd. Turning to the queen, Portia's stomach dropped even further—the queen was pale and gripping the arms of her throne. The king consort looked nearly as disturbed.

There was something very bad about Callac. About Cecilia. Portia stared at Cecilia, who looked frightened and surprised at the outburst. Mark, Portia, and Cecilia stood in the middle of a storm.

The unusual chaos went on for minutes on end until the queen held up a hand for silence. The court slowly came to order.

"Are they relations?" Queen Lorica asked while motioning to Portia and Cecilia.

This time the spirit answered much more quickly. "The daughter is always part of the mother."

Mother! Portia whirled to stare at Cecilia. Her mother! Dizziness overcame Portia, and she collapsed in a heap with only Mark's arms keeping her head from dashing upon the tiles. Cecilia rushed to Portia's side, her face ashen.

Cecilia is my mother, Portia thought just before blacking out.

13

People in deep blue robes flew above her, silhouetted against the brilliant sky. Portia squinted her eyes at the vision as she came back to consciousness. Wasn't she inside? Her confusion cleared when she realized it was an intricately painted ceiling above the couch she was laid upon.

Sitting up, Portia looked around. The couch was in a large room with tall ceilings but still much smaller than the throne room. The queen and king consort were conferring with some advisors over a massive wood table in the corner. Cecilia was sitting in another chair nearby, her head down. Two advisors stood near her, conversing and stealing covert looks at Cecilia's bowed head. The rest of the court was gone.

"You passed out," Mark said, his voice coming from behind her. He was sitting on a chair watching over Portia. "It was surprisingly difficult to rouse you, so they brought you back here." His eyes glittered as he looked around the rich room. "It's much cozier. At least they could lay you on the couch." He gave her a half smirk.

"Why do you look like an elf in a rosebush?" Portia asked quietly while sitting up slowly. Everyone else was distracted for the moment.

"A what?" Mark gave her a confused look.

"Elves love roses... never mind. Why are you so happy?"

"Because you found your mother!" Mark whispered, then gave her a poke before Cecilia, who had noticed Portia awakening, reached them. "And she's a big deal!"

"Portia, are you better?" Cecilia asked. Her face was drawn, and she kept glancing back at two royal advisors who looked like they wished to come and retrieve her but didn't dare while Cecilia was by Portia's side.

"I am, I think." Portia sat at the edge of the couch and leaned forward. It eased the pressure in her head. It felt odd to feel so ill. It's not as if someone had stabbed her.

The queen and king consort approached. Mark stood quickly and bowed. Portia attempted to rise, but blackness crept on the edge of her vision and she wavered for a moment. The queen quickly motioned for her to sit, and Portia gratefully lowered herself to the couch again.

"We have sent for a healer, young Jack," Queen Lorica said. "Until then, do not move from that couch."

Nodding seemed like a bad idea, so Portia inclined her head the smallest amount possible. "Yes, Your Majesty."

It was deeply uncomfortable to sit in front of the queen, especially when no one spoke further. Portia glanced up. The queen was staring at Cecilia, who was looking anywhere but at the royal's face. The king consort's hand rested gently on the queen's upper arm.

"What is going on, if I might be so bold," Portia asked. "Who is Callac?"

"You, apparently," the queen answered, a touch of bitterness and some other emotion in her voice that Portia could not place. The queen shook herself. "This knowledge could have picked a better time to come out, with war coming for us."

What knowledge? Portia wanted to scream but didn't dare, both because that was not the proper way to talk to a queen, but also because her head hurt so much.

It was not needed though, because after a moment the queen's tone dropped and she continued. "Callac was the royal house of Haulstatt, before the great war that splintered off Jukhnovo and Lusatiana. All humans were under one kingdom then."

Mark blew out sharply and muttered, "Royal."

Portia shot him a glare. He closed his mouth quickly, but his body throbbed with energy.

Ignoring Mark, the queen sat down on a great wooden chair brought by an attendant, with the king consort finding his own seat brought by another attendant.

"Why is nothing mentioned of them... the Callacs?" Portia asked, unable to stop herself.

"The Great War almost destroyed humankind. We needed unity. The other races were not happy at our presence and watched for our self-destruction. Things are better now. A little," King Consort Aldis said gently. "There is nothing evil about the Callacs. It is just an opportunity for strife we do not need."

The queen shot the king consort a quick look that made Portia suspect there was something he was not telling her. She'd seen a reference once before to the house of Callac. It was in a tiny yellow book from the special library, but Portia couldn't remember exactly what it said about them. It was time to visit that library again.

There were too many secrets in this kingdom.

A commotion by the door caught Portia's attention. Commander Korja, Captain Ross, and Myra had arrived. Captain Ross and Myra wore the blue uniforms of the Magic Academy guards, while Commander Korja, a tall, thin man, completely bald, wore the gold and purple of the Coverack guard, his uniform decorated with lengths of gold braid.

The group approached the queen and bowed. Captain Ross snuck Portia a wink as he stood. Portia relaxed a bit at his teasing familiarity. Portia knew Captain Ross and Myra from the Magic Academy guards, but Commander Korja was unknown to her. He stepped forward.

"We might have traitors in our midst, Commander," the queen said.

The commander's face fell at that, deep lines growing in his forehead as the corners of his mouth turned down. "That is ill news."

"Indeed. These traitors think to sell our people to invaders as slaves. They dare to subjugate my people."

"Slavers," Captain Ross murmured, death in his voice.

"Exactly," the queen said. "Commander, your task is to

rectify that. I've asked Captain Ross here so the Academy guards can coordinate efforts with you. You may ask Portia more questions when she is better, but until then my scribe has notes of the current information. Please, go." The queen motioned to the large table spread with parchments.

The commander nodded and led the others to the table. Just as they were walking away, Portia noticed a shadow stretch out from behind the doorway under the arch of the entrance. Heart racing, she reached instinctively for her knife while also concentrating on ice magic, ready to shoot at whatever was coming.

The queen noticed Portia's reaction and turned to the shadow and held up a hand to Portia. "Do not interfere."

It took all of Portia's self-control to not lash out at whatever the shadow was, but she obeyed. A shimmering held over the shadow, then it fell away to reveal a figure in long dark robes with a deep hood pulled forward to hide its face. The figure approached the queen and then bowed, standing upright only upon the acknowledgment from Queen Lorica.

"Welcome, Spymaster Grania," the queen said.

Slender hands pulled back the hood to reveal an older woman who stared at Portia, her black eyes glinting in the dim room, before returning her gaze to the queen. "I have news, Your Majesties."

"Then share. All those present may hear it," the queen said.

"I stayed behind in Lusatiana after Mark and Portia fled with the captives."

Mark and Portia exchanged glances. Portia's face burned

while blood pounded in her ears. They had been followed. What else had been hidden from her?

"This one showed great bravery in the face of danger. There were times it took all my skill to keep up with her," Grania said, pointing to Portia and grinning.

Despite the words of praise, anger and unease boiled inside Portia. She stood abruptly; her arms stiff with anger. "You had us followed?"

The queen looked at her and tilted her head. "Of course."

"Don't you trust me?"

"Trust has nothing to do with it. Only a fool relies on a single source when others are available. And if others are not available, they find ones." The queen's voice took on a dangerous tone. "You are not calling me a fool, are you?"

Flustered, Portia blew out air and stammered, "No, of course not, Your Majesty... but you could have told us. Warned us."

"Why? So you would reveal our agent if caught and risk her life too?"

"No, I just meant it would be good to know." Portia suddenly felt foolish. What the queen said made perfect sense. "I would not reveal her," she added, her voice sounding petulant and young. Portia's face burned red at the sound of her own words.

"You can resist a truth cube?" the queen asked.

"No," Portia admitted.

Mark pulled at Portia's arm, trying to get her to sit down again. Portia glared at him, still a little angry and a great deal embarrassed.

"It's for the best I'm sure," he said quietly. "What if something really bad happened? There was at least someone watching out for us. When has *that* happened before?"

"Not often."

"Your young friend is growing on me," King Consort Aldis said.

Portia's heart sank a bit. No one else thought it was bad that they had been followed. Not only had she objected, she had interrupted the queen and made a fuss. When would she learn to not just say whatever she was thinking?

"No one likes being spied upon, no matter how it is for the best," Grania said dryly.

Portia nodded, unwilling to raise her eyes to make eye contact.

The spymaster turned to the queen and continued. "The invaders are gravely unlike ourselves. Their language unknown, except now for Portia. Perhaps she can share that knowledge." Portia glanced up to see the spymaster giving her the intent look of a cat. Was she intending on thieving the knowledge from Portia's head? The skin on Portia's back crawled, and she breathed a sigh of relief when the spymaster once again turned to the queen. "A large force came off the strange metal boats then split into two. Those two forces are slow going, having large-wheeled vehicles that are difficult for horses to pull, appearing to be heavy and easily stuck in ruts in the road. They were making poor time. This is a blessing in our favor since one of the forces is headed directly for Haulstatt and possibly Coverack. There were more ships in this attack than we had heard of in Jukhnovo. They also brought the tools of a land battle, another change since Jukhnovo."

The queen grimaced. "Where is the second force going?"

"I was unable to tell before having to flee back here to give warning. Most of the ships removed themselves and went back out to sea. Presumably to the portal again."

"For more soldiers," the queen said.

"Most likely. Or more supplies." The spymaster looked grave. It was devastating news to have to bring to court. "It would be logical for them to attack us next. It's unclear why the ships struck at Rodaine after taking Juknovo instead of just moving south down the coastline."

"So war is coming, and fast," the queen said. She turned to Portia. "We will need all your magic now, if the prophecies are true. Somehow, you are here to save us from this. We shall prepare our armies just in case."

Cecilia, who up until that time had been silently watching everything, gasped at this and looked at Portia.

"You did not tell her," the queen said.

Portia shook her head.

"Tell me what?" Cecilia asked, then quickly corrected herself. "Your Majesty."

"Portia is a Jack of Magic. They come into existence only when the kingdom will be in dire need. Apparently, that is now. As a Jack, she can do more than one tree of magic, something no other human can do."

"I fear I can't do it very strongly, Your Majesty."

"It must be enough," the queen said firmly. "Jacks are our sacred warriors and our champions."

That was a certainty Portia wished she had. Two kingdoms had fallen already. How could she, a young girl, stop this entire force?

Portia studied the floor tiles. Their only hope was if they kept more invaders from coming. They were so large and powerful and had such strange weapons. If they could at least limit the number, then there might be a chance. But Grania spoke of armies and wheeled machines. Could it possibly be too late already?

"But she's so young," Cecilia said, protesting.

"She's our champion," Queen Lorica said firmly. "She has taken up the charge."

Cecilia stared wide-eyed at Portia, who looked up to nod in return.

"It is my duty," Portia said, and then she turned back to the queen, mustering the strength to lift her head high. "Your Majesty, if we are to succeed against these invaders, we need to stop them from coming. We cannot allow the numbers to increase, or we will be overwhelmed. I ask that I be given a ship and a crew so we can go directly to the portal and stop it."

All talk in the room ceased. Somehow Portia's words had carried, and even the group conferring over the table paused what they were doing to look and watch.

"We need all our ships to defend the city," the queen said. "Protecting the people is my first charge and my duty."

"But, Your Majesty, would that not be easier if we kept the numbers of invaders down?"

"Perhaps, but we know the attack on our city is imminent. We do not know how far away the splintering is. It might be a week's voyage or more. How could we give you a ship that is a significant portion of our defenses right before an attack from those that wish to enslave us, thereby putting our own people at risk? Worse yet, we could also then lose that ship, and you as well, since it would stand no chance against any it might encounter upon the open sea since we cannot spare an escort for you, not if we must to put forces to the southern border too." She shook her head. "No, Jack, there is some wisdom in your words, but we must wait and defend the people first, and then if a ship survives, we will send you to the splinter."

"But what if there is not a ship left and we are utterly run over? Your Majesty, what then?" Portia pushed on, fear of the coming catastrophe making her overly bold.

The queen's eyes darkened as her brows pushed together, her mouth forming a frown. An advisor came upon her right elbow and, with her nod, whispered in her ear. The rest of the room waited in tense silence. The queen held up a hand, and the advisor stopped talking abruptly then stepped back. Another few moments passed. It felt an eternity to Portia. Finally, the queen spoke.

"We will wait until the invaders are within our sight and the main battle engaged. As soon as it is clear the city's defenses will hold, and only then, we will send off a ship under the cover of the chaos of war. Your ship, Portia. Fight well so we have the opportunity to send you to do the final battle."

"Yes, Your Majesty," Portia said gratefully. The thought of war frightened her, but less than the thought of those huge creatures running through Coverack and attacking everyone she knew and cared about. It could be even worse if they were anything like the bloodthirsty author of the small book she had found.

AN ATTENDANT TOOK Cecilia away to the quarters in the palace. Portia was uneasy leaving her there, but Myra would not allow her to stay with Portia in the pyromancy house without orders from the elders of the Magic Academy. "It must be authorized by them," was all she would say about the matter.

The third watch bells rang out as Portia returned to the pyromancy house. Most students were sleeping, and it was dark and quiet. Her growling stomach demanded that she raid the cold closet for meat and bread, but it took all her energy to chew the small sandwich before passing out in her bed. Ella snored and spoke in her sleep, oblivious to Portia coming into their room so late.

Despite only a few hours of sleep, Portia woke before dawn, thoughts of her sword waking her from a deep slumber. Rather than fight her restlessness, she rose and bathed, then went to the practice room to train yet again. Better to be productive than to fret in bed.

By the time she finished, the clatter of dishes and din of voices came from the dining hall. Portia wiped down the blade and stowed it in her room before going to find breakfast.

"Portia! How nice of you join us here at school!" Ella

called out sarcastically, her broad smile softening the reproach.

"Hello, roomie." Portia set down her loaded tray at the table Ella shared with Mia. Their plates were empty.

"You'd better hurry if you want to eat all that," a deep voice said from behind her. Richard stared at Portia, Liam at his side. She'd only been gone a short time, but Liam already looked different yet again. Rainbow stripes colored his hair.

"Where have you been?" Richard sat next to Portia and stole a piece of bacon off her plate while Liam sat next to Ella.

"Didn't you already eat?" Ella poked at Richard. "Leave her food. Look how thin she is. They must not have had food there. Portia is always off doing important stuff, aren't you, roomie," Ella said, an edge to her voice.

"Yes, she is." All eyes turned to Professor Hilda. Dark circles showed under her eyes. "We've all been briefed on her work early this morning. Far, far too early. It seems you've been busy, Portia."

"I have." She ducked her head to avoid their curious eyes.

"So let her eat. You'll all get the news soon enough," Professor Hilda said. "The commanders have sent down the battle plans. Classes are canceled until further notice. We have a meeting as soon as the bell tolls."

"About the invasion?" Ella's eyes rounded.

"Let's hope it does not come to that, but yes, we have our orders." Hilda drew her hand down over her eyes and over her mouth. "I hate this. We are a school, not a phalanx. But we must defend our home."

The jovial mood was gone. Suddenly, the food in front of Portia didn't look so appetizing.

Hilda noticed Portia's stillness. "Eat, child. We have a lot ahead of us. You must be strong. The rest of you get ready. We're going to the harbor. Ships have been spotted." Hilda left without waiting for acknowledgment.

"No more practice, I guess." Richard's voice was subdued. None of them had been in battle before. Practicing on campus was not nearly the same, they knew, without Portia having to tell them anything of her own experiences. History class had told enough bloody tales.

"Let's go face it," Liam said, rising and grabbing Ella's tray for her. They left Portia to eat in silence. As savory as the food had been a moment ago, it now tasted like dry grass. Forcing herself to finish, she rushed out of the dining room to grab her weapons and meet the rest of the students by the portal door. They would leave for the harbor from campus.

Students crowded the docks while merchants and residents boarded windows and packed up wagons to move further into the city per royal decree. Frantic citizens pushed by guards and mages wearing blue robes setting up defenses on the shoreline.

Out in the harbor, a line of large ships faced outwards, their white sails billowing. Further out in the sea, shadows and dark smudges gave away the positions of the enemy's metal ships. They circled quickly, taunting the large and cumbersome defending vessels stationed closer to shore.

More ships were still in the dock, but they were mostly merchant ships and ill-suited for a battle, being wide, flat, and far from agile. Sailors frantically loaded supplies and worked the decks, making room for the guards and mages. Other guards and mages worked together to prepare attacks from land. No one wanted the enemy to reach shore, but they had to plan for it, nonetheless.

Hilda looked out at the ships in the harbor and swore softly under her breath. "As of last night there were no ships. Our plan of attack must be modified because they are constructed of metal. Fire will not be as effective in stopping them. They are still vulnerable to being heated, though I doubt any of you have the energy to burn the entire ship red-hot."

"That would be decisive if we could," Liam said.

Hilda nodded wearily. "If only we would be so blessed. Further, they don't have portals on their sides that would be vulnerable to attack. These ships of theirs are terrible things for us."

"No portals? However do they travel in the harbor without oars?" Mia scowled at the enemy ships. Of all the students, she was the only one who had traveled by clipper, voyaging with her father to the Hidden Isles off the coast of Coverack. Were those isles under the control of these invaders as well?

"They have no oars nor sails and still they travel faster than any of our ships," Portia said.

"How do you know this? Where did you go *this* time?" Ella asked, her hands on her hips.

"We don't have time for this. Please stop." Hilda held up her hand and waited until it was quiet. "However they move, they do so without vulnerabilities in the sides of their ships. We need to find a way to stop them even so. Rather than spread our efforts too thin, we will concentrate on one ship at a time. Other houses are doing the same and we will communicate with them with flags. Those of you versed in node magic will first lay traps along the harbor and shallows, as many as we can. It will not be easy to come ashore, not by our will. Rodaine was overconfident in their wall. We will not follow their lead."

"Rodaine? Has it fallen?" Mia gasped, and turned to Portia, reading the answer on her face. Tears welled up in Mia's eyes. "Rodaine too!"

"Don't think of that now. We have our own battle to face," Hilda said. "If their ships make progress into the harbor, we will have to send the magic to them. Only advanced mages are on our ships... for now."

"If advanced mages are at the front, how can we do better?" Richard asked. He was never the most confident of students.

"We must," Hilda replied. "At least we must try. The alternative is unthinkable. This city is not designed for defense from the sea. All the citizens depend on us."

Liam clapped Richard on the back. "Not a problem. These metal shipped outlaws haven't met us yet."

After her journey to Rocabarra, Portia thought it foolish that Coverack, originally an Elven city, was not better prepared to defend an attack from the sea. Wasn't that where the humans had come from? The humans that had displaced the Elves and sent them fleeing into the interior? If nothing else, those interlopers should have upgraded the defenses themselves after capturing the city. The arrogance of their conquest showed in the lack of preparation for another invasion from others behind them. She shook her head.

The node pockets of magic would at least slow them down. The nodes could be roughly set to go off by the size of something passing over or through it. They were crude, but the only way Portia knew of to store magic for an attack to go off where the mage was not there to do so.

Laying the nodes in the harbor was done cooperatively between the houses, mostly the pyromancy and cryomancy houses, with a few from the lightning house. Portal magic was not amenable to nodes. It would have been useful to have a gigantic door to send the invading ships far away but there was nothing to anchor the magic to out in the harbor. Freestanding portal magic was a sub-magic of splinters, and only the elves knew how to create those. Or one elf, she corrected herself. Even the Elves struggled with splinter magic.

Nor was time magic possible with nodes. They were reduced to brute force methods such as fire and ice. A wooden ship would buckle and strain with ice and burn with fire. But the invading ships were metal. They did not know what effect their magic would have on the invading ships, but they had to try.

Hilda paired Portia with Magisend Lucy from the cryomancy house. Their job was to layer fire and ice nodes in the shallows of the harbor while a lightning house student placed charge nodes on the far end of the harbor.

Magisend eyed Portia. "Time to earn your keep *commoner*."

"I could say the same to you." Portia said, sick of the hostility. "You know I can run magic circles around you. Shall I demonstrate?"

Magisend's eyes widened for a second and then she glanced around before she drew herself up impressively high for such a small girl. "Just concentrate on your work. We have more important problems than your social climbing."

Portia huffed but turned to do her work. Magisend's attitude problem could wait for another day. Portia felt no need to keep her powers secret any longer—not when the enemy was breathing down their throats and war imminent. Magisend's bullying days were numbered.

Going by the rough drawing a representative of the guard had handed them, they only placed the nodes in set channels. This way the defending ships would know where to avoid, for the nodes would damage them as well, probably worse than the invaders since all the Coverack ships were wood. A mage could stop the nodes from going off but only if they knew of the nodes first. Human mages could not see them. Only elves could, and there were no elves present to help. Portia grimaced. Why hadn't she brought some back with her? Surely King Magnus would have agreed to that. Without them, the defending ships would be sailing blindly through the now deadly waters.

Without telling Magisend, Portia doubled the amount of nodes in the channel, both of ice and of fire. The ice magic was exhausting for Portia, but she pushed through the buzzing in her head and the accompanying dizziness. Conjuring the memory of the threatening invader and the hate burning in his eyes was motivation enough to keep going. She doubled the amount of magic she stuffed in each node for an extra blast, something only she could do.

He would never get her. Never.

Portia didn't realize she was swaying so far to the side until she lost her balance and sprawled on the dirt. Breathing heavily, she willed the darkness to go back from her vision. The battle hadn't even started yet. It was too early to be this tired.

"Portia, are you all right? What happened?" Hilda's concerned eyes looked down at Portia.

"Nothing happened. I don't know. Perhaps I'm pushing too hard."

Magisend snorted, earning a black look from Hilda. She turned back to Portia. "That's understandable, but this battle could go on for quite a while." Hilda's face was set in grim lines.

Portia nodded. *If we are lucky. If we are not, they will quickly crush us.* It was too much to hope for that they would defeat the invaders easily and send them packing. Reaching up a hand to Hilda, Portia stood with her instructor's assistance and brushed off her breeches.

Before she could say anything else, a crackling explosion of wood from a nearby building shook the ground. A scream came from that direction as people scrambled and ran. The invaders had struck the building in the city from their location far out at sea.

"Run!" Hilda exclaimed, pushing the students to take cover further away towards the other end of the harbor curve, away from the buildings. They scrambled over the dirt embankment and hid behind a low hill to watch the action. Sailors on the ships still in dock hurried to unmoor the lines and move the cumbersome vessels into the harbor. The beater screamed the count as the oars dipped into the waters in time. If the enemy could strike from such a distance, all the ships at the dock were sitting targets. They needed to move. Quickly.

Blood pounded in Portia's ears. Had they struck from so far away in the Rodaine battle? She was there and should have noticed, but they had been some distance from the city freeing the slaves when the attack occurred.

Another booming explosion shook the ground. Peering over the hill, Portia saw one of the larger ships with a gigantic hole blown in its deck. Sailors on board were screaming and shouting and jumping overboard. The ship began to burn, black acrid smoke filling the air over the harbor.

"Is that magic?" Ella screamed in Portia's ear. Panic shone in her eyes. Ella was always composed so to see such fear was almost more terrifying than the ships themselves for Portia.

Portia grabbed her roommate by the shoulders. "I don't think so. Calm down."

"That's not magic? That's even worse." Ella pointed to the destroyed ship in the harbor, her finger trembling. "How are they doing that?"

Portia shook her head. She didn't know exactly how they did it, but it was the same as in Rodaine. "They shoot large metal balls from their ships."

Distant cries and yells caught Portia's ear. The guttural horrible language of the invaders rang out across the waters of the harbor, booming and echoing. The voices were unnaturally loud and could be heard throughout the harbor. The city ships relied on flags and visual signaling and were at a disadvantage if there was smoke or fog or other impediments. But the invaders had a different system—one that didn't rely on sight. They had no reason to fear the humans would understand their commands. It was a miracle they hadn't used that advantage to attack at night.

It was a stroke of good luck they didn't know Portia could understand their language.

Holding her finger to her lips to quiet Ella and all those around her, Portia cocked her head to hear better. The echoing made it difficult to understand what they were saying but she could pick out a word here and there. One of them was 'dock', another few words about 'the buildings' and 'move'.

Portia looked around. There were no city commanders nearby, nor even an Academy guard, but Hilda was still close. She must know how to get word up the line. Portia crouched down and ran to Hilda while keeping her cover behind the hillside.

"They're going for the docks next, either for strikes, or moving close," Portia said to Hilda, pointing emphatically at the invaders.

"How do you know this?" Hilda asked, surprised.

"I know their language."

Hilda stared at Portia for just a second, her mouth

opening and shutting again. She nodded. "Tell the group to fire on the ships using the long-distance techniques we practiced. I'm going to tell the commander. Our most powerful mages are next to him. They need to attack now. He needs to know."

Hilda pushed Portia towards the other students, then ran down the line, circling back to an area closer to the docks where the commander must be located. Portia ran back to the other students and passed on the commands. Richard looked a little ill at her words. Of all the students, he was the one least prepared for a long-distance attack and could do little to help the others except watch for nearby ambushes and protect them as they worked.

The lobbed fireball and ice bomb nodes flew across the harbor but stopped short of the ships just past the defending line. One especially large fireball nearly hit one of their own. Liam paled at the near catastrophe, having sent the ball flying himself. He pursed his lips and gathered another fireball, his back and arms stiff with the effort.

Portia grabbed his arm to stop him and pointed to another set of invading ships further in the harbor, flowing between defending ships towards the field of magic nodes waiting for them. He nodded curtly and aimed for a spot in front of the lead vessel, a small patch of water without a defending ship. The fireball landed precisely on the prow in the metal ship. The prow glowed a soft red then quickly faded into a dark metal gray again. The ship did not slow at all. Liam panted heavily as he helplessly watched it come closer.

The first invasion ships quickly reached the line of nodes set by Portia and the other mages, the waters churning darkly. How did they move like that? If their commanders wondered why the defending ships did not move to block them, they did not let those questions stop them from moving forward fearlessly.

Portia held her breath as the first ship hit the nodes. The water boiled as fire and heat hit the hull. The ship struck another node—an ice one—and the water dropped noticeably in the front of the ship as the boiling water cooled quickly, sending the craft bouncing up and down. This process repeated several times, and even from a distance the dull red glow of the hull could be seen every time it hit a fire node. Those nodes had been set by powerful Academy mage teachers who had decades of experience and far more natural magic reserves than Portia. While she could do all sorts of magic, individually each type was not that strong. This was not the case for most instructors.

After the fourth round of hits, the ship slowed as if its propulsion method was broken. The others behind it kept moving forward, sliding across nodes the first one had not hit. One ship crashed into the stalled lead vessel.

That was enough to do the lead ship in. It sank in slow motion, invaders jumping from the craft and attempting to swim to other ships. Cruelly, the other ships did not slow to rescue those overboard. The students watched with their mouths in small circles of shock as ship after ship did nothing to stop their own from drowning. The creatures quickly sank into the dark waters, even those who had shed their armor before fleeing the ship.

"Lay more nodes!" someone shouted. Portia shook herself out of her trance and sent more nodes in front of the other ships passing into the harbor. There were still many unactivated nodes in the water, but not enough to stop all the ships. Portia laid node after node in front of the new ships while those around her did the same, as well as sending fireballs and ice and lightning down on the ships.

Lightning was especially deadly if it struck after ice and fire had first hit the ships, dousing the invaders on deck in water and allowing the lightning energy to flow through the huge invaders, charring them from the inside out. Portia gritted her teeth and thought of her people enslaved to strengthen her resolve as the screams of those struck filled the harbor.

The number of incoming ships seemed relentless. Even

after they sank ship after ship, there were still more behind them. Portia's energy flagged and she fell to her knees, still throwing magic at the ships. But soon even that was too much effort, and she had to halt, watching helplessly as yet more ships poured into the harbor.

One of the foreign metal-clad ships finally reached the docks. It smashed into the wooden structure, barely slowing its approach as it pushed the dock to one side, cracking the moorings. The wood gave way with a horrific screech. Invaders wearing heavy plate armor jumped from the ship to the swaying dock and ran towards shore.

The invaders were on land.

As more came off the ships, the invaders formed a line just off the dock. They held oddly shaped shields and spears. More invaders filled out the rear, but these carried enormous crossbows.

The city's defenders rallied to try to stop the invaders from completing their formation. The invaders responded by sending a volley of arrows from their crossbows. The bolts easily reached the defenders and pierced their thick leather guards. The power of the crossbows was immense. Men and women screamed.

Bile pushed at the back of Portia's throat. Those were city and Academy guards being struck down like blades of grass. They needed help fighting the enemy. She rallied her strength and shot ball after ball of fire at the huge wall of attackers. Her magic was not strong enough to disable them, but the bursts of flame interfered with their aiming. She harried them the best she could while others stronger in their magic were able to strike decisive blows and fell a few of the invaders.

Another of the metal ships landed, creatures streaming from its deck to replace those falling in the fighting. There were so many of them. The defenders continued to fall in much greater numbers than the invaders. Fear balled in a knot in Portia's stomach. They had to do something differently or the city would be lost—perhaps the entire kingdom.

Pushing their advantage, the invaders in the front line rose from their kneeling position and marched forward, leaving a space between each one of them for the crossbows behind them to still continue to shoot. The force advanced to the first line of buildings while the defenders fell back, scrambling through the streets and throwing garbage and any debris they could behind them to stop the march of the soldiers.

It had little effect.

The invaders stomped on, brutally killing anyone foolish enough to stop and fight hand to hand. The long spears outreached any sword. Only the most concentrated of magical attacks could fell one of them—and the city only had so many mages to use in the battle.

The only advantage the defenders had were their pell-mell tactics. They scrambled up onto rooftops and behind barriers, attacking in a wild and uncoordinated manner to distract the invaders. The students concentrated on shooting towards the invader's faces to blind them. Anything to slow their forward motion.

Just as another volley of arrows shot towards the defenders, landing deep within wood walls and the soft bodies of the defenders, a clanking sound came from behind them, the distant noise rising in volume as it grew closer. It was the approach of supplemental additional defending forces; forces clad in thick plate armor. Portia breathed a sigh of relief and hope. They could not move fast under the heavy weight, but it was much more protection than a piece of leather against a crossbow bolt.

Portia and Mia scrambled onto a rooftop with a good view of the relief soldiers, for they looked more like soldiers than guards.

"War armor." Mia looked at the forces with a strange expression on her face.

Portia followed her line of vision. "Is there something special about that armor?"

"After the Great War... it was forbidden. They must not have destroyed it."

"Lucky for us." Portia bit her lips with anxiety. "There is a lot of it."

Mia nodded then turned back to the invaders, sending more of her fire magic to the nearest invaders. Her magic was some of the strongest of the students and could send a single invader flying and, with any luck, break his neck. Mia's red hair flew as she worked frantically throwing ball after ball. One of her missiles struck a figure in the chest and blew off his helmet as he flew back. A curse escaped his lips in a voice Portia recognized. The acrid black smoke from Mia's fire cleared and his face came into view—a face with a purple mark around one eye.

It was the invader who had hissed his threat at Portia.

He was here.

He knew common and could understand them. He could talk to the commanders, if only they could force him to do so.

The defenders had to know that in case anything happened to Portia. She was the only one that could speak their language. If she was struck down, that creature was the only key they had to communicate with the invaders, beside the unmistakable communication of war.

"Where are the commanders? Or a guard, anyone?" Portia asked Mia. They searched until they saw two blue uniforms a block over. "Right. See that invader?" Portia pointed to the one who had threatened her. "He knows common. We need to capture him. Keep him there but don't kill him."

"Will do," Mia said grimly. She shot a wall of fire around the guard, heating his armor. Portia wondered if he was stubborn enough to roast alive inside the hot metal or would he tear it off. She didn't have time to stay and watch though, so she scrambled off to reach the guards for assistance while Mia kept the creature contained. Mia was strong, but they had been battling for hours. It would be good to not test her limits.

To Portia's relief, the guards nodded and followed her instructions, running to face the creature. They ran along the street below the building Mia was perched on. With a nod to Mia, they timed it so that when she dropped her pyromancy attacks, the guards ran in to grab the creature, now dizzy with heat and smoke inhalation. Portia struck his head with the butt of her knife just be sure. He went out cold.

Mia scrambled down from the rooftop to join them. They gingerly pulled off the pieces of his armor, still blazing hot, before tying him for capture. The scales on his body smoked. The guards dragged him towards a nearby building that was only slightly damaged. He was a prize to be protected for later.

The sounds of the battle changed, retreating back towards the harbor again as the new guards with their thick plate armor pushed back at the invaders. Few of them fell, and their numbers grew, overwhelming the new creatures.

The streets were slick with blood, littered with the bodies of invaders and defenders. Portia felt ill, but there was no time to think about it. Academy guards cut off a section of the attackers in an attempt to capture a ship, but they lacked the strong armor of the backup guards and were unable to hold the creatures as they fell back. Several Academy guards jumped into the harbor to get out of the way of the retreating invaders when it was clear they could not hold them.

The creatures scrambled over the gangplanks to get back on their boats. One slipped in its haste and fell into the water, grabbing at its companions only to pull them into the harbor with him. They quickly sank under the weight of their own armor, ignored by their companions rushing past to escape. The ships backed up in their mysterious way, churning the waters as they went, and turning to the center of the harbor.

The fleeing ships hit more nodes in the water, bouncing as the first had as fire, ice and electricity shot through the water and slowing their escape.

Spells from the mages on shore flew after, further slowing them. One fleeing ship fired a few more cannonballs towards the city and the defending ships, but it was a scattershot method. The other ships didn't even manage that. Soon, many of them were sinking. The ones that did manage to pass through the harbor bumped against the defenders' wood ships and pushed through. The invaders' decks were empty and sealed. Somehow, they were sailing the ships blindly from below.

A city commander swore under his breath as he watched the last of the foreign ships leave the harbor. "They'll be back, of that I have no doubt. What it would've been worth to have one of those ships still afloat. To know their capabilities." Another soft swear followed when he turned to survey the wreckage on the street of the harbor.

The street was oddly quiet, with only the odd moan of pain from a man here or there struck down and wounded. Survivors walked the streets in a daze, checking bodies but otherwise silent.

Portia looked around for her classmates and Mark. Mia was nearby. A few minutes later, Mark ran towards her from further within the town. He was covered in dust and debris.

"What happened?" She looked at his filthy clothes. There was no visible blood at least, besides a few scratches on his arms.

"A wall collapsed from one of the strikes. I was nearly hit by one of those horrid metal balls. Dang effective and scary too." He brushed off some dirt. "The guards are sweeping the streets now for stragglers. We didn't find any. Hopefully none are hiding in that mess." He pointed back to the wreckage of the buildings that once formed a beautiful harbor walk. "Not that I wouldn't give much to have one captured for a little grilling."

"We did get one."

Mark's eyebrows shot up. "Alive?"

Portia nodded.

"Nice work. Where is it now?"

Portia pointed to the low building they had taken the captive to. The battle around them had died down; the guards had things under control nearby, and the invading ships that had survived the battle were now too far at sea to strike from shore. It would be too much to hope for them to leave Coverack for good, but at least they would most likely not attack again any time soon. The city had not proven so vulnerable as Rodaine, even without a seawall.

"Shall we go see?" she asked Mark. She had not told him about her ability to speak its language.

Mia shook her head at Portia's invitation. "I'm going to find Ella and the others. I think Richard might be hurt."

A stab of pain hit Portia's heart. She wanted to help Richard, but she was the only one that understood the invaders' language—at least that they knew of. Time was crucial to stop more invaders from flowing in. So instead she nodded stiffly at Mia and pulled Mark after her towards the low building.

The captive was on the floor, his hands tied behind his back. He was too large by far for any chair constructed for a human. Even the floorboards groaned ominously under him whenever he shifted his weight. He stared forward with a fierce glare, ignoring the surrounding humans.

"Just like that one on the dock in Rodaine." Mark stared at the creature.

Spitting out the strange sounds, Portia told the captive to look up. The guards in the room jumped at the sounds coming from her mouth, as did Mark by her side.

The brief surprise on the captive's face was quickly replaced by hatred. He snarled at Portia. "*How dare you ssspeak to me again, you filthy creature.*"

What was the deal with calling her filthy all the time?

"*Enough insults. They bore me.*" Her throat hurt to use its language. "*What is your name?*"

It just stared at Portia.

"Answer her question," a voice said from behind Portia. It was one of the city commanders, an older one with a crisp uniform and a chiseled face. The commander pulled his sword to communicate his intent to the creature.

The captive narrowed his eyes at the newcomer but did not answer.

"*You are too cowardly to speak?*" Portia asked, trying a different tactic. She had not the stomach to see how brutal things would get if the commander decided to use interrogation tactics to bend the captive to his will. She held up a hand behind her back to the commander, hoping he understood the signal to let her try things her way.

Silence was the response from the commander. She would take that as a yes.

"*You are afraid of filthy things? Is that why you were left behind?*" Portia teased the captive.

"*Ssshut up!*" it said to her. She'd touched a nerve. How far would that go?

"*You are afraid to even hear my words, much less speak to me? How unclean are you?*" Portia backed up a half step and brushed off her clothing as if he had contaminated her just by being in the room.

"*I fear nothing, leassst of all you, you tiny whining little dirt piece.*"

Dirt piece?

Its eyes burned red-hot hate. Portia was suddenly very glad it was securely chained with guards nearby. It was a powerful creature, and she was exhausted from the long battle.

"*Then tell me your name if you are so brave.*"

"*Acrux.*"

"*Acrux. What are you doing here? This is our home and you've not been invited.*"

It laughed at that, a surprisingly light sound for such a huge creature.

The others looked at Portia, questioning looks on their faces. "His name is Acrux. He think it's funny that I told him they were not invited into our home. I think he's a bit rude," Portia explained.

The commander leaned forward as if he wanted to take over but then leaned back again and gave Portia a tight little smile. She had a bit more time to work on the prisoner.

Acrux stared at Portia with an odd expression. She knew he had understood her speech to the commander.

"Isn't that right?" Portia asked him in common. Acrux's

expression did not change.

Fine, Portia thought, *we shall see how well you play that game.*

Switching back to his language, Portia squatted down so she was face-to-face with him. *"Why are you here?"*

"It is time to take this world. It fitsss the needs of our emperor. His will isss our command."

"Your emperor has been here?" Portia asked, surprised.

"Of course not, not until it has been cleansssed. He makes his judgmentsss from our reportsss and has ordered the gatesss created."

"Gates?" Portia could not quite pick up on how this word was used in Acrux's language.

"Our door to this world," Acrux said, contempt written on his face for her not knowing the term.

A splinter. They called them gates.

"I will close that gate," Portia said. She lifted her head to look down her nose at Acrux. She didn't feel so confident, but he was not going to know that.

"You will fail and die. The gates are opening asss we ssspeak."

"There is more than one gate?"

"Yesss. The wizards are creating a sssecond one now for our warships. They will crusssh your force like vermin underneath our feet."

"There is only one place known to have a gate in this world. You lie." At least that was what Professor Aelric had shared in history class.

"Ha! Our wizardsss found that weak spot. But we are

creating one splitting the water and air so widely that our largest dessstroyer ships will pass through. Your fear will be without measure when those vesselsss come into this world. You will learn your placcce in thisss world."

"I don't believe you. You are the liar. No such thing is possible," Portia retorted, pretending to examine her fingernails.

"*I don't lie.*" Acrux spit out the words. "*Our new gate is closer. I saw it with my own eyes on our journey here. Defeat will come quickly to you.*"

Portia held back a smile. The location of a second gate was the information they needed, and he willingly handed it over because of his pride.

"*Not possible. Your leaders know not what they do.*" Insults in that language were even harder on Portia's throat than the normal speech. There were also a lot of them. These creatures had twenty ways to say they hated another. Portia picked one at random and used it, not quite sure what it meant. There was not an equivalent in common, at least that she understood. It meant 'mice toes', although how that was insulting she didn't understand.

But it was. The captive's eyes grew larger than Portia thought possible.

"*Our emperor's war plansss are beyond reproof!*" Acrux spat the words.

Portia repeated the insult, then looked Acrux in the eyes and spoke intently. "Yet here you are as my captive, totally within my power. Your emperor knows nothing," Portia retorted.

"I will *kill* you!" Acrux shouted.

Everyone stared at him with jaws hanging down. All except Portia, who stood and crossed her arms. She had said her last statement in common and he had answered back in the same language. "He speaks common. Be careful what you say around him."

Acrux growled in rage and spat at Portia. She danced back, easily getting out of the way. "*You will not sssave anyone—*"

Portia held up a hand to stop him. "I know, I know, because I'm a filthy creature." Suddenly she felt very tired. The room spun a bit until she realized it was she that was swaying.

The commander came up and put a steadying hand on her back. "Thank you for your assistance. We can take it from here."

Portia nodded, strongly desiring fresh air. "We need to speak to Queen Lorica."

"That can be arranged, Portia," the commander answered. Portia wondered what he knew about her. It didn't matter though, if he could get her quick transport to the palace.

MARK ACCOMPANIED her to the palace. They rode in the carriage the commander had managed to find and lead through the battle zone.

Portia leaned against the window frame and looked out at the sprawling city. So many people lived here and depended on her. She sighed heavily. Her stomach answered with an embarrassingly loud rumble.

"Impressive." Mark laughed at her from the other bench.

"Not funny. It seems like breakfast was days ago."

"That's true. I didn't have much time to eat at the palace." He pulled out a pouch from within his jacket and extracted two long pieces of dried meat and handed one to Portia.

Portia grabbed it quickly and shoved it in her mouth. She hadn't realized how famished she was until she saw the food. "How was Cecilia this morning?" Portia said around a mouthful of jerky.

"Didn't see her. I think some advisors had her cornered even before breakfast and were grilling her. The name Callac does make them dance."

Portia frowned at this. An uneasy feeling swept over her for leaving Cecilia alone at the palace. For leaving *her mother* alone at the palace. It still did not seem real that Cecilia was related to her, much less her mother.

The smoke from battle covered the city. It burned in Portia's nose even as they reached the top of the hill where the palace stood and hung like a dirty stain over the city.

The queen and king consort did not receive them in the throne room. Instead they were shown to a much smaller room in the back that was lined with low bookshelves and walls filled with maps. Several high-ranking military officials were meeting the royals and their attendants when they arrived. The military officials bowed and filed out, leaving Portia and Mark alone with the royals and their advisors who were standing at the back of the room.

Portia curtsied, her skills having improved a bit, while Mark bowed.

"We have heard news of the battle. Thank you for your service." Queen Lorica sounded as tired as Portia felt.

"I'm only grateful to have helped hold them off. We have bought some time." Portia took in a deep breath. "Many of our ships survived. I've come to see if we can attack the splinter. We have the location of two of them."

"Yes, a messenger informed us already." The queen motioned to a table filled with small scrolls and maps. "The commanders at the dock sent word. They have selected a clipper for you. We are sending you off with a phalanx of guards and a full crew at first light. They have a distraction planned for your escape from the harbor if such is needed. You needn't have made the trip up here." The queen rubbed her eyes.

Portia felt foolish. Going directly to her bed to rest would have been better, but no one had told her. "Thank you, Your Majesty."

"Portia, our Jack." The queen stared intently at Portia. "Be careful. We have every confidence in you. Closing the splinter is critical." The sadness and worry in her face reflected the large numbers lost that day.

"Yes, Your Majesty."

Mark and Portia exited and then stood outside the shut door of the conference room for a moment, the guards there studiously ignoring them.

"I think they just told you to save the world," Mark said softly.

15

The next morning dawned clear and cold. The smoke had long ago cleared over the battle scene, revealing wreckage everywhere. Portia gingerly stepped over the remains of a building wall to pass down the street to the docks. Fortunately, more than half the docks had survived intact.

One ship, a small clipper, was crawling with sailors preparing to make way. It was the *Dancing Queen*, the ship Queen Lorica had given to Portia for the journey. Polished wood beams shone even after the battle, and the thickness and fineness of its construction gave away that it was of the royal family's personal navy. The mission was dangerous, true, but it still felt surreal that she would finally get to go on one of these beautiful vessels. Her life on the street seemed so far away.

"Moved up, haven't you?" Mark smiled at her from the

dock next to the ship. She hadn't noticed him nor the other students from the Academy.

"What are you guys doing here?" Portia stared as Mia, Ella, and the twins, Richard and Liam, smiled at her. Richard's right arm was in a sling, but everyone else looked unharmed from yesterday's battle.

Ella stepped forward, pushing Mark out of the way as she did. He half scowled but didn't look nearly as angry as Portia would have expected. "We're here to help. Your friend here let it slip last night that you have a mission. An important one."

"What? How?" Portia glared at Mark. "Why?"

"Why not? You could probably use the help."

"Yes, but this is dangerous. And it's my duty."

Mia folder her arms and gave Portia an intense stare. "Why is it yours alone?"

"I, er... because," Portia said lamely.

"I stopped taking 'because' as a reason when I got here and away from my parents. You're our friend. This is our world. We don't want to be enslaved any more than anyone else." Mia was not taking no for an answer. The rest of the group nodded in agreement.

"I think it's a good idea," a deep voice said from behind Portia. She jumped and scolded herself for letting someone sneak up on her so close. What had happened to her street sense?

Professor Aelric stood behind her, his usual blue campus robes replaced with a fitted set of leather armor. He also had a sword and thick pouch covered in magical scribings. He was equipped for the journey. Checking behind her, Portia saw that the rest of the students were also dressed for battle. They all wore leathers. Portia's eyebrows rose.

"Portia, you need to reserve your energy for healing the splinter. We will help get you there," Professor Aelric said somberly.

"We've been busy practicing while you've been gone," Ella smirked. "But don't worry, this is definitely high-class armor." Leave it to Ella to care about the status of the clothes. What mattered to Portia was that it was practical and the students were armed. Even the mild-mannered Richard had a blade strapped to his belt.

"We're coming. No arguments." Liam's hair was uncharacteristically dark, matching his black leather pieces. He folded his arms to match Mia's, and soon Portia faced a wall of determined faces from her friends with Professor Aelric joining them on one end.

"Okay, fine." Portia threw up her arms and turned to the ship to hide the small smile that slipped across her face before she could suppress it. Warmth filled her chest. The sun seemed just a bit brighter.

"Good choice." Mark clapped Portia on the back and turned her to the gangplank.

The ship itself was spotless. Most of the sailors' work in preparing the sails and oars was done, and they looked expectantly to Portia as she stepped foot on the deck.

An officer wearing the purple and gold of the house of

Coverack stepped forward. "Welcome aboard." He saluted. "I am First Mate Sayer."

Portia nodded awkwardly, unwilling to try to return the unfamiliar salute. "Thank you. Can I please speak to the captain?"

The officer's mouth worked as he stared at Portia. All the other sailors were still, watching the exchange. Finally, he spoke. "Well, that would be you, Madam Captain."

"I DON'T UNDERSTAND; why am I the captain?" Portia paced the small cabin that she, Aelric, Mark, and Sayer had retreated to after the initial confusion on deck.

"It keeps the line of command clear if we go into battle. You are to decide our direction."

"But I know nothing about sailing a ship!" Her voice cracked in a definitely uncaptainly way.

"You don't need to," Sayer said reassuringly. "I will command the actual workings of the ship. You will decide our overall plan."

This did not reassure Portia.

"It is the queen's command," Sayer said.

Well, that decided it. Portia nodded. She would just have to be as captain-like as she could. At least there would be no argument about where they were going. The power was hers, as well as the responsibility, if something went wrong.

It was all her responsibility.

Portia had never thought about the downside of being in

charge until now. It was not something she wanted to learn about this moment, with the stakes so high, but there was no choice. She was captain. They had to succeed.

Nodding to Sayer, Portia took a deep breath. She could do this. "Okay then, let's go. We are going to the Well of Tears. There might be ships stationed before then that we have to watch out for."

"Yes, Captain," Sayer responded. "We have some luck in that all the attackers from yesterday are gone. At least we can get out of the harbor."

Portia nodded. "We also need berths for all those I've brought on board. Do we have room for everybody?"

"Of course."

Portia looked around at the maps on the walls of the room, as well as rolled in tubes stacked in a wall cupboard. They were in the captain's quarters. Her quarters. A large polished box was attached to one corner of the desk. Flipping over the lid revealed a beautiful metal contraption marked with angles and sight lines. She gave Sayer a questioning look.

"The ship's compass. It's used to guide the ship's direction."

She had no idea how to work a compass, or whatever that thing in the box was. Pointing to it, she stared at Sayer. "How does it work?"

He smiled. "I can show you later, once we are on our way, but it is not critical."

"How could it not be critical?" Portia asked, surprised.

"I know the sea well, and my power is pathfinding."

"So we better not lose you then." His confidence bothered her for some reason.

Sayer nodded. "No, Captain, but I can show you the compass just in case."

Yes, you will, Portia thought grimly.

They rejoined the rest on deck. Citizens and guards worked on the damaged buildings while other ships were in the harbor trying to clear the wrecks from the previous night's battle. They had only raised a few of the wooden ships; the enemy's metal hulled ones still sat at the bottom of the harbor. Portia wondered if there were any survivors other than their captive. If he hadn't been so strong and large, it might have been useful to bring him. As it was, he was too much of a danger on a small wooden clipper.

"Depart." Portia pointed awkwardly to the harbor entrance, summoning her best version of a captain who expects her orders to be followed.

They were.

Sayer raised one eyebrow but called out the proper orders to the waiting sailors. The sailors untied the thick rope from the mooring and pulled it on board, leaving it in a tall coil on deck. Other sailors below decks rowed. The full sails would not be deployed until they were outside the mouth of the harbor and had fewer obstacles to navigate, a good policy, especially now that there were so many wrecked ships close by, as well as untriggered nodes scattered in the waters.

The clipper slowly made its way through the harbor. Portia and the other Magic Academy students lined the railing, watching the other ships slide by. The wind picked up and blew Portia's hair wildly in her face. The air smelled of salt and the tang of moisture. Large sea creatures swam next to the ship, their blue-white skin barely visible, pulsing darker then brighter as they dove and rose within the waters. The buildings in the harbor shrunk on the horizon as the ship ventured further to sea.

A tinge of anxiety pulled at Portia. There was nothing to protect them for vast stretches except the ship, whose wood hull, once so solid on shore, now seemed flimsy and thin. Waves whipped up by the wind rocked the boat, some violently so. The anxiety in her stomach turned to nausea. Mark's face showed he was also feeling a bit ill, having turned a shade of green that reflected the green of the water.

Portia growled in her throat at Ella, Liam, and Richard, who laughed and joked further down the deck as if nothing bothered them at all. If anything, the sea made Ella positively glow with happiness and she chattered on unrelentingly.

"Seasick," Mia said. The tiny redhead was right at Portia's elbow, her brows knit together with concern.

"What?" Portia asked. A small burp escaped her lips and she turned away from Mia. Somehow it seemed like a good idea.

"You're seasick. From the motion."

Portia nodded, unwilling to open her mouth unless she had to.

"Take one. These always help me. I thought it might be needed, so I brought extra." Mia's outstretched palm held a few long thin sticks. "Chew on it. It will help, I promise."

Portia gingerly picked up a thin stick then pressed it

between her lips. Just a little taste melting on her lips pushed back the worst of the dizziness, enough that she could relax her jaw and push the stick in further to chew on it slowly. The nausea in her stomach relaxed and faded. Breathing came easily once again. Her belly unclenched, and slowly she stood up straight, not realizing how hunched over she'd been until that moment.

Mia gave Mark one of the sticks, as well as Professor Aelric, who had been even greener than Mark but had refused to sit down or hang over the railing, instead standing straight like a tortured but determined sun plant refusing to back down.

The sticks helped them too.

They were a miracle. Portia hoped Mia had brought a lot of them.

After the land behind them became a blur on the horizon, Portia looked around at the ship and the crew. There appeared to be nearly eighty men on board, plus the Magic Academy members. She had no idea of its defenses or how to handle an attack. She was the captain and knew nothing about how to handle the ship if there was a conflict, or even what its resources were.

"Sayer," she called to the officer who was standing by the man holding the wheel.

"Yes, Captain."

"I need you here." Portia motioned to the Academy members as well.

Once Sayer joined her and the others, she spoke in a lower voice. "I need to know the resources of the ship and how it fights. We were told little yesterday except our own magical tasks. How does this ship work?"

Sayer looked confused at the question. "I don't understand, Captain. It floats on the water."

He was not really being that difficult, was he?

"How do you fight other ships, such as if we run into one of those invader ships?" Portia forced her tone to be pleasant and not show any of the irritation she felt. It was a challenge.

"Ah, fighting. For that we have a few Magic Academy graduates. A very small few are assigned to each ship so they have their own mages. Of late, those have been even fewer and fewer." Sayer cleared his throat and looked at Aelric, who stared back placidly. "We have asked for more but were told it was not necessary since peace has ruled for hundreds of years. There *are* still pirates though. It has been an ongoing, ahem, negotiation."

One that Sayer and the others in the navy had been losing, judging by the glare he directed towards Aelric.

"The need was only for enough to deter pirates, not to create an arms race with our neighbors," Aelric said acidly. "I'll not condemn our people to life aboard ship merely for bragging rights of the navy."

Fury covered Sayer's face. He turned away momentarily, his lips pursed to thin white lines.

Aelric's lack of tact surprised Portia. The navy was Sayer's life. Did Aelric not see that? Was something else going on here?

Portia quickly stepped between the two men. "Right, well

things change, like now. We're here now." She gave Sayer a quick smile. "What do you do against pirates?"

Sayer relented a bit at Portia's deferential question. "Usually we have a fire mage and that is enough. It's more effective if we can strike the ship at some distance, otherwise we put our vessel at risk. In the cases of close combat, ice is more effective. Or straight sword work. All the sailors have some training in hand-to-hand combat."

They had a great crew for fire combat. All her classmates there were members of the pyromancy house of the Magic Academy. Aelric's magic was ice. That was a good combination. Mark's magic of light could be used for distraction.

"Are there any other mages on board now?" Portia asked.

Sayer shook his head. "Our last one left to have a baby, and we had not been given a permanent replacement. Members of the Academy took her place for the battle yesterday."

Portia was suddenly grateful her friends had decided to risk this journey with her. A ship with eighty men would have been a lot to protect while also focusing on healing the splinter, something that could blast them all to their watery graves if she did it wrong. Just a small error on a tiny piece of wood in Rocabarra had ended with splinters flying and a charred tabletop. What would happen if she lost focus while healing a much larger object? Shaking her head, she banished the thought from her mind. If she ruminated on it too long, her nerve would vanish.

"Ship!" a lookout called from atop one of the masts.

Sayer ran to the raised deck where the wheel was for a

better look. Another sailor handed him a spyglass, and he peered in the direction the lookout pointed. Portia and the others joined him. He handed the glass to Portia. The ship was the tiniest dot on the horizon. The lookout must have incredible vision.

Taking the glass back again, Sayer looked at the ship and then scanned the rest of the horizon. "It looks to be a solo patrol ship."

"Whose?"

Sayer looked again more intently. "Judging by the strong shine from the sun, it is metal-clad. The invaders. I see no others. We're in luck that it is facing away. I suggest we get some distance and avoid it. Most likely they have not seen us yet."

Portia nodded. "Let's do that."

Sayer called out the orders. Men ran along the deck, pulling at the rigging and swinging the sails. The ship moaned in complaint as the adjustments forced it into a different direction. Once the turn was complete, the crew stood in silence, waiting. Only the lap of waves breaking against the hull sounded as Sayer watched through the glass at the offending ship. Finally, he lowered it. "It's gone."

Portia exhaled and nodded. She did not want a battle. Their job was to heal the splinter that was open between the worlds allowing these huge monstrous creatures in. That would never happen if the *Dancing Queen* was captured, or worse yet, sunk.

"At least we have clear seas and much warning. Things

can happen quickly when the sights are shortened." Sayer handed the glass back to a sailor.

"Shortened?" Portia asked.

"When fog holds the sea. Why haven't you illustrious magic folks mastered the art of making camouflage for our ships?" Sayer had a bit of a smirk that he directed to Aelric.

Aelric drew himself up and gave a tight smile. Camouflage was not in the magic arsenal, for now.

When Sayer had excused himself to reassign some men, Portia looked at her group thoughtfully. Could they do something like that, or even create fog itself? She could try the invisibility spell, but the ship was so large, and she was to conserve her strength. No, it was best if it was something the others could do.

"Professor Aelric, would it be possible to do something like fog?"

All the students looked at him expectantly. Liam didn't wait for an answer and instead shot his fire into the ocean next to the ship. It only succeeded in boiling the water in front of him and creating steam that quickly rose up and dispersed. Not to be outdone, Mark sidled next to him on the rail and made his own attempt. Flashing the water with his light beams, he made tiny puffs of steam that dispersed even quicker.

"They are demonstrating our problem right there." Aelric leaned over the side and watched the water bubble, chewing on the anti-nausea stick. "It would need a combination of pyromancy and cryomancy, and a great deal of it, for fog is cold and hangs in the air. It would require heating the water to get the moisture into the air and then cooling of the air itself for it to condense again and probably some other conditions. At least two mages would have to work together on it, and two strong ones at that, unless you want a small patch of fog moving around suspiciously like a ship. That wouldn't work well in the middle of the seas with nothing else around."

Portia had the combination of magic to do it alone, but she was not exceptionally powerful, and she was supposed to save her strength. It would take tremendous energy to create fog to cover the ship, much less to flow all around it. The puffs Mark and Liam were making were barely as big as one of the long boats stowed on the ship. She chewed on her own stick. They had to find a way to get to the splinter without drawing notice of the invaders. One ship with student mages was not enough to fight a war.

"Bummer." Ella's normally bright face had an edge of fear on it.

Mia patted her on the back. "How about a little fighting practice? We might need it."

"Oh, that's so much work." Ella sighed and looked at Liam and Mark, who were still attempting to make fog. The fear on her face melted away into irritation.

"You have something better to do?" Mia asked, her hands on her hips.

"Oh, no, I guess not." Ella pulled her knife and jumped into a defensive fighting stand with her feet awkwardly placed and her balance unsteady.

Ella needed a lot of practice. Portia fervently hoped it wouldn't come to hand-to-hand combat on deck.

They spent the rest of the day practicing their weapons. Mark showed some tricks he had learned on the streets, even impressing Aelric. He scoffed at their rules.

"The only rule is survival, don't you know?"

Richard snorted at that but leaned in to see more clearly the wrist twist Mark used to disarm Liam in a few seconds flat.

Portia practiced with her sword. She still had her trio of knives but more and more the sword called to her. There was something special about this blade, plus it didn't seem to like when it was neglected for other weapons.

Aelric pushed her harder than he ever had before in their practices, but he could not get through her defenses. Her skills had increased, as well as her ability to be in tune with the weapon. After a flurry of movements, she tapped him on the shoulder with the flat of the blade. If it had been a real fight, she could have gutted him.

Suddenly the light dimmed. The sky was clear blue, not a cloud in it, yet the day grew dark. A cold breeze whipped up sideways and cut across the deck, blowing Portia's hair in her face. Goosebumps rose on her arms.

"Whoa." Liam dropped his fighting stance. Everyone looked around. The air shimmered for a second and then darkened further.

"This isn't the Well of Tears, is it?" Portia asked.

"There is no island anywhere close," Aelric answered, a scowl on his face. The island of the Well of Tears was the location of the splinters in the past, and from what their captive said, the location of their main one too.

The air turned icy while the sun faded in the sky. Blue sky faded to the darkness of night, revealing stars that should have been hidden. A shimmering hung around them. The back of Portia's neck tingled, and then stabs of pain zapped her between her shoulder blades. The shimmering was caused by magic. Strong magic

Could this be the location of the new splinter the captive, Acrux, mentioned? It was powerful. Portia's stomach clenched. Should she be working on this one too? He had said it was not functional yet.

Just as quickly as it came over them, the strange disruption faded, leaving a sunny, clear day. Portia shook her head at the rapidness of the change. They had to go back and deal with it.

She ran to Aelric's side. "We should—"

"Ship!" the lookout called. He pointed in the direction of the setting sun.

Portia swore. It was difficult to see that way because of the glare.

"Glass!" Sayer called. After a moment looking, he called to Portia. "Captain, it's coming at us. We've been spotted.

"Can we outrun it?"

Sayer looked again. "We can't beat that speed, no. It's fast. There is little wind to work with." He glanced up at the stacked sails above them.

The sails were full but not straining. The gentle wind was good for making way in a leisurely fashion but not effective enough to make full speed from an enemy.

"We'll have to fight." Sayer looked at the mages meaningfully. Their best chance was if Portia and the others could disable the ship from afar. Otherwise, they were at a huge disadvantage, being a wooden ship against the metal of the other. If the invader's craft had the formidable weapons they saw the previous day, then they had to defeat it from far away indeed or risk getting a hole blown in the hull. A shiver ran down Portia's spine. Dying in the middle of the ocean somehow seemed worse than dying on land. Neither was something she wanted.

"Run directly away, if possible, we want a thin profile. No sense giving them a fat target." Portia hoped that was enough of a command. Sayer could deal with the details while the mages planned the assault.

The second possible splinter would have to wait.

The ship turned, narrowing its profile to the foreign ship. As if sensing their advantage, a boom rang out across the water, followed by an enormous splash about halfway between the ships. The ship was firing on them.

"That wasn't even close," Liam said.

"Range finding perhaps?" his brother answered.

"Or just trying to intimidate us." Mark snorted.

"Most likely that," agreed Aelric. "Come, we'll follow the plan we came up with. Portia, hold your fire unless things get really dire. We need you fresh to fulfill your mission."

Portia bristled at Aelric's command but had to admit he knew her. Her first instinct was always to jump in when help was needed. But this mission was playing a long strategy—as long as they survived this encounter and continued on to heal the splinter, they didn't need to crush this enemy, much as they might long to.

Mia and Liam lined up with Aelric. Mia was nearly as strong in the pyromancy as Aelric was in cryomancy. After much discussion earlier that afternoon, the plan they had come up with mirrored what they had done in the battle yesterday: they would alternately heat and cool the hull of the ship. In between strikes, Liam would heat the ship with thrown nodes of fireballs so Mia didn't have to work so hard. Aelric was on his own since Portia had to conserve her strength.

Mia and Aelric sent off their first strikes. The enemy ship was so far away that they could not see where they were striking with their bare eyes so Ella checked through a glass after each shot.

"Lower. You're above the water line." Ella kept the glass in place and watched as the second volleys went off after Liam's blast of fire nodes landed just in front of the ship and blasted hot steam that was visible even from their distance. "As soon as it clears... Yes, I can see the red-hot hull just below the water line. Shoot again like that."

They continued to work methodically while their own ship raced away. Sayer had been right—they could not outrace this strange ship with its unseen propulsion methods, but they were doing damage. The cannonballs they kept sending out to the *Dancing Queen* landed closer and closer. There were only minutes left before one of the enormous hunks of metal blew a hole in their hull.

Portia narrowed her eyes, squinting at the ship getting

dangerously close. She would never heal the splinter if they sank to their graves. Concentrating on the suggestion spell for invisibility, she extended it over the three masts and sails of the *Dancing Queen*, a massive area compared to just covering herself. It just had to be enough to interfere with the aiming of the soldiers on other vessel.

"Sayer, veer!" It was an unsailorly term, but Sayer understood what Portia meant. He called out commands, and the ship suddenly jerked to the right and tilted into a tight turn. The hull screamed in protest and everyone had to grab hold of the deck to keep from being thrown into the dark green waters.

The moment the ship entered its turn, Portia concentrated on the invisibility spell, pouring energy into it. Aelric would be furious if he knew, but that would be okay as long as they were all alive for him to even be furious.

The ship wavered and shimmered.

"What the heck? Portia, are you doing this?" Mark called.

Not daring to speak and break her concentration, Portia held up a hand and closed her eyes. Her head throbbed. It was hard to breathe. All the energy in her body flooded into the magic she tried to wrap around their ship to hide them. *Please, please, no one else talk to me.* Blessedly, they didn't. She could hear grunts from Mia, Ella, Aelric, and Liam as they worked methodically at striking the other ship's hull while the sailors raced around to maintain the ship.

A whine of another cannonball ripped through the air. If the enemy aimed correctly, it would hit their hull and destroy them. Their only chance was if Portia's magic had worked.

The whistling missile of death came closer and closer. Portia braced herself and forced her eyes open. If the end was coming, she could at least face it. But the ball reached its apex and fell to the left, where the *Dancing Queen* had been. Not where it was now.

The *Dancing Queen* itself shimmered in waves that matched the waves below. Wide-eyed sailors went about their work, continually glancing at the half translucent wood they trod on but not stopping their tasks, a testament to their discipline.

An enormous splash reared up when the ball hit the water. They didn't have much time. Portia could not sustain the magic for much longer, and even if she could, the other ship was gaining on them. The invisibility was only a suggestion and would not survive close scrutiny. They would be doomed if the other ship reached them.

"How's it going?" Portia called out, hanging on to the spell the best she could. It was slipping away. Her head ached with the effort.

"Nearly there." Aelric gritted his teeth with the effort of speaking and working his magic.

"Throw an ice ball at it!" Portia called.

"What?" Mia panted. She had just warmed the hull again. The red glow was now white-hot. Steam spit from the water hitting it, hiding those on the enemy ship. It was getting too close, close enough to see shadowy figures on the other side of the steam.

"If the hull is weakened, all it needs is a swift kick. Use an ice one!" Portia practically screamed. Her heart was going to burst if she had to hold this much longer. They had to finish it.

Aelric didn't answer. He turned to the water and motioned upwards. A stream of water flowed up into the air and froze. Following a hand motion from Aelric, the ice twirled in the air. More water surged to it and froze on the ball, increasing its size. Aelric spun the giant ice ball faster, sweat beading on his brow.

Portia's grip on the suggestion magic slipped. The *Dancing Queen* dropped into sharp focus, every bit of it crystal clear. A yell from the other ship said they had seen it. The sound of metal grinding on metal came across the water. It must be machinery to focus their weapon. Whatever it was, it was not good news for them.

"Now, Aelric, now!" Portia yelled. She dropped her efforts at the broken concealment magic and used every last bit of energy she had left to help throw the ice ball towards the other ship. It needed to hit hard and fast if it was to break a hole in the weakened hull. Portia's neck tingled again as the others helped as well. Every last bit of fire and light and ice magic they had flew towards the ship.

The ice landed smack in the center of the red-hot hull and stuck there, then slowly slid down. It had not been enough. Tears pulled at Portia's eyes.

Sayer furiously called out commands for the ship to turn yet again. They did not want to be a sitting target. Portia felt rooted on the spot, staring at the other ship. It didn't feel real. Not the noise, not the sailors running on deck, not her classmates there with her.

They had given it their best, and it wasn't enough. Now they were going to die—Portia and those closest to her. It was about to happen.

Dimly, she heard Mark and Aelric yelling but couldn't move.

Then, the other ship split open with a scream of metal, starting where the massive ice ball had hit it.

16

Their magic had worked. The enemy's ship was taking on water through the massive crack opening in its hull and sinking fast.

Distance opened up between the ships as the *Dancing Queen* pulled away while the other ship shuddered and slowed. The torturous noises coming from deep within it told that whatever propelled it was failing—and fast. Several of the terrifying creatures fell into the water at its abrupt faltering.

"Should we help them?" Portia asked. It was one thing to fight them off; it felt another entirely to leave them to drown.

"No." Sayer pointed to the ship. "They have smaller boats that they're dropping now. They might yet come after us—we have no idea the capabilities of those other vessels. The best thing is to make speed for our final destination." He gripped his hands together tightly. "We don't want those at the splinter to get warning that we are coming."

"That would be disastrous. Yes, let's go." Portia put a

brave face on it, but a small part of her felt terrible at leaving them stranded in the vast sea.

"They shouldn't have come, at least not to conquer and be cruel to us. Don't feel bad," Ella chided Portia. "I know you. Stop it."

Portia nodded. Ella was right. She was always so pragmatic. She had to be as a poor villager in a school of well-off nobles.

At least four small boats dropped from the enemy craft, crawling with the huge invaders. Much to the relief of everyone on board, they did not pursue the *Dancing Queen*.

Portia found Aelric sitting on the deck, leaning against a pile of thick rope. "We barely won that. It took all of us."

He nodded. "It was far too close a thing. All that for one ship. The metal gives them a serious advantage." Grimacing, Aelric stretched out his legs. "We need to find out how they shoot those balls."

"I don't feel any magic from them."

"Feel? You feel magic?" Aelric's intense stare bore into Portia. She turned away.

"Just sometimes. Don't you?"

"No." Aelric sighed then leaned his head back on the rope and closed his eyes. "I don't want to know right now about another new thing you do. Tell me later."

They sailed on. Sayer assigned two lookouts to try to prevent another surprise sighting, but it was not needed that day, for they encountered no more ships. Either the ship they had disabled had no way to call for help, or they had just been lucky enough to miss any support craft rushing to its rescue.

The night was crisp and clear. There was no moon to take away from the stars, and they shone down brightly, more brightly than Portia had ever seen.

"There are so many." The sky was almost white with a blanket of stars.

"Stargazing was always my favorite part of sailing. It made up for all those hours of boredom during the day listening to my father or someone else lecturing about noble duties." Mia lay back on the deck and rested her head on her folded arms. "I don't know why, but the sky always looks so different out here. They used to navigate by stars, you know, before they found wayfaring magic. Just looking at the night sky could tell them where they were and what direction to go."

"Do you know how to do that?" Portia asked. Mia never disappointed with her vast knowledge. She must not have done anything before the Academy than study.

"Possibly. A tutor showed me once, but I never got to practice."

When Portia came back with the ship's compass Mia was able to figure it out and showed Portia how to line it up to the stars. "You need a map of the night sky though, or knowledge of the stars. Some sailors probably know them by heart, but not I."

"There must be a map below decks. I'll search for it tomorrow."

Portia dreamed of the stars that night.

THE NEXT DAY was cold and chilly. The blue skies were gone, replaced with clouds and an ominous glowing red in the eastern sky. The day was not welcoming.

A nightmare had woken Portia before the others, so she'd gone topside and practiced making fog in the early morning light. If the sailors knew she shouldn't be able to do such a thing, they did not let on, instead ignoring her while sleepily going about their own tasks. A few sea creatures stopped to visit and dance in the fog but swam away when the sun grew higher. Or perhaps they ran from Ella's booming voice calling good morning across the ship's deck to all the sailors she saw.

"Did you know that we have a birthday today?" Ella asked Portia, startling her.

Portia quickly dispersed the magic she'd been using to make fog. Hopefully Ella wouldn't notice the white mist hanging in the air just a few lengths from the ship. Portia didn't feel up to explaining about her abilities.

"A what?" Portia turned to face her, leaning casually against the ship's railing.

"One of the sailors, Brasta or something. It's his birthday today. We should celebrate."

Portia stared at Ella, her eyes wide. "Ella, we are on a dangerous mission and might all *die* if we're not careful." Ella blanched at the word 'die' and Portia regretted saying it for a second but pushed on. "We can't go around celebrating birthdays and having a party."

"Why not?" Ella asked, flipping her hair but her expression serious. "I mean, maybe now is the time to celebrate because there might not be a tomorrow."

"You just want a party."

"That's true too." Ella shot Portia a mischievous grin.

"We need to put the time into practicing our skills so we're ready."

"Oh, you and your practice. Practice fancy script reading, practice swords, practice magic. Don't you ever get tired of practicing?" Ella's lower lip stuck out in the way that often got her what she wanted.

Honestly, no, Portia thought. Getting to learn everything in that great Academy was a dream come true. She would do that as many hours as she was awake if she never had to go back to stealing for a living again. Ella wouldn't understand that. "Think of it as survival preparation. That way you'll survive to attend many more parties."

Ella shrugged. "Fine, we'll do it your way. I'll go get my knives."

"They should be on you at all times," Portia said, chiding.

Ignoring her, Ella walked back to the stairway to below decks.

"How do you know that it's someone's birthday, anyway? We've only been on board for a day!" Portia yelled after her.

The only response she got was a wave from Ella as she walked away.

The rest of day flew by with all the students practicing. The sea seemed to go forever. The morning had started out gray, and the day only grew darker as the hours passed. A distant rumbling warned of a storm, but they only saw a few flashes of lighting as the darkest part of the dangerous weather swept sideways across the horizon. Smatterings of raindrops whipped their faces while they concentrated on weapons practice. There was little room below decks, so it had to be conducted outside.

As Portia returned to her cabin to retrieve a whetstone, Ella's complaints brought a painful realization to her mind. She had been so diligent at practicing sword work and other magic, but she had not been practicing the healing she'd learned from the elves—the skill critical to sealing the splinter into the invader's world, one that she had barely mastered and had such dire consequences if done improperly. Attempting to heal a splinter large enough to allow these ships in, and then failing, would have deadly consequences not just for her but for all those people around her. Her hand stung just at the thought of the last time she had messed up that magic. She did not want to imagine the destruction that would be unleashed with poorly done work on an enormous splintering.

Her heart pounded at her oversight, and her face burned red at the shame even though there was no one around to see it. She should have been practicing that magic this whole time. Could she even perform it anymore? Or would the words flee her mind and her throat refuse to sing it properly?

By the time she reached her cabin Portia felt like she couldn't breathe. Shutting the door, she sat on the bed and tried to calm herself. That didn't work, so she leaned forward and let her head hang down between her knees and focused on her breathing. After a moment or two, she felt better.

Besides, there was too much blood in her head to keep sitting that way.

Grabbing a piece of parchment from the desk, Portia

ripped it in two, placed it on the desk, and then trilled the elf magic needed to heal it, singing it as fast as she could. The paper pieces flew together and zipped up the tear while it vibrated wildly on the table. The vibrations in the paper were diminishing when a bang on her door startled her. Portia stopped singing and the paper pieces burst apart with a loud popping noise and fluttered over the desk, leaving a charred spot where they had been. *No good.*

"What is it?" Portia said angrily under her breath. She wasn't angry at the interruption, only her inability to ignore it.

"Ships. Lots of them. Huge ones." Mark's voice sounded small from the other side of the door. "What was that noise?"

THE MASSIVE SHIPS were small dots on the horizon. There were three at least. The cloudy, dim day offered some protection from being spotted, so Sayer was not as concerned about them being seen but still held the ship at some distance.

"How do you know they are huge?" Portia asked after giving back the glass to Sayer.

"Because they are by the cliffs of the Well of Tears. The cliffs are five stories high."

The ships' decks had been level with the top of the cliffs.

Portia looked down at their own ship. The deck was some three measures above the surface of the water, a measure being roughly the height of a full-grown man. Those ships were at least three or four times bigger than that.

Those massive ships were guarding the Well of Tears, and they had to get by them if they were to heal the splinter.

At least Portia had to.

"We cannot fight them," Aelric said, cautioning.

"I wouldn't dream of it," Portia said. His look said he didn't believe her. "I just need to get around them."

"Could we distract them?" Liam asked, rubbing his hair and glancing in the direction of the ships. "Something showy."

"We don't want showy," his brother said.

"Not to reveal us, but a distraction somewhere else."

There was nothing around them but open seas and the Well of Tears island surrounded by the huge ships. They didn't have another ship to throw magic for them and distract the enemy. And there was no way to win in a fight if that enemy spied them. They would just have to make sure they weren't seen.

"How about sneaking up in the dead of night?" Portia said, thinking out loud.

Mark grinned at Portia's suggestion. He had once told the queen Portia was good at 'sneaking' so she wasn't making a liar of him.

"This is not an ideal sneaking vessel," Sayer said. "It is rather large."

It was rather large, having three masts, a dozen sails, and close to a hundred people on board. And other boats hanging from its sides.

"So I'll take a long boat." Portia thrust out her chin.

Liam whistled. "Bold."

Aelric shot him a dark look. "It will still be spotted, and its size will only make it less capable of defending itself." Portia didn't like his tone but schooled her face while he continued. "Besides, you couldn't control it on your own. We'd have to go with you, and I have no desire to provide target practice for those giant metal balls."

"Are you giving up?" Ella said at Portia's shoulder, making Portia jump. She hadn't been there a minute ago. Mia must have roused her from her nap.

"No, we are *not* giving up," Portia said, looking meaningfully at Aelric. His caution surprised her.

"I'm not suggesting we give up, *Student Portia Harris*, just that we come up with a better plan—so it works and we live."

He hadn't called her Student in a long time. Portia crossed her arms and scowled. She was captain of this ship, although it didn't feel like it right now with such a surly and unamenable crew.

"I'll go," Liam said, unfazed by Aelric's words.

"I will too," Richard said quietly.

Ella, Mark, and Mia nodded as well. The students faced Aelric, who huffed at them.

"How about we find a good way to be stealthy first before volunteering to die." Aelric practically spit the words at them.

"I can create fog around a long boat."

All eyes turned to Portia.

"You can what?" Mark asked. A glint of jealousy and betrayal shone in his eyes. He'd practiced for nearly an hour and failed. Portia had not even offered a whisper of a hint of how to do it, much less told him of her skills.

Portia blushed at his rebuke and looked down for a second.

"For how long?" Aelric asked quietly.

"For long enough. Once I start it, it seems to stay around for a bit, at least an hour. I can put it around a long boat, and we can sneak in right under their noses. It's already cold and cloudy. Fog would fit right in. And they can't be so sure of knowing our weather just yet, being that they *are* from elsewhere."

"It will soon be night," Sayer offered helpfully.

No one said anything as Aelric thought about what Portia had said.

This is ridiculous. I am captain, Portia thought. She stomped her foot to get everyone's attention. "I'm doing it. We've got no choice. It's why we're here. And if this," Portia pointed to the ships on the horizon, "is what they have brought over in such a short time, then it makes it that much more imperative to stop them before they can go further. We nearly lost that battle with the small ship. How could the navy stand against more of those monster ships and all the invaders that must be on them? Jukhnovo and Lusatiana have already fallen. These creatures must be stopped before Haulstatt is just a distant memory." Portia pulled herself taller. "I'm captain on this ship, Professor Aelric, by command of the queen, and what I say goes."

The ship was silent. Not even the sailors manning the oars moved.

Finally, Aelric nodded. "Yes, Captain."

As much as everyone pressed to go on the dangerous mission, only four could safely fit on the long boat. Portia chose Mark to come with as the second mage, since they knew each other so well and had spent years sneaking around and communicating silently. Sayer insisted on going with his wayfaring ability, and Portia agreed to let the fourth be a ship's guard whose skill with weapons was above all others. He also had powerful shoulders, which would be much needed for the long row ahead of them.

Night fell quickly, and it was blessedly dark thanks to the new moon and the thick layer of clouds hiding the stars above. The plan was that Mark or Portia would send up a flare if they ran into trouble, and the others would attempt to rescue them without getting caught themselves. Portia thought it would be better if they ran, but none of the others would agree to it. The next best thing was to insist that they come up with a plan. So far, all they had was sending bright nodes of fire magic away from the ship as far as possible to lure the enemy away while sneaking in with a second long boat. They were gambling that Aelric with his ice magic and one of the pyromancy students could figure out how to make fog in time. Liam and Aelric were practicing off the side of the boat as the first boat was prepared, and all that had happened was some steam, a small blizzard, and a lot of cursing.

Once the four of them were all settled in the long boat, Portia created fog around it. Conserving her strength, she created only a low patch that extended just a measure or so beyond the boat. The moisture in the air chilled her arms, and she pulled her jacket in tight.

Sayer looked around appreciatively then stood up. "I'm out of the fog. It isn't very high."

"Does it cover us while sitting?" Mark said from deep within it.

"Yes."

"I don't want to push too hard. There is still the splinter to heal," Portia said while concentrating on keeping the fog around the boat and not drifting off over the sea.

"Right. Everyone stay seated then." Sayer sat down heavily. He nodded at the guardsman and then each picked up a heavy oar. They looked like dark shapes within the fog. Portia only knew who each shape was by where they were in the boat. A bead of water ran down her nose. They were going to be soaked by the time they got to the large ships. Pulling her jacket even tighter, Portia hunched down to stay warm.

Sayer and the guard slipped the oars silently through the water, rowing towards the larger ship. Occasionally Sayer would issue a quiet correction. His wayfaring magic allowed him to find his way to the Well of Tears. The fog seemed to hold in all sound. Portia heard her breathing as if it was right in her ear, while Sayer's commands and the occasional drops of water from the oars sounded far away, as if from the other side of a soft wall of cotton.

They rowed for hours, the rhythmic pacing of the oars hypnotic. Even while holding on to the fog magic, Portia felt her eyelids lower. She wanted nothing more than to lie down on the bottom of the boat and sleep. A flash of pain from pinching herself worked for a short time, then her eyelids drooped once again.

A hand came out of the fog towards her, holding a piece of jerky. "Eat. You'll need the energy."

Portia took the food gratefully while Mark handed out more to Sayer and the guard. Some bread followed. Her energy returned as she chewed. It was just in time too, for as she swallowed the last bite, two dark shapes loomed on the other side of the fog—massive dark shapes that seemed to go up nearly to the sky. It was only up close that Portia could understand the true scale of the enemy's ships. It was as if the palace had grown a hull and was floating on the sea. They were terrifyingly huge.

The fog magic faltered as her grip loosened in shock at the sight of the ships. It took some energy to pull the fog back to the still moving long boat.

Sayer motioned for the guard to stop rowing as well.

They sat still in the quiet, straining to hear anything. Portia's stomach tightened as her ears tried to latch onto a sound coming from the great big ships looming ahead of them, but there was nothing. The drip of water from the guard's oar sounded as loud as a slammed door. Her scalp tingled.

"They are incredibly close. We would not dare position our own ships so," Sayer whispered, but it sounded like shouting to Portia.

"Splinter." Portia pointed ahead. It must be on the other side of those two ships. No magic tingled at her yet. They were not close enough.

Before Sayer could answer back, Portia held up one finger

to her lips while leaning in so he could see her. He took the hint and responded with a nod.

Picking his oar back up, he motioned for the guard to row as well. This time, rather than give verbal directions to the guard, Sayer steered with his oar, handling all the corrections himself. Slowly, oh so slowly they made their way between the two huge ships towering above them. It was like going into a deep cavern where the walls kept coming closer and closer together.

Despite knowing the ships could not be touching, and that they had been immobile the entire time the long boat had been there, Portia had a sudden fear that they would be crushed between the foreign vessels so thoroughly that no one would even know they had been there. Splinters of wood and crushed bone would sink unnoticed to the bottom of the sea floor. Forcing herself to focus on her breathing and the fog magic brought her heart rate down, but only just a little.

Tiny waves from their passage splashed up against the metal hulls of the great ships, echoes bouncing back and forth. A distant grinding voice drifted from the deck above and down to them. One of the creatures was on deck and speaking that guttural and aggressive language. Portia strained but could not make out what it said. Croaks that could have been laughter floated down after it. The crew had no idea they were there.

Suddenly, something sailed down from above and landed with a splash just ahead of them.

The smell told Portia what it was. She pinched her nose.

They were dumping their waste overboard. Blessed be the stars that it had not hit them.

They continued onwards. More noises drifted down from above.

Finally, they neared the ends of the ships. The looming darkness opened up as more of the cloud-filtered starlight was able to reach the waters.

Portia thinned a bit of the fog ahead of them so they could see what they were moving towards. She had expected to see the cliffs of the Well of Tears ahead of them or at least some rock outcroppings and partially submerged boulders. But no rocks or cliffs were visible directly ahead. Instead, the waves that came from their long boat flowed ahead of them and lapped towards a huge, partially submerged oval that reached up into the air just higher than the ships above them.

It was the splinter between worlds.

This was the door these invaders had used to reach their world. Portia's eyes opened wide staring at it. Mark had the same expression. Humans had come to this world ages ago, before the Great War, and no one alive had seen a splinter like this before—one that opened to a foreign world that was not of their own creation. Those rare occurrences were marked by the gigantic Elven hourglass.

The oval was a milky white, reflecting light—what little came from the dim night sky—onto the water below. Despite its opaque color, the waves seemed to wash into it and disappear. They did not bounce back again as if it was a solid object. Each crest of water entered as if there was no substance to the oval at all.

On impulse, Portia grabbed a bone button from her jacket, ripped it off, and whipped it low into the oval. Holding her breath, she waiting to hear a splash as it hit the water but there was nothing. The button had not landed in the water, at least not in their world.

Goosebumps crawled up Portia's neck and scalp. The others breathed out heavily.

The splinter was open.

All eyes in the boat turned to Portia. "Keep the boat still," Portia said so quietly she wondered if they had heard her. Sayer nodded, and he and the guard put their oars in the water and adjusted its position, keeping it where it was as best they could.

Portia began the healing magic, singing the Elven tune as quietly as she could. When she started, she could barely hear her own voice, but something happened as the first tendrils of magic reached the oval; the milky whiteness on its face swirled into motion, and it vibrated. Soon Portia's voice rang out louder, sent out by the oval itself. Portia snapped her mouth shut in shock at the unexpected result, but then the oval began to vibrate more violently, reminding her of the consequences of stopping the healing before it was done. She had to resume singing—stopping the spell early was not an option if she wanted them to live through the night. So she sang once again. And once again the oval sang her own voice back at her. The longer she continued, the louder it got. The oval shimmered in a strange way. The reflected song began to take on the tone of a shriek.

"What are you doing? Stop it!" Mark said to her in a low panicked voice.

She shook her head but didn't stop singing. This had to be completed once it was started. Comprehension came into his eyes. He swore softly and looked away. She had to continue, and they would not be able to hide.

Soon her voice echoed over the waters and bounced off the metal hulls of the ships, creating even more echoes. Yells came from the ships' decks, and the clacking of armor and weapons rang through the night. Torch lights bounced on the decks as creatures ran with them. A few torches were held over the edges of the ships' decks and waved around.

The fog around the long boat drifted partially off now that Portia was fully concentrating on the healing spell. The long boat was visible to those on the decks above. One persistent torch held above them let it be known they had been spotted.

Another torch flew down to the boat and nearly hit the back of Portia's head. She saw the light coming and ducked to the side at the last minute. Instead of hitting her, it landed on the bottom of the long boat, blinding them all with the sudden intense light. Sayer and the guard stomped it out. Fire on a wooden ship was deadly.

But what came next was worse.

The thunk of an arrow made her jump, burying itself deep in the hull close to Portia, but she continued singing with only a glance at the arrow. It was a crossbow bolt. If that had hit her it would have gone clean through her body. Another glance above showed rows of faces peering down at them from the heights of the ships' decks above. There were too many for them to fight. She had to finish this spell and then they had to run. If only they would be so lucky as to have the disappearance of the splinter be enough to distract these boatfuls of angry invaders.

Sayer and the guard moved the long boat towards the oval, trying to get some distance from the weapons on the ships. Portia motioned for them to stop, but they were too frantic to notice.

A second bolt whizzed over their heads. The guard pushed his oar towards Sayer and pulled a huge, metal bound shield from where it had been stashed in the front of the boat. Pushing his way to the back of the boat, the guard used the shield to protect the four of them the best he could, sweeping it from side to side as the arrows came. It was not large enough to cover them completely, especially when being shot at from both ships.

Portia gripped her fists tight, thinking only of the words she was singing while their little boat vibrated with the arrow strikes. One went into the bottom of the boat and a small trickle of water seeped around the arrow shaft.

Mark boiled the water around them, making steam. It helped hide them a bit, but the steam rose too quickly and left them exposed once again. Shifting his attention to the other boats, he sent light motes in concentrated streams to the decks, trying to light fires, but there was little flammable material on the ships except the clothing of the creatures themselves. He could not blind them all with his light magic, being so far outnumbered, but he did his best to flood their eyes with light and start their clothes on fire. He had to duck out from under the shield to aim then pull back again before an arrow found his face.

The guard's arm flagged, and he switched his hold on the shield. Sayer tried to keep the boat still, but the force from the arrow strikes was enough to keep nudging it towards the milky white and rapidly vibrating oval.

Sweat poured from Portia as the stench from burned flesh, steamy sea water, and refuse filled her nostrils. All she thought about was the words, the most important words she'd ever known in her life, coming from her mouth in the Elven melody she'd learned in Fife's kitchen.

A stinging heat burned across her belly. Looking down she saw her jacket and tunic ripped, a bright red streak of blood and flesh showing where an arrow had torn across her body. A finger's width closer to her and it would have killed her. Portia closed her eyes and held her arms tight over her belly, while continuing her song.

Mark swore when he saw her wound. Switching to attacking the bolts as they came in helped until more of the attackers could aim without his harassment of their eyes. Arrows rained around them, the sea splashing up with each landing.

Sayer docked the oars and scooted to Portia. He pulled his jacket off and wrapped it around the wound, pressing down to stop the flow of blood. Pain washed over Portia.

Fighting dizziness, Portia opened her eyes to keep from falling. The milky whiteness of the oval was fading, becoming more and more translucent. It was also shrinking. No longer would one of the large ships behind them fit inside it. As if noticing it themselves, the arrows from behind increased in a desperate volley, along with more thrown torches. They knew she was doing something to the splinter.

Pushing even more energy into the healing spell, Portia slid to the bottom of the boat and curled into a ball, all the while still singing.

The boat jerked with a sudden movement and Sayer swore and pushed back to the oars. "We're caught in a current!" He rowed desperately, but the boat moved inexorably towards the remaining oval of the splinter.

A cry of pain came from Mark. Portia opened her eyes. Mark screamed at her, "Don't stop!" An arrow stuck out of his arm. She continued singing, tears coming to her eyes.

Then a cold wave went over her body. Looking up from the bottom of the boat she saw the milky arch pass over her. The front half of the boat had gone through the splinter with her in it.

Then the splinter pulled together with the speed of water through a drain and snapped shut.

17

The boat sheared off where the closing splinter sliced through it like a woodcutter's saw. Portia's half of the boat sank into the water, and she paddled and shut her mouth to keep from drowning.

There was no need for singing anymore. The splinter was healed.

But with Portia on the wrong side.

Mark and the others were on the other side, being attacked right now. Tears threatened to drown her in addition to the water. It took a great force of will to calm herself so she could keep swimming. There would be no opportunity to help them if she let herself die.

A thought chilled her even more than the water; she would never see her mother again. To be ripped away like this after she had just found her was too unfair. Anger pulsed in her veins. Portia treaded the water with determination. She would not die on this world. There had to be a way back to Haulstatt.

It was daylight around her with a blue-white sun low to the horizon. She was in a cove with several large ships and scattered smaller craft. A stretch of white sand glinted in the distance. The land looked too far to make swimming in her heavy clothes.

Kicking off her shoes and unwrapping Sayer's jacket from her waist, she let them fall into the depths of the water. It was easier to keep afloat after that. The land was still too far, as she was already exhausted from casting the splintering healing spell. A nearby ship would have to do.

No one seemed to have spotted her, for no cries rose from the ships. Conversation floated over the water, but it sounded like it was from a large ship at the far end of the cove. Several smaller boats clustered around it.

Choosing a medium-sized boat that was partially hidden from the large ship with the voices, Portia swam towards it as quietly as she could. If she pushed her panic down and forced her breathing to even out, the going was easier, and the splashing reduced.

When she reached the boat, she paddled alongside it as quietly as she could and listened for any sound betraying someone inside. There was nothing. Finally, she reached a ladder attached to the side and slowly climbed onto it. The rungs were so far apart she had to pull herself up to go from rung to rung. It was not designed for someone of her small size.

She lifted her head to peek over the side. There was no

one on the deck nor in the windows of the small cabin. Climbing the rest of the way on board, Portia crouched low and ran to the cabin, going inside and out of view of anyone from another boat.

An enormous wheel and some equipment she didn't recognize filled the empty room. There were stairs leading to below deck.

Downstairs was empty as well. There were crew quarters and a room that must have been the captain's room, for it was filled with maps just as hers had been on the *Dancing Queen*. Portia dug through them. She spied a map lying flat with weights holding it down on a large table in the back. It depicted a curve of water surrounded by land. On a hunch she unfocused her eyes and was rewarded with an understanding of the written text of the map. The librarian's spell worked for this language as well as for Elven. Portia slid the map from under the weights and rolled it up to fit in her inside jacket pocket. It would get wet, but there was no choice for that. She muttered a wish that the ink on the map would not run.

Putting the map in her jacket jostled her injury. Blood soaked the front of her tunic. Pulling the top linen from the long cot lining the exterior wall, Portia wrapped it around the wound. It was drier than her own clothing and would have to do for now.

Looking around for anything else that might be useful, Portia found a piece of parchment under where the map was. It spoke of a lunch on another vessel. That must be where the crew was. She had to hurry. The only things that looked promising were some scattered coins along a shelf over the bed. Scooping them up, she put them in the small bag still across her chest. She had not thought to ditch it in the water and was now grateful for that oversight.

A trill of fear ran down Portia. She had to get off this boat and to land somehow without being seen. Ideally without having to go into the water again. Who knew what creatures lived in the seas of this strange land. A shiver swept over her.

Running back up the stairs, she examined the deck. There was a tiny craft hanging by hooks at the rear of the larger craft. It could have fit several people, but Portia guessed it was only big enough for one of the invaders. The boat, while small, was all metal, as were all their craft, and far too heavy for her to lift off the hooks despite her trying.

Panting from the effort, Portia looked around. There were no other options unless she wanted to swim for it. Almost crying in panic, Portia looked at the hooks holding up the small boat and then blasted one of them with pyromancy magic, heating the metal just as they had done in Hilda's class. The metal took the heat. It seemed forever, but eventually the hook turned red, then orange, then white-hot. Portia gave the boat hanging from it a yank and the hook slowly straightened, letting that end of the boat drop to the water. But it didn't fall all the way down. The boat hung by the tip of the hook on the other side. Portia gave the boat a kick with all her might and it was just enough to bounce it off the hook and send it crashing to the water below. She held her breath as it fell. It landed right side up. It would have done her no good if it had landed upside down.

Sparing a glance to the sounds coming from the ship at the far side of the cove, she saw no one coming. If anyone had heard the boat fall, they had not set off an alarm. Quickly, she jumped into the little boat before it drifted away and out of reach. Her ankle turned at the heavy landing, but she held in the cry of pain.

A strange device sat at the back of the boat that reached into the water below. It probably had something to do with how their boats moved, but she could not figure that out. Blessedly, there were two oars in the boat, and she set up in the middle, paddling with both of them, her arms barely long enough to reach and her legs dangling from the high bench. She rowed as fast as she could away from the sounds in the harbor. It would take longer to reach shore, but this way would keep her out of sight for as long as possible.

It took a many candlemarks to reach the shoreline. Her shoulders ached in complaint, and broken blisters oozed blood on the handles of the oars. But she made it to the rocky shore, the beautiful white sands going far down the coast as she had fought the currents to reach land.

Reaching the land just as the blue-white sun set on the horizon again, Portia crawled to shore and fell asleep in the brown dirt and rocks.

THE BRILLIANT MORNING SUN beat down on Portia, waking her from slumber on the rocks. Faint squeaking echoed along the shore, a sound she hoped was harmless wildlife. There were no buildings around, nor roads. The boat had drifted away in the night since she'd failed to secure it in her exhaustion.

Her head ached and her stomach growled. She'd not eaten in nearly a day nor drunk water since then either.

Stumbling around in the heat of the sun, Portia came across a deep break in the rocks at the bottom of which came the gentle tinkle of water. Half walking, half falling down the opening, she stumbled into the stream itself and stuck her whole face in the water and drank deeply. Her mouth watered and her head ached as her body registered the precious fluid going down her throat. Finally, she stopped drinking and pulled her head from the water. Nausea filled her, but she didn't care. There was water.

After more drinking, Portia sat in the shade until the throbbing in her head abated. Pulling out the map from her jacket, she was relieved to see it had survived getting wet. The ink had not run at all. There were several cities down the coast from the harbor where she'd landed. One of them should be close by.

Her knives had been lost to the sea, but her sword was still with her. Pulling it from the waterlogged sheath, she checked it for rust. There was none. The blade gleamed just as pristincly as it had when it was first gifted to her. Portia cleaned it with the bottom of her shirt. She laid the baldric and scabbard out in the sun to dry.

Looking at the linen she'd wrapped around her waist, an idea came to her.

It didn't take long to fashion the long piece of linen into a cloak and hood, much the same as the one worn by the invader they had seen on the dock. It was even the same color, a dull brown—the color of raw linen. She was tiny by their standards, but at least she would be dressed the same and have her face hidden.

The hood also kept the blazing hot sun off her head. Portia gathered her things and set off.

Walking straight inland, it didn't take long to find a road. The map showed the closest city to the left, so she chose that direction and set off on the wide road. The city soon appeared on the horizon. From afar, it looked just like any city in Haulstatt or Lusatiana, but when she got closer, a huge difference made itself apparent; wagons flowed in and out of the city with lines of beings walking behind.

Getting closer revealed them to be humans, connected by neck chains and overseen by a gigantic creature dressed just as she was with a long cloak and hood.

Enslaved humans.